Mortals As They Walk

Markus McDowell

RIVERSONG
BOOKS

An Imprint of Sulis International Press
Los Angeles | London

ISBN (print): 978-1-946849-68-7
ISBN (eBook): 978-1-946849-69-4

Published by Riversong Books
An Imprint of Sulis International
Los Angeles | London

www.sulisinternational.com

Receive a free collection of short stories
by Markus McDowell from your favorite
retailer by visiting
https://books2read.com/mcdowell-such-chaos

Contents

*...the way of human beings is not in their control;
mortals as they walk cannot direct their steps.*

Jeremiah 10:23

ADAPTATION

Pate
(January 2019)

Do the next thing.

That's always what I told myself when I found myself overwhelmed or feeling helpless. There was always *something* to do. *Something* I could control, even if I felt powerless in the current situation.

Tonight, I could only think of one thing to do.

Exposure to the bitter cold should do it. Here, in the dark, on the sidewalk. I wonder how soon before I pass out, never to wake up again.

Do the next thing.

I threw off the dirty ragged blanket and yanked off my threadbare coat, tossing both against the building. The chill hit me like a stinging wave. I pulled off my shirt and began shivering. Oh, this is dreadful. Do I have the willpower?

"Hey, get up. You can't sleep on the sidewalk."

I looked up to see one of our proud men in Blue.

"Come on, pal. Move it." He poked me with his nightstick to emphasize the seriousness of my violation.

I staggered to my feet, pulled my shirt back on, and picked up the coat and blanket.

"What are you trying to do, freeze to death? There's a shelter on East Third halfway down past Second Avenue."

I shuffled out of the alley onto East Seventh. Guess my heart wasn't in it. I thought I'd hid from passersby. But authorities have eyes everywhere. As I well knew.

Only a few cars were traveling Seventh, a contrast to its usual congestion and life. The city was sleeping—as much as it ever did. Which was not much. Like me.

"This blanket smells really bad," I said aloud. I had retrieved it from the trash bin behind a clothing store near the Park. I assumed it was reasonably clean of bodily fluids and insects. But it still smelled rotten.

After a half mile, I turned onto East Second and found the shelter in the middle of the block. As he entered, a young man sitting at a table on a folding chair bolted upright, as if he'd been asleep. College-age, doubtless volunteering for college credit or to impress a girl. When I got my degree, we got credit through becoming experts in our field—although a Master's of Information Technology didn't offer much in the way of volunteering.

"Hi. Need a bed? Food?"

"Yeah, both. What time is it?"

"Two forty-five. Here, sign this sheet, then come on back, I'll get you a bowl of soup and show you where to sleep." He wrinkled his nose. "And I'll get you a clean blanket."

Eris
(January 2006)

The little girl opened her eyes and then squinted in the bright antiseptic light. It hurts. So much—

A motion to the side caught her attention. "Gramma? Why are you here?"

"Hello, Eris, my dear." Her face was pinched and worried; she looked like she had not slept. But Gramma lived in Dallas. What was she doing here—

Eris jerked upright. Mommy. Daddy—

"Eris, dear, I have some bad news."

"Where are mommy and daddy?!" Tears formed in her eyes.

The old woman took the girl's hand and shook her head. Matching tears appear in her eyes. "I'm so sorry, little one. They did not...survive. They did not suffer—"

Eris screamed and tried to get out of the bed. Two nurses appeared to hold her down, while a third inserted medication in the tube which led to her arm.

"Eris, Eris, please," croaked her grandmother, "let them help you." She stopped to take a breath. "It is terrible, terrible, I know. But we will be okay. You'll come with me to live."

Eris did not agree that it would be okay. They couldn't be gone—they *couldn't!* She squirmed under three nurses' firm grips.

"Now, now, Eris," one nurses said in an irritating soothing tone. "We're just giving you something to calm down. Relax, honey."

It couldn't be. It couldn't be.

Her grandmother was speaking, but she couldn't understand the words. A rushing sound filled her ears, and she felt like she was going blind.

As she began to drift off, she heard her gramma tell the nurses, "We have no other family. The poor little thing."

Salim
(June 2032)

He loved walking on the cobbled streets of Old Town. The earliest had been laid down over a thousand years ago, his teachers had told him. Of course, they'd been replaced many times. But streets were ancient. The one he was on now, for example, Plock Strasse, had been 'Plock Strasse' for over two-hundred and fifty years. He liked to imagine the tens of thousands—perhaps millions—of people who had walked this street throughout that time.

He looked up at his father, walking beside him. His father looked down. "You okay, Salim?"

Salim nodded. People often asked him that. Salim didn't mind.

He enjoyed the buildings that crowded the narrow streets. All butted up again each other. Most were three stories high, making the old road seem like a man-made canyon. Some buildings were as old as the road. Many of them were the traditional half-timber construction, others were made of cut stone. Squeezed in between, here and there, were newer-style structures: concrete, glass, and metal. Old signage, painted or carved wood, right next to glowing screens and moving holo-signs. A strange hodgepodge of materials, decor, architecture, and time. Salim thought it all fit together well. Like an artist who created a montage, it came together to portray a unified "feel." The city had personality. A sense of a hoary entity, yet still very much alive.

Part of that aliveness was the people. Though his home town was a small town, it was a popular place for both travelers and tourists. They were drawn to the twelfth-century castle, the old stone bridge (part of which had been bombed by the Nazis under the advancing Allies), the Nazi amphitheater across the way (where Hermann Göring had once spoken), the prehistorical Celtic hillfort at the top of the mountain. Except during the winter, the town teemed with a piebald, writhing mass of humans. Some townspeople didn't like it, decrying the "commercialization" and "touristy" characteristics that the town fathers often pursued—and the overwhelming summer crowds.

Salim liked it. He enjoyed watching the dance of pedestrians, bicycles, tiny security drones, carts, robot cleaners, and the occasional driverless vehicle, as they moved and weaved through and among and in and out of the streets and the buildings. It might seem random to most observers, but he saw the patterns. Once, for a school project, he sketched it out, using different colors and thickness of lines to represent the variables. To depict the variations over time, he used vellum layers. He still blushed at the memory of the teacher looking at it, confused, even after he explained it. Which was hard anyway using sign language. He tried it out on his dad later, but he just smiled and said, "That's way beyond my capability."

His dad spoke again. "Salim, I want to run into this store and buy some newspapers before we go to Schafheutle. Today is a very important day. Do you know what it is?"

His dad often tested him like this, for as long as he could remember. Usually, the questions concerned some historical, political, or religious event. Rarely was it a birthday or something personal.

He knew this one. "The 88th anniversary of D-Day when the Allis stormed the beaches at Normandy. It led to the victory over the Nazis and the liberation of the concentration camps."

His father nodded with pride.

They had visited Nürnberg three years ago. Salim wasn't allowed into some parts of the museum and walking tours, but they had a special library for children that told them about the camps. Salim figured it must have been pretty terrible for them to want to keep it from the children. He learned, for the first time in his life, that humans are capable of doing some pretty horrible things to each other and found creative ways to rationalize it.

"I want to get old newspapers," his dad said, "with the front-page stories about the event, and some new ones the commemorations happening in Germany, Poland, and the Czech Republic."

The old store had worn wood floors and walls. The detritus of the ages lay upon it like a dark cloak Salim smelled the mustiness as he scanned the single room filled with wooden racks and shelves, wire racks, and plastic baskets. Each piled with magazines, newspapers, tourist books, with a smattering of toiletry items and a few snack foods. Such a contrast with the glowing screens and wireless purchase stations, which stood like contrasting monoliths casting judgment on their ancient ancestors.

His dad tapped 'search' one of the screens and spoke a few keywords. He scanned through the list of items as Salim looked around.

It was a typical shop carrying cheap items for residents and tourists, though the number of real books and newspapers was a bit unusual. Once, he heard an American call it a "drug store." In German, a "drug store" was a place to buy medicines and drugs—a Drogerie. The incident led Salim to read about the differences between cultures and subcultures. He learned that language differences are sometimes about the peculiarities of history, but sometimes are about a people's worldview and value system.

"Ah!" His father exclaimed. They have a hard copy facsimile of some of these!" He pulled out his tablet and tapped to order.

A woman came out of the back to the counter, and Salim sensed she was irritated at something. When his dad stepped over in front of her, she retrieved the print copies from behind her and dropped them on the counter in silence.

"It's a great day, isn't it?" Salim's father said, as he waved his credit over the payment console.

She tapped a screen on the counter, harder than necessary. "The electronic version are downloading to your device now," she said without looking up.

"Eighty-eight years," his father said. Salim wished he would stop.

She looked up. "It's not a great day. Won't they ever let us forget?"

"Whatever do you mean?"

"It was eighty-eight *years* ago!" Salim examined her more closely. Elderly. Her clothes were worn. Perhaps she was a little girl back then. More likely, it was her parents and grandparents who were involved in some way. Perhaps they were killed. Or maybe they supportive of the Nazi regime until they discovered the truth and were shamed forever. "When will they let us forget those horrible days and move on?" Her mouth trembled slightly. Definitely a personal connection of some sort, thought Salim.

His father drew himself up. "I hope we *never* forget!" Part German, part French, his dad felt like he had a stake in what had happened so many decades ago. His grandmother, as a child, ran in the streets of Paris alongside American tanks; his uncle was a member of the White Rose; and his cousin was a preacher in Germany who renounced the Nazis and was executed for it. "We must remember so it will never happen again. We just let events play out then, and we should have taken control and stopped it!"

"We were not even there! Hitler was an aberration! We cannot change history or fate. Yet Europe wants to rub our noses in it forever!"

"Well," his father said, "*that* attitude is part of what got us there, if you know history."

"I know my own history, young man. The world cut us off and punished us so severely our economy collapsed. Many starved, or were forced to do terrible things to survive—" She paused. *That was it,* thought Salim. Her parents suffered in the aftermath, he'd bet. "What the victors do is never criticized, even though it had the same results. And there was nothing anyone could do. Forces much great than us were at play" She shook her head.

His father often got into such debates—and this was an old one. Usually, he debated with Herr Doktor Weissweich, their next-door neighbor. He'd been a professor at the University, and was the only person Salim ever heard argue both sides of an issue with the same passion. He did so because he believed we have no control over our own biases. "The only thing you *can* control, my friend," he would say to Salim's father, with a wink to Salim, "is to make sure you enjoy good bratwurst and beer!"

His swept up the print newspaper from the counter and headed out, Salim trotting to catch up. The woman muttered, "... punishing us for the sins of our fathers..." as they left.

"What a myopic view of history!" Salim's father said, almost running into a man as they hurried out the door. Dressed in all black, he had a long, thin nose and a very white face. He turned quickly away from his father's wrath.

Salim knew he was young and did not know much. His father believed that even a single person could shape history—and it could just be any regular man or woman—if they thought carefully and acted with honor. Herr Doktor Weissweich disagreed, though whether he actually disagreed or was playing the devil's advocate, Salim did not know. The Doktor often said that "...most political and historical scholars were blind monkeys working in the dark and had no clue how humans affect events." Salim always laughed at that image.

Then Salim's dad would say that he believed that leaders, scientists, politicians, and lawyers had the best interest of all people in mind, and that Hitler and his kind were rare.

"Beware of anything that sounds too good to be true!" Herr Doktor would say, holding a finger in the air, "and especially beware if anyone or any group tells you they are doing anything for the good of others!" Then he would laugh and take a large gulp of beer from his mug.

"Ah, well," his father said, shaking Salim out of his reverie. They had arrived at the café. "Not to let it ruin our outing, right?! Your mom should be here waiting for us."

Salim nodded as they entered. As they stepped onto the patio entranceway, Salim caught a glimpse of the white-faced, beak-nosed man walking behind them, near the corner of the building. Salim tapped his dad's arm, but when they turned back, the man was gone.

Pate
(January 2019)

The restaurant was around the corner, part of the Bowery Hotel, which was much fancier than my usual haunts. The waitress enthusiastically told us that they had the best Eggs Benedict in the city. I ordered two plates of them. Rolf thought I was ordering one for each of us, but I set him straight. I added a side of bacon, wheat toast, orange juice, coffee, and another specialty, lox with a house-made bagel. Rolf had a cup of coffee and a breakfast roll. He watched as I devoured my feast.

"So tell me, Rolf," I said between bites, "How did you find me?"

"Our clients seek people with certain characteristic. They do a wide search of many databases to assemble a list. They hire my company to find you. I did."

"That's not 'how.' That's 'why.'"

"Yes. It took time, because you are homeless. But my company is the best in the world."

"Best Eggs Benedict. Best trackers. This is a day of bests, isn't it, Rolf?"

"We start in San Francisco, we follow your trail until it led us here to find you in New York City and determined you were homeless. So search every shelter every day."

"Thorough. This bacon is excellent. Smoky maple, but something else, too. Not sure what it is. Try one, tell me what you think." I held out a floppy piece.

He shook his head. "No, thank you."

"You said you were 'sent over.' From where?"

"Vienna. My client makes a research project with great funding. They are my exclusive client for this time. If you agree to volunteer, you can learn more about the project, which is secret."

"Volunteer? Secret? Those words make me want to finish eating, tell you to get lost, and go to my hotel. But finish eating first."

"It is not volunteer like charity. You are compensated a large amount. You will never worry for anything again. The project is...they say 'ground-breaking' because it is for many industries, governments, universities, and more. It is worth a lot, so must be kept secret. Non-disclosure agreements for everyone."

"Curiouser and curiouser."

"Pardon me?"

I pushed away the plate, now only surface glistening with a thin coat of hollandaise and egg yolk. I picked up the last piece of bacon. "Let's stop talking around the edges. What is the project and why am I such a perfect specimen?"

He set his cup down and leaned forward, his face coming alive. "I cannot speak of details, because I do not understand many and because I cannot tell you until you agree. The project combines biogenetics, bioengineering, synthetic biology, computer science, and more. It is very exciting and very new."

I was surprised. This had nothing to do with my degree or my experience. "To what end? I thought human genetic engineering was illegal? Wasn't there some big hoopla in China years ago, some guy engineering the DNA of babies?"

"It is not illegal, but restricted by both national and international laws. It is why this project is so important. One of the few that can proceed. It is why so many organizations want to fund it with big money."

"Lots of money."

"Yes. It is as I say."

"Okay. So why me? I know nothing about those areas except computer science. Even so, nothing with biological applications."

"You are not selected for your expertise. You are selected for your biological characteristics."

"Biological characteristics."

"Yes. The project is primarily a medical study. It requires test subjects."

"Test subjects. Like—"

"I will finish, please. The study seeks to learn and increase positive human characteristics. Health, mental, emotional, more. Everything that makes human. You have a unique set of biological characteristics in the twenty areas they seek."

"Ah. So they want to clone me because I am such a specimen of manhood?"

"No cloning. Human cloning is even more restricted than genetic engineering. But not the purpose of this project."

"So what is the purpose?"

"To make better humans."

I shook my head. "Sounds like some bad superhero movie."

"No. You misunderstand me. It is a problem of language. I speak English not as good as you."

"As well."

"Yes, very well."

I shook my head. "Try again."

"Okay." He sat back. "Today, many humans suffer from genetic disease. Or are...easily contract some disease. Some have mental deficient. Some have problem with emotional control. Many things. But some people have less problems. It is all built into the genetic code. I am no expert. But it is to learn from the humans who have the best characteristics, and, using the new technology, to use genetic engineering, biotechnology, nanotechnology, to help everyone be as good.

"Still sounds like Nazi research. And you are from Germany." I knew how rude that was, but I was rather put off. I was hoping someone wanted my skills so that I could contribute what I was good at and enjoy. Not some passive subject for some short test.

He sat back as if I had hit him, and his face flushed.

"I...I do not know why you say that. It is much insulting. How do you know I am from Germany?"

"Your accent."

"I could be from many Baltic countries. But I told you I was from Austria."

"No. You told me you were *sent* from Austria. Your accent is less Austrian and more mainstream German. From the central or northern area, would guess. Also, your specific vocabulary choices and grammar. The food and amount you are eating. The label on the inside of your jacket is from a high-end clothier that is only located in Berlin. None that is definitive, of course, but makes it more likely than not are a German native."

A big grin spread across his face and he nodded. "It is good! This is the example of your genetic characteristics. Your observation skills and ability to analyze." The Nazi insult was apparently forgotten.

"Flattery will get you nowhere. What does the successful end of this project look like?"

"Ach so." He leaned forward. If nothing else, this guy believed in this project and did not seem to be trying to manipulate me. "Genetic modifications, maybe *in vitro* modifications, maybe biological nanotechnology on infants or fetus, maybe modification of bone marrow production DNA. This is what the experiments are for—to find the best way. To someday provide procedure to increase the quality of physical, mental, emotional, and spiritual quality of life."

"Sounds illegal. Or should be."

He looked hurt. "No. If you think it, then you do not understand what I am saying. Perhaps we have a language problem. My English is not best."

"No joke."

"It is not joke. This is how it was explained to me at the beginning. You know how we optimize technology, a computer for instance? We strive to make the best components, out of the best material, to be most efficient and durable, and to work best with all components. Imagine the way to make people like that. Instead of a drug or a surgery to fix problem—disease, genetic flaw—we use advanced medical technology to make better so there is less disease and weakness. It is a simple explanation, but I am not an expert. My expertise is in data analysis and systems research. My company researches and finds the best subjects based on the criteria provided by clients."

"And this is so important, and you are so excited about it, that this project is your only client now?"

"Yes. They pay well. I don't need other clients."

I could not deny that what he was telling me was fascinating. I knew a lot about the technological advances in general, as a related field to my expertise and kept informed. When you are homeless, you can spend a lot of time in the New York Public Library.

"I don't know, Rolf. I see the benefits to medicine. But I can imagine that the processes will only be available to the wealthy. Or those in power. Or that it will eventually fall into the wrong hands."

"Yes, yes, all things that are discussed by the project leaders. I am not part of it, but they have told me—many times again—that it is not to be the way. The primary researcher—Dr. Androvich, an academic—is very insisting on this. It is all his theories, so he directs the projects."

That was encouraging—a primary academic researcher in charge instead of someone from a medical corporation or a government division. I knew full well how those who provide the money can corrupt a worthy and innocent idea.

"Okay. Let's say I agree. What's next?"

"You and I fly to the research center."

"Where is that?"

"I cannot say unless you agree."

"Okay. What happens when I get there?"

"As I understand, they will map and analyze your DNA, and a comprehensive study of your genetic makeup. Tests of mental and physical skills. Psychological testing. If it all makes you a best candidate, then you are accepted into the full program and will learn more about it."

"Let's say I am the best candidate. What's next?"

"You will learn more after. All I know is that your DNA will be subjected to the testing procedures and, depending on the results, used to do some modification *in vitro*."

"Wait wait wait." I said back. "*In vitro*?"

"Yes. You are not the only subject, of course."

"That's not what I am asking. That sounds illegal."

"I tell you it is not. Doctor makes sure we are in compliance."

"Alright, I'll let that go for now. So there is a female subject as well?"

He held my gaze for a moment. "Yes, of course. If the project is to succeed, it cannot only be for males."

"But you said '*in vitro*.' That means you intend to produce a child."

"It is not necessary. It is only one possibility of the project. But we are at the area where I am not qualified to speak—"

"Is there a possibility that this project will produce a child from my DNA?"

"It is a complicated—"

"Stop it. Answer the question."

He looked at me with what I think was pity. "One possible outcome is that offspring will be produced from your modified DNA. Not your DNA directly."

I dropped the piece of toast I was holding onto the plate. It did not have the impact I wanted. I wished I'd been holding a fork. "My offspring."

"In a manner of speaking. A female subject would also undergo the same process, of course. If the result and experiments lead to a believing that *in vitro* is best, more than genetic build or engineering, then it may be so. But not the subjects direct DNA. Modified and even further modified *in vitro*. It is one of the unique processes that Dr. Androvich discovers: to combine natural and synthetic procedures that may be a success that other—"

"So you are going to produce a child from me and this mystery woman?"

"Maybe. But not really your child. Only based on your DNA but changed."

"And who will this child belong to? Who are his legal parents?"

"Mr. Williamson, those are questions I do not know answers. It can all be explained and answers given if you agree. I am only—"

"Out of all the people in the world, you chose me? What are the chances?"

He seemed confused. "Small chances for any given individual in populations, but very high to the people who fit the criteria." He frowned. "I would think you would be intelligent enough to understand that. The probabilities are only high or low in context. From the—"

"Never mind, I get it." I noticed his English got better when we were speaking about his area of expertise.

"But you are the only one. There are many. Some are rejected. Some did not want to spend a year. But part of our research—"

"A year?"

"—is also in life circumstances. More likely to agree. You fit almost all the criteria. After college you followed your friend, Mr. Parmalee, to startup a big company. You were frauded by an international investment group that preys on young, smart, inexperienced people. We know Parmalee had joined them to use your ideas. Very smart ideas, by the way, I say to you. We know your fiancee left you because of it and refuses to talk to you. We know your parents died in a car accident when you were—"

"Enough! I get it." I shook my head. Anyway who understands modern technology knows all the information is out there about us, but when it sits across the table and recites it... "I think you and your people are bastards. Okay. Tell me the bottom line, right now."

"If you are not interested, I pay for breakfast, you go to your hotel, you never hear anything again. If you agree, then we look over the contract. If you sign, we fly to the research facility, where you will undergo procedures and have your questions answered. It will be about a week. Then you decide it you want to continue. For this, you will be paid one million U.S dollars."

My heart lept. "You have got to be kidding."

"It is no kidding, Mr. Williamson. As I say, the results of this project will make rich many biotech, medical, technology, and much more companies rich. It is well-funded. It makes the quality of every other human organization better, businesses, military, education, and so on. And better human lives for everyone.

I was having a hard time holding still. A million dollars? Of course, it could make me un-homeless for the rest of my life. But it could also allow me to start up a company— my way.

Yet it also sounded too good to be true; and there were still questions about moral and ethical issues.

"What if I decide not to continue after the tests, even if I am a good candidate?"

"You keep one million dollars and we fly you back home. If you decide to continue after the first phase, you commit to one year at most, and other payment is made. Considerably more than one million."

"How much is considerably?"

"I cannot say."

"You don't know or you are not allowed to say?"

"I know, but not exact. I am not allowed to say." He leaned forward. "I say you will faint when you see."

I stared at my empty coffee cup. A million dollars would get me out of every mess I am in. Still…

I shook my head. "This is too easy, Rolf. Things that sound too good to be true always are."

"Not always. Only rare."

"Be honest with me. What's the catch?"

He sat back and sighed. He turned and looked around the room, caught the waitresses eye, and motioned for the check. "There is no catch. It is not sweepstakes or lottery ticket. We are not the scam company that ruined your life —I understand you might be worried. This is a business proposition. You have something we need. All involved get rich—researchers change the field of bio-genetics, investors make fortune, the university—"

The waitress placed the bill at his side. "More coffee, gentlemen?"

"No, thank you," Rolf said, without looking up.

"What about the child, Rolf? I mean, it's *my* child. And hers. Whoever she is."

"I say I don't know these details. And it is not the child from your direct DNA."

I didn't like the way this felt. It was so much like what happened before. A man appears out of nowhere, a supposed acquaintance of Parm, offers us riches—just to use my ideas, had a contract, everything above board, all legal. This was exactly like that.

I shook my head. "I was burned once before."

"Is it no? I will go to next candidate and you go back to street."

The abrupt willingness to dismiss me after so much pressure caught me off guard; the reminder of my current situation was manipulative.

A million dollars. For a few tests? It didn't make sense. Some consequences of the program might be immoral or unethical. I was not a bleeding heart—companies are in the business of getting rich. But I did care how they got that way—and what role I might play.

Still, I'm not responsible for other people's bad acts. If they are willing to give me million—

"Mr. Williamson?"

"I don't know. I need some time to think about it. Give me five days." I smiled.

He reached into his pocket and pulled out a wad of cash, extracted a few bills and placed them on the little receipt tray. He stood.

"I have decided you are not a proper candidate. Thank you for your time. Enjoy your hotel." He turned away.

"Wait, wait! Can't I even have twenty-four hours?" I jumped up. He was almost at the door. "Rolf?!"

He left without a glance, leaving me alone with the detritus of breakfast.

Salim
(June 2032)

The room was warm. To Salim, it felt like love. He treasured this room where his family always gathered after dinner to talk about their day, relax, and allow their food to digest. More important, dessert was forthcoming.

His dad had lit the fire, and it was popping and crackling, like a puppy playing with a bouncy toy. The floor and walls reflected the light—old wood, showing the wear and tear of decades of use by his family and many others before. Salim knew that the building, which housed several other apartments, was almost one hundred years old. It had been renovated, additions built, and the new wireless electricity had been installed a couple of years ago, though they'd left the old metal electrical conduits running along the floor and up the walls, for some reason. It all added to the charm of the place for Salim: it was like an old grandfather, all worn and sage—but still well-kept: warm and inviting.

His father was telling his mother about the woman at the store. Salim loved it when they discussed politics and history. His dad was so full of passion and idealism; his mother was just as knowledgeable, but more dispassionate and logical. She was playfully baiting him now, with a little twinkle in her eye.

"But you know, my dear, she has a point. While we should not forget the lesson of the War, we don't have to rehash the people, events, and places associated with it in as way that feels abusive to people today who had nothing to do with it."

His dad leaned forward. "Yes, yes. The Americans say the same about their history of slavery and affirmative action." He adopted a smarmy American accent. "Let me say that we cannot replace the prejudices of our ancestors with a new prejudice of our own. I just want to say that we've just replaced one discrimination with a new one, you know..."

Salim and his mother laughed. His dad continued. "The wrongs of the past must be righted, even if it means the current descendants must suffer a little shame for things they did not cause. It's *that* important!"

"Maybe so," she said. "But how far do you take this noble idea? Shall the Americans pay restitution to the American Indians? What form would it take? Should the English make restitution to the Scots and the Welsh for Longshanks' atrocities? Should Italy offer something to the Jews for the destruction of their Temple in the first century?"

He laughed and sat back in his armchair. Salim loved to hear him laugh. "Now you are being silly. This was a mere eighty-eight years ago."

"But that's what woman was asking: how long? It really is a different question than the one you are answering."

His dad cocked an eyebrow. "And what question am I answering?"

Salim's mom was so insightful and had a way of cutting though convoluted discussions and complex arguments.

She found the core truth. Salim was good at that too and assumed he inherited it from her. He could often see answers or paths of logic before others did, based on less data.

Salim wished Herr Doktor Weissweich was with them now. His work in history and law, he added perspective to these discussions. His dad had passion and breadth of vision, his mom had the calm ability to see all sides, and the Herr Doktor had the benefit of great historical knowledge. Salim always just listened, but if he could speak, he would wish to be like his mom: direct, concise, and insightful, without any rancor or deceit.

His mother stood up and smoothed her dress. "Let's have cake and coffee first, and then I will tell you." Salim clapped his hands. He knew it seemed silly for a twelve-year-old boy to clap like a little kid for cake, but he didn't care. His father had taught him that it was important to celebrate and enjoy the pleasures of life. Besides—it was dessert. His mother smiled at him.

"Yes," said his father, "Kuchen ist das Heilmittel für alles!!" They laughed and went into the kitchen.

Salim knew his view of life was idyllic. He used to wonder if other families had it this good. As he grew older, he realized that his parents orchestrated certain "fairy-tale" events, such as these evenings. There an unspoken rule—though perhaps it was spoken between his parents—no arguments, only expressions of love and support, even in debate. His parents argued sometimes, like others. Sometimes his dad was frustrated with work and a bit irritable. His mom complained of bouts of "the pain" in her legs and arms, and she would take to bed, or go away for a weekend to the baths. But they had amazing control over the general tone and aspects of their life.

And it made Salim happy.

Still, he had questions. Once, when he was ten, his parent went out on a long evening. His babysitter fell asleep, and Salim spent an hour going through drawers, cabinets, and tablets, trying to find documents or pictures of him as a baby. There were none. It seemed strange, but it was a minor aberration in a larger picture that was quite good.

Salim smelled the toasty aroma of coffee and heard the oven door open as his mom took out the cake she had begun making earlier. His dad pulled plates and cups out of the cupboard. Salim went to the pantry and set out napkins and a bowl of sugar cubes.

His mother touched his father on the arm. "Dear, would you take the garbage out to the bins while I get it ready?"

"Of course. My favorite thing." She laughed, he gave her a quick kiss and took up the plastic bag from the bin in the kitchen. Salim heard the front door open and close—a heavy sound that made him feel secure.

Their home was one of many small apartments in a larger building, with similar buildings on each side, stretching the entire block on both sides of the street. The apartment doors of the lower floors opened onto a narrow sidewalk which ran down an equally narrow street. The upper apartments were access through narrow stairways between each of the lower apartments. Salim once saw a show about American homes and he was amazed at the space between them, which was filled with grass, gardens, and fences or walls. And the streets were so wide! It would be scary to live in such an open area, so isolated from one's neighbors. How could one control exit and entry? Anyone could just wander up.

He watched his mom cut neat slices of chocolate cake, each the same size. The aroma of the sweet confection filled the kitchen. Salim breathed deeply through his nose as he watched her heat raspberry sauce in a pan. Once ready, she expertly spooned the viscous liquid over each of the three slices of cake, creating a design that seemed both random and artistic.

Salim poured the coffee into the three mugs and helped her take it to the table. He sat down and picked up his spoon, playing with the raspberry sauce, watching the red, thick liquid drip slowly back onto the plate.

"Don't play with your food, Salim." She looked back towards the door. "What's taking your father so long? Would you go check while I get some napkins?"

Salim nodded and set down his spoon down on the plate, making sure it wouldn't slip and splatter the sauce. In the salon he opened the front door, stepping out into the cool night down the two steps to the sidewalk. He peered up the street where the common trash receptacles were located, about fifty or sixty meters away. He could see dark shapes moving in the late dusk.

As he stepped in that direction, a figure detached itself from the shadows, running towards him, weaving in and out between lampposts and signposts along the sidewalk. At first Salim thought it was his dad, but the person had long hair which bobbed this way and that as he ran. Salim's heart jumped. He turned and ran back inside, colliding with his mom coming to the door.

She grabbed him to keep him from falling.

"What is it, Salim?"

Before he could answer, a commotion outside caused them both to whirl towards the door. A man stood inside the frame, dressed in black, with a scarf about his face. He held a thick pole or bat.

He came at them without hesitation and swung in one smooth motion. Salim ducked aside and fell, heard a crack, and saw his mother go down in a heap. He scrambled to get to his feet, but the man leapt over and pinned him to the ground.

Two other men appeared inside. "Get him bagged and let's get out of here. There's someone walking a dog down the street," one said. He wore a black, hooded coat, and was tall and thin. His nose stuck out of the hood like the beak of a bird.

Two of the men taped Salim's and wrists together. One was quite large, and the smell of alcohol and body odor was pungent. To his shame, he felt a warmth spread between his legs.

"The little bugger pissed himself!"

It didn't matter. Salim knew his dad would come through the door any moment, and with a yell, would beat these men up and save him.

The men flipped him over, his face and cheek pressed into the ground. He was inches away from the back of his mom's head. He watched as a red, viscous liquid below her dark hair stained the floor.

One man, larger than the others, lifted him up as another pulled a cloth bag over his head and down to his legs. The big man hoisted him into the air and slung him over his back—jostling as he walked. The man's shoulder dug into Salim's stomach. His fear did not keep part of his mind from observing that they turned right, towards the trash receptacles.

Right towards his dad. Perfect.

After a moment of jouncing, Salim heard the doors of a vehicle open and he gasped as he was tossed onto a hard surface.

One man spoke. "What do we do with *him*?"

"Leave him by the bins. Someone will find him in the morning. Requiescat in pace."

Eris
(January 2019)

She sat, reading her book, ignoring the other patients. A little boy was attempting to get the attention of his mother by reaching out and pinching her leg every few moments, but his mother never looked up from her magazine. Eventually the boy gave up and sat on the floor, tearing the pages of another magazine into tiny pieces, which he placed in a piled under his mother's chair.

The office door opened, "Eris? She's ready for you."

She tucked the book into her backpack and followed the receptionist through the narrow hallway to a door on the far left. She could have found it on her own, having been here so many times during so many years.

As she entered, Doctor Petty came around from her desk to take her hands. "Eris, how are you feeling today?"

She always said that at the beginning. Not, "How are you thinking?" Only, "How are you feeling?" How many sessions had they had? It had to be hundreds.

"I'm doing well, Doctor."

"Have a seat. I understand you told the receptionist that this is your last appointment?"

Eris sat on the couch, with its throw pillows and stuffed animals. Memories from a decade ago flooding her mind. *Pretend the bunny is your dad. What would you say, Eris?*

"Yes, that's correct."

"Well, I cannot say I am surprised. You are doing quite well, and have made excellent progress, especially in the last two years. The nightmares are gone—or mostly. You believe your life is worthwhile, that you have something to offer, and you have completed a major step by finishing your master's degree. I agree you don't need regular visits. Of course, you can always make an appointment if you need to, even just to check in."

Eris picked up a pillow beside her and held it on her lap. "Yes, I know."

"How did the job interview go? Did you feel good about your demeanor? Did the practice sessions help?"

"Oh, yes. I felt comfortable, qualified, and confident."

"Excellent! When will you find out?"

"I already did. The answer was no."

The doctor looked surprised, then concerned. "Oh, I'm sorry, my dear. That must have been a blow after all your preparation."

Eris shook her head. "No, I'm fine. They went with a more experienced candidate. That's no reflection on me."

The doctor raised her eyebrows. "That's exactly right. A healthy attitude." She seemed a bit surprised. Eris imagined rolling her eyes at her. *I'm an adult now, not a little girl suffering a trauma.* "Well, then, what's the next step for you?"

"That's part of the reason that this is the last session. I am moving to Vienna."

"Vienna? That's a long way. Do you know anyone there?" She leaned forward, as if to hear the answer more clearly.

"No. But I have a job. Not exactly a job. It's a study that pays quite well."

"A study? Like a psychological study?

"Yes, but this is a biological testing program. It has to do with genetics."

"I see. But it pays?"

"It pays very well. It will set me up for life."

The doctor opened her mouth then closed it. "Eris, I—"

"Doctor, I know how that sounds, but I've researched it vigorously. It's legit. It's a prestigious research program at the University of Vienna, deeply funded by corporate and government interests. The scientist in charge is considered *the* expert in the specific field. My genetic makeup is exactly that they are looking for."

Doctor Petty smiled. "Of course. Sometimes I forget you are not that scared, withdrawn girl—"

"I know you do."

"—but you have always been the brightest and most resourceful patient I have ever had." Eris nodded at the compliment—knowing it was not mere flattery. "I do worry about you leaving your friends and community here, to a new place where you know no one, and—"

"Doctor, you know I have no real friends here. The last of my family died when Gramma passed ten years ago. I have acquaintances, and I can make those just as easily in Vienna as here."

The doctor paused. "True, but I must voice my concern that you know well. People need more than just acquaintances. We need intimacy, we need—"

"I know. We need intimacy, trust, loyalty, and deep human connection." The doctor smiled at her own words parroted back. "As I have said, I am not avoiding that. I am not afraid of it. I would even like it. But this place...this was the place of my healing, my education, my preparation to go out and be an adult. I'm ready to go out and make that start. I need to get away from here, if I ever am to find those things."

Doctor Petty nodded, smiling. "That makes sense. I hope you find a community that's right for you."

"So do I, doctor. If not there, somewhere else. But I need to take control of my life. And I am doing it."

After a few more niceties, she took her leave of the doctor for the last time. She even hugged her before leaving the office.

Pate
(January 2019)

"Hey. Wake up."

Why won't the world leave me in peace? I peered out from behind the fresh clean blanket drawn up to my eyes. It was the kid again.

"Some guy here to see you. I can't let him come back here—you have to go out front."

"Police?" Shouldn't be. All my legal troubles were civil—that's what happens when you choose the wrong business associates. They don't imprison you for violating business codes, they just take all your money and assets.

"Not police. This guy's dressed really good, looks rich. Drove up in a Bentley."

I snorted. "He's got the wrong guy."

"No, he asked for you by name. Maybe a long-lost relative. Or you won the lottery!" Big grin. "Gotta stay positive and show up!"

I stared at the naïve child for a moment, then slid past him into the hallway.

He *was* impeccably dressed, a stark contract to the shabby reception room, holding sunglasses in one hand and a cell phone in the other. He looked foreign, though I am not sure why I thought so.

He looked down at his phone and back up at me. "Pate Williamson." It wasn't a question. German accent?

"Yes? Who are you?"

He smiled. "I am here to change your life."

I turned around to the kid who had followed me out. "When's breakfast?"

The man was suddenly beside me, holding my arm. "I am sorry, I did not mean to be...what is the word...'flippant.' I have been a long time looking for you. My employers know you and what you have been happening, and they have an offer. Will you listen? Only listen?"

I looked into his eyes. He seemed sincere. Might even be telling the truth. But that's what I'd thought about our investors, too.

He held out his hand. "We start again. I am Rolf. Please accept an apology, I should not joke and consider what you have experienced. I was only trying to break ice."

"Break the ice," I corrected.

=He smiled. "Break ice, yes. Hear me explain. Allow me to feed you breakfast. There is an excellent diner down the street."

"How does your employees know me? And how the hell did you find me?"

He nodded. "I understand the hesitation. My employer is large organization. Funds university and private sector re-searchers, quite generous. You may be suspicious because of the past, but this is legal and genuine."

So he *did* know what had happened to me. My spidey-senses were active. "Can you prove it, Rolf?"

"'What can be shown cannot be said.'"

"Excuse me?"

"Wittgenstein."

"I studied technology and business, not philosophy."

He reached into his suit pocket and extracted a card from a leather wallet. I took it from him. High quality card stock, professional design, clean printing. It cost a a lot, not the stuff of scams, though it did not have much information.

Rolf Sadler, Leiter der Untersuchungen
Österreich Untersuchungstechnologien, GmbH
Wein: +43 7242-95030
Deutschland: +49 089/12345-123
United Kingdom: +44 (020) 774-0001
United States: +01 132-726-0594

An investigative agency from Europe. The word 'investigation" made my stomach tighten. How did he find me *here*? I didn't even know I was coming here until the middle of the night.

Still, I doubted he was here in a Bentley to kidnap me for my organs.

I stuck the card in my pocket. "You buy me breakfast. I hear you out. What if I just want to walk away?"

He shrugged. "I find someone else. My employers want *you*. But neither of us can make you. It is your choice."

"All right. Still have my concerns. Tell you what: you buy breakfast *and* a hotel room for a week. Nice hotel. With no guarantees."

His eyes narrowed. "Three nights."

"Five."

He nodded. "Okay. You navigate hard bargain." He laughed.

"Drive."

"Yes, I drive. We go now."

I rolled my eyes. "Fine. Hotel check-in first, then break-fast. Not letting you scam me out of this."

"We have a deal, Mr. Williamson."

Salim
(June 2032)

The van bumped and jostled as it made its way through the narrow streets. Salim felt as if he were in a dream—strangely calm after his brief bout of crying. It felt as if, at any moment, something would make sense of it all. It was as if he was supposed to be *doing* something.

He realized that he'd been subconsciously keeping track of their progress. Apparently one of the men was actually driving instead of using the AI, which was strange, but made it easier to envision each turn, how far they went before turning again. Humans drive less smooth than AIs. *Now we're at the light at Neckarstaden. Right on Rohrbacherstraße. Just passed Bizmarkplatz. The van turned onto Kurfürsten-Anlage. Towards the train station.*

No turns for a bit. His mind began to wander. The man had said, "Leave him by the bins, someone will find him in the morning." That had to be about his dad. Salim's lip trembled. Salim didn't need to recall the year of Latin he had to know what the phrase the man uttered meant.

He couldn't be dead.

Then he thought of his mom lying in a pool of blood. He shook his head and focused back on his current circumstances. The vehicle had been stopped for a while, probably at Römerstraße right before the roundabout. If they went straight, they were likely bound for the train station. He'd know for sure at Mittenmaierstraße. Left or right, to the major freeways out of town. Straight, it was the train station. Salim could heard traffic and crowd noises, and the van engine idling. The men up front had not spoken.

His dad said kidnapping happened all the time in America, because it was a land of lawless and violent people. But they were rare here. (His Dad also said that America passed so many laws every day that eventually everyone would be in prison. Salim wondered how it could be both lawless and stifled by laws.)

A cold sweat made him shiver. Were they going to kill him, too? Probably not—otherwise why kidnap him? Cold sweat beaded up on his skin. Were they going to take him away and kill him? And if they wanted something from his parents, they would have taken it. Or kidnapped them. Was it a child trafficking ring?

It made no sense. He and his parents were ordinary, plain, unremarkable people. Sometimes his dad joked about how they were invisible.

He began working through the facts he had. Part of his mind knew that his penchant analysis and cold reason was a way to keep distracted and calm. It also gave him courage, because he knew he was good at it. He would observe, listen, and evaluate. There would be an opportunity to escape. People always underestimated him.

He heard voices now from the three men up front, but it was just a mumble with the van noise and the bag he inhabited. The fat one was driving. He was not sure how he knew that. Sometimes he just knew things.

He turned his attention back to his body. The bag was not tied shut. He could wriggle out. His wrists were taped. Perhaps he could rip the tape on something sharp in the van.

He twisted his hands back and forth. The tape was made of cloth, flexible and not too sticky. As he did so, the fibers of the fabric stretched. He continued the motion until it was loose enough to pull one hand out and then the other.

Were there handles on the inside the van? This was an old van, perhaps not even retrofitted for self-driving.

As he wriggled, the van slowed again and stopped. Salim used the momentum and the noise to push with his feet and slide out of the bag.

The van was bare inside, and dark, with only a little illumination streaming in through two small side windows It was a cargo van. He squinted at the back door. At the bottom of each was a lever.

The van jerked to a stop again. Mittenmaierstraße, for sure. Now he'd know where they were going. After a short wait, the van drove straight ahead—towards the train station. Unless he'd missed a turn. But he was sure he hadn't.

Why a train? Why so public if this was something sinister?

Salim thought ahead. Hands out, leap to the door, open both levers (in case one was a stationary door), and jump out. Of a moving vehicle? No. They'd be stopped soon, anyway. He'd have to wait.

The car swerved to the right and squealed to a halt. He grabbed the bag and pulled it over his head. The engine stopped. They were at the Hauptbahnhoff. He could hear the kidnappers better now with the engine off.

"You stay here. We'll go inside and find Pablo. We'll come back and get him once we have the tickets." Salim replayed the voices from earlier. It was the man with the big nose, telling the fat driver to stay.

Doors opened and slammed. It was too quiet to open the doors. What now?

A door opened then slammed shut. Silence. The driver had gotten out. To smoke a cigarette? To watch and guard? This might be his chance.

He wriggled out of the bag, but before he could make a move, the door it opened.

 The fat man stopped and stared. "How…" He shook his head. "No matter." He reached in and pulled Salim out, to set him on the ground. The man leaned down into his face. Salim estimated he was in his 40s. Scars on his face. Clear blue eyes. Rather kind-looking. "This will be confusing to you, but I don't have time to explain. Do as I say if you want to escape. Go into the train station. Don't run, don't draw attention to yourself. Keep with a crowd. Get on a train—any train that is not heading towards Frankfurt. You got money?"

Salim blinked. What was going on?

"Kid! Focus! Do you have money?!"

Salim nodded. He didn't have money, but he knew how to ride trains without paying, like most boys his age.

"Don't go to Frankfurt, don't come back here. This is more important than you can imagine. Go!" Without waiting, the man turned and ran down the street, away from the station.

Salim hesitated. Why couldnt' he just go back home? He looked back down Kurfürsten-Anlage towards the old town. Why trust a kidnapper?

Because the likely explanation was that the man was not a kidnapper, but a mole. At least he had his own—or someone else's—agenda. The "why" and "who" were unknown, but irrelevant at the moment.

Salim headed to the entrance, finding knots of people to walk close behind or beside. He kept his eyes on the entrance, watching for the other two men. If they came out, he'd have to move—without drawing attention—to put crowd members between him and them.

It was good luck that it was a busy night. Cars, vans, and taxis were pulling in and out, parked vehicles with travelers and taxi-drivers unloading luggage, while a steady stream of people flowed in and out of the station. A tour group of about twenty filed out of a bus. Salim found his way over to a family of five. A little girl struggled with her rolling bag.

"Excuse me, may I help?" He said, nodding to the parents and taking the suitcase.

"Thank you, very kind of you, young man," the mother said. The father gave him a nod. They entered through the large doors, with letters above proclaiming "Hauptbahnhof." His dad always liked to say that it was the only Bahnhof in town—of course it was the Haupt! He said it every time they came. Salim smiled at the thought, then felt a pang of pain.

Inside, a mass of people were moving and weaving through the walkways. Vendor stands dotted the concourse, sitting like rocks in the middle of a river of people.

His adopted family halted just inside to scan the large trains schedule board mounted high above and across from the entrance. They seemed befuddled by the occasional clacking and flipping of the numbers and the letters on the board, as trains left, arrived, or—rare in Germany— late.

Where should he go? He'd been to Strassbourg the most of any other town—his parents had friends there. He had an aunt in Hamburg, but he'd never been there. He'd only met her once, when he was little. All he remembered was that she had a French accent when she spoke German. He didn't even remember what she looked like or her name.

As he looked down the station, he spotted the two kidnappers passing in front of the ticket booths, with a third man now accompanying them. They were fumbling with papers and talking. He moved over behind and beside the little girl, next to the mother, keeping his eyes on the men. They turned towards the entrance, peering here and there. Their eyes passed over him without a hint of suspicious or recognition. People are not too observant when they expect things to be a certain way.

He didn't have much time. When they got back to the van and discovered him missing, they'd come after him. Would they search inside the station, or assume he'd left the area? If it was him, he'd split up three ways—one to the station, the other two in the most likely directions.

He set down the suitcase. "Have a nice trip." Trying not to run, he moved towards the platforms. Faint "Thank you's" floated after him.

He passed through the arch into the platform area: a wide, elevated walkway with glass walls on both sides which crossed perpendicular to the twelve tracks underneath. Stairs provided access down to each of the twelve.

He walked near the stairs, looking down at the signs. The first three were headed north: "Mannheim-Frankfurt," "Mannheim-Mainz-Düsseldorf," and "Frankfurt-Leipzig."

He glanced back and was surprised to see one of the men, just crossing under the arch, walking and scanning the crowd, some sort of communication device in his hand.

They'd split up, obviously. He needed to get below before he spotted him and alerted the others.

He took the next stairway and saw the train was already waiting. Excellent. The sign read Baden-Baden-Stuttgart. Leaving in three minutes.

He took the stairs two at a time, slowing as he hit the platform, dashing through the thinner crowd outside the cars, up through the first door of the passenger car, then made his way back, stopping at the far end of the third car, where the luggage racks and bathroom were located. He could duck into the bathroom when he saw the conductor enter the car at the front. He took a seat near the racks on the aisle, away from the window.

He was fortunate to have found a train going south that was ready to leave. If he'd had to wait ten or fifteen minutes, they'd surely have caught him. Once underway, they would have no way of knowing which train he took. Or if he had even gotten on a train.

Three minutes seemed like ten, but the alarm sounded, the door closed, and with a puff and a whoosh, the train lurched forward. Salim watched the platform flow by and disappear. Baden-Baden was about a thirty-minute trip. All he had to do was stay out of the way of the conductor. Once there he could decide where to go.

The door behind the racks whooshed open. Before he could turn and look, someone grabbed his arm.

"Don't move." He looked up into a pale face and beak nose.

PRODUCTION

January 2019

I didn't bother to check out. Though Rolf had paid for my stay, and I had no money, I had ordered room service that morning. What were they going to do about it? I walked through the buffet as I left to grab more food and stuff in my pockets. I wrapped the rest of my stash in the blanket

I was still angry that Rolf wouldn't let me have some time to think about his proposal.

"Mr. Pate?"

Hotel staff. Envelope in hand. Uh oh.

"Yes?"

"This was left at the desk when you checked in, with instructions to give it to you when you left."

"How did you know I was leaving?"

"I...was watching..." she became a bit awkward. "...the instructions said you might try to leave without checking out, but that you'd eat breakfast."

I laughed without humor and opened the envelope. Five $20 bills. "No letter or note?"

"Only the sealed envelope and instructions."

"Thank you." Must be Rolf. Nice of him, I guess. Above and beyond. I'm still angry, though.

I stuck the money in my pocket, refilled my coffee cup, adjusted the blanket around my shoulders, and said good-bye to my brief home.

π

I forced my eyes open. They hurt.

Florescent lights. Beeping sounds. Soreness and pain in my face and neck. Arm. Ribs. Pretty much all of me.

Hospital room. How did I get here?

"Are you awake?"

A nurse. Large, sweet-looking face. Antiseptic.

"Yes." Croak. Dry throat. "How did I get here?"

"You were brought by ambulance. You got beat up pretty bad."

Flashes. Sleeping in an alley. So cold. Yelling. Faces, yelling, grabbing. Pain.

Four or five guys. Punching, kicking.

"Where?"

"I don't know. A police officer is on his way to interview you."

I nodded. "How bad?"

She smiled. "Severe, but nothing permanent. Three broken ribs, cracked collarbone, contusions. Scrapes on the face and head. One head wound required fifteen stitches. Possible concussion, but tests were inconclusive. We'll want to do some more tests now that you're awake."

I nodded, then grimaced at the pain. "How long?"

"How long have you been here? They brought you in last night. It's three in the afternoon now."

"What hospital?"

"New York-Presbyterian in Lower Manhattan." She smiled again. "You had no ID."

"No. Homeless."

"We figured. I'm afraid you'll have to leave tomorrow morning, unless you exhibit severe concussion symptoms. Then we are allowed to keep you longer. The closest shelter is on East Third, about a mile and a half, if you have nowhere else."

"Thank you."

"Do you need anything at the moment?"

"Thirsty."

"I'll get you some orange juice and order something to eat, you should be hungry. I'll send the police officer in when he arrives, if that's okay."

I couldn't tell the officer much about the men who attacked me. He acted as if I was wasting his time. If you are going to get beat up, at least give some evidence of the perpetrators. Otherwise don't bother, I suppose.

"Anything else you can tell me? Any idea *why* they would attack you."

"No. I can't think of any reason. Other than the fact that I was homeless and outside at night. Maybe they thought I had booze or drugs."

He shook his head. "No. Doesn't fit the modus operandus. Did you have anything of value on you?"

I shook my head, both to his question and the misuse of Latin. "Oh—wait. I did have $100 in cash."

"Well that might have been something to tell me up front. Probably a simple robbery. Happens all the time."

"Is the $100 gone?"

"I'm sure it is. Anything else you can think of?"

I shook my head. He left and I buzzed the nurse.

"Yes?"

"What belongings did I have when I came in?"

She turned to a little cabinet. "Everything is in here. Do you wish to look?"

"Yes, please."

She pulled two large plastic bags out of the cabinet and opened one. "A blanket. Rather nasty—I can provide a new one for you to take with you." She set it aside and opened the second bag. "A blue and white checkered shirt; khaki pants, pair of Nike sneakers."

"Anything in the pockets?"

She fumbled with the pants. "No—wait. A business card. Nothing else."

"I had $100 in twenties. Nothing?"

"No. I will check the log, though. Sometimes we put valuables in a safe. But usually there is a receipt inside the bags."

"I'm sure it's gone."

At least I get a new blanket.

π

I left the employment office and pulled my blanket tight around my shoulders. Another cold night. My last in the hotel. It had been a wonderful reprieve and included a continental breakfast in the dining room. I had been filling my pockets with extra food to store in the room for when I left. Plan contingencies.

Beyond that, it had not been a good four days. This was my second trip to the employment office, both unproductive. People were hiring, but I was over-qualified for anything they had. And the places that needed my skills wouldn't hire me because of my company's public disaster.

I had even gone to the recruitment office. They said I was a prime candidate age-wise, so I took the physical, but my history with a concussion and a hernia surgery disqualified me. Not forever, perhaps. They told me to come back in six months.

There had to be something out there. Somewhere. I was smart, educated, and hard-working. Perhaps I should leave New York. Some place warmer would be nice. Fly south for the winter. Actually, I'd have to hitchhike—but that was how I got here from San Francisco.

Maybe I should go back there. To the university. People still knew me.

As I approached the hotel, I pulled the blanket from my shoulders, folded it, and tucked it under my arm. The hotel staff didn't like their guests walking through their lobby looking homeless. I stepped inside and strode across the large lobby.

A man intercepted me halfway across from the lounge area. I moved to allow him to pass, but he stopped.

"Pate Williamson?"

Oh, no. I turned. Big man. Dressed in jeans, black t-shirt, thick leather jacket. "Yes?"

He handed me an envelope. Instinctively, I reached out and took it, then was immediately sorry. "Ugh."

"Yes." He smiled. "Thank you." He turned and exited through the front doors.

I stared at the envelope in my hand. I didn't know what the subpoena was for, but I could guess. Of course, I *had* no records left, or no access to them. But they could get to me testify. Incriminate myself, even though I was the one scammed. You're still an accomplice, even if unwitting. Well, mostly unwitting. I got caught up in the headiness of success, and I didn't want to know the details.

What's the worst that could happen? Huge money judgement? Probably. Never being able to start a business again? In that field, most likely. Perhaps not being hired for any serious jobs—after all, accomplices to fraud, embezzlement, and unfair business practices rarely garnered the interest of employers.

I went to my room and opened the envelope. It was as bad as I thought, with a few extra baddies thrown in that I hadn't considered.

π

I stepped out of the hospital into a blizzard. Perhaps not a blizzard in meteorological terms, but it sure felt like one standing in it. High winds, snow, biting cold. I hesitated on the step just above the sidewalk level. Cars, with windshield wipers going, crept along like metal varmints stalking prey. People walked on both sides of the street, like staggering pillars wrapped in cloth, arms hugging themselves, leaning into or back against the wind.

The homeless shelter was over a mile away, and little piles of snow sat on the blanket over my shoulders. The wind cut through the cheap blanket and my flannel as if they were sieves.

I went back inside the hospital lobby.

"Can I use your phone?"

"Yes, there is a payphone through there."

"I don't have any money. I just checked out of here because I was attacked on the streets. Can I use your phone?"

"Hang on." She reached down and pulled a jar filled with coins and ladled a few out. "Take a few more—you'll need some warm coffee out there."

"Thank you."

I took the card out of my pocket and set it on the little ledge below the payphone. I called the U.S. number.

"Guten Tag, Österreich Untersuchungstechnologien. Wie kann ich dir helfen?"

"Do you speak English?"

"Yes. How may I help you?"

"May I speak with Rolf, please?"

"Rolf Sadler?"

"Is there another Rolf?"

"No."

"Then yes, Rolf Sadler."

The phone rang, made a funny beeping sound, then rang again with a different cadence. Click.

"Rolf."

"Rolf, this is Pate Williamson. Please reconsider. I'm all in. I'll do anything."

"No, Mr. Williamson. You had your chance."

"Please. I'm begging. I have nothing else. Nowhere to go."

Silence. Then, "Where are you now?"

"At a hospital. I was attacked."

"That is unfortunate."

"Look, I'll take half the money. Hell, I'll do it for room and board."

"Do not promise what you regret later. No free subjects. I will pick you up in ten minutes. Make that fifteen. It's really bad out there."

I hung up and realized that I had not told him which hospital I was in.

January 2019

Once seated in Business Class on a departing flight from New York, I asked Rolf questions about where we were going in Vienna. His answer to each was, "When we get there, you will have all your questions answered."

I had better luck asking the steward for a blanket. My wounds made it difficult to get comfortable, but I took one of the Percocet given to me by the hospital and slept most of the nine-hour flight to the Wien-Flughafen airport.

I had never visited Vienna, though I had traveled throughout Europe in the summer after my sophomore year at college. The city was charming and felt a bit like a dream. The concourse with German signs, German architecture, and German cars. Or, rather, Austrian. I learned that even though the inhabitants spoke German, ate German food, lived in German architecture, and acted German, they are not German, and will remind you of that fact.

Rolf took exception to my line of thinking when I mentioned it to him. "It is racist. You would say Chinese look the same."

"It's nothing like that. And that's not racism, anyway. Wrong word."

"English is difficult. Austrians are not German."

"I think history would beg to differ."

"Prepare to get beat again during your visit, then. Different food, different language, it is different everything."

"I didn't know Viennese were so violent."

"No. Quite peaceful. It was a figure of speech."

"That's not the right phrase. It's—"

"Silence, Pate. I like you better as a homeless man."

Neither of us had luggage (I didn't even have a carry-on), so we made our way with speed through customs and onto the concourse. We passed a McDonald's and Rolf, while expressing disgust, agreed to buy me a coffee and breakfast sandwich.

"I don't see how people eat them."

"'It.' Eat 'it.'"

He made me walk while I ate. After a twenty-minute walk, we arrived at "Parkhaus 4," where a car with a driver waited.

"Why didn't he just pick us up outside the concourse?"

"Those were not his instructions."

The drive was close to forty-five minutes, north-north-west as near as I could tell. The driver told the car something-something "Arbeitsgebäude." My guess was the University of Vienna, which I knew was a center of research into innovative technology with a large medical university nearby. I wasn't even sure why I knew that—must have picked it up along the way somewhere. I had learned to trust what was stored in my mind, even if I didn't recall the source. It has always proved reliable.

"Can I sleep when I get there, Rolf? I've had a rough couple of days."

"Not probably." He fished in his bag and pulled out a packet. "Eat this, it will help."

I unwrapped it. "What is this? An energy bar?"

He laughed. "No. Much better. Banana bread."

"Banana bread will make me sleep."

"Not this banana bread. Made from eggs laid by genetically modified chickens. Contains medical compounds to combat fatigue, boost immune system, and increase metabolism. Best cure of hangover in the world."

"I've never heard of such a thing."

"It is not for purchase."

"People would pay a lot of money for—" I stopped. He grinned at me.

Twenty minutes later, I felt as if I had slept for eight hours and eaten a healthy meal. Even my injuries were less bothersome. I would not give Rolf the satisfaction of letting him know, however.

"Can you tell me anything about what will happen when we arrive?"

"You will meet with senior researchers and administrator. They will explain to you and answer questions. But first medical examination. It will leave you wishing you were back in an alley of New York." He looked over at me and smiled.

"You have an excellent bedside manner. Have you ever slept in an alley in New York in January?"

"No."

"Then you have *no* idea what I can endure."

π

When we arrived, they whisked me off to a medical lab. Rolf wasn't far off about me wishing I was back in an alley in New York. I cannot imagine that astronauts get a more thorough assessment in one day. Three hours of extensive examinations, some of it expected, but also some unrecognizable instruments and intrusive prodding that was not only painful but embarrassing. But I would not flinch. I'm a rich man now. Or will be soon.

When the lab technician and doctor finished the final test, I stood up. "That was it?"

The doctor peered at me over his glasses. "That was just the initial assessment. Much more to come."

I followed an attendant to a large conference room. He sat with me, silent and unresponsive to my questions while others began to enter one at a time and in groups. It was a diverse crew: men and woman in suits, others in lab coats, still others dressed in business casual, and two dressed like they had just come from the gym. Ages ranged from thirties to seventies, I guessed.

A woman approached about halfway through the room-filling process. "Pate Williamson? I'll be guiding you through this process for the next week or so, and, if you pass, the next year." A light French accent. Light, angular features. She appeared to be in her late 30s. Dark hair in a no-nonsense bob.

I nodded. "Okay. And you are?"

"You can call me 'Director.'"

I purse my lips. I'm not a fan of affectations. But the money reminded me not to care.

She took a seat beside me. "You've had a brief physical. We don't expect any complications, we have a pretty good basic workup on you from accessible databases, anyway. This meeting is with the primary staff to acquaint you with the process and answer questions. Then we'll get to it."

I scanned the gathering. Twenty-two people. Twelve men and ten women. More than half had to be over sixty years old. Two-thirds plus one had folders or notebooks in front of them. A silver-haired man at the far end, dressed in an elegant suit, caught my attention. His demeanor said he was in charge. People were avoiding looking at him. No nonsense. Little emotion. Doesn't suffer fools. By the ring on his finger, he was married.

Poor woman.

A man got up and shut the door, and the silver-haired man looked at me for the first time.

"Welcome, Mr. Williamson. Thank you for joining our project. This meeting is to orient you to the project and answer questions. Dr. Androvich will begin." He waved toward an elderly man to my left, seated about halfway down the table. White lab coat. Reading glasses on a thin chain around his neck. A pile of tidy papers and folders in front of him.

A Russian name, confirmed as he began to speak. But the accent, his ease of use with the English language, and his idioms revealed he did not grow up in Russia. An Eastern Block country, perhaps, with immigrant parents or at least in a Russian community but around a lot of English-speakers.

He welcomed me warmly, used my name, and smiled a lot. But when he began talking about the project—he called it "Project Pacem"—he became the college science professor that most students tried to avoid taking. Overly detailed, far too many side trips, a pacing and structure of sentences that made the flow of thought difficult to follow, and far too much technical jargon for an introduction. He was enthusiastic, though. Embarrassingly so. Occasionally, the man to his right would tap his arm, as if they had a pre-arrangement. Dr. Androvich would pause and then return to the main road he left behind in his excited wanderings.

The content was fascinating, however. He began by describing his original doctoral work in genetics and bio-engineering as a means to create a DNA-level cure for some disease I never heard of, peppered with asides about the administration not understanding the importance of his research, and his frustration with the narrowly focused research of his doctoral colleagues and the university researchers. His post-doctoral work frustrated him, too, because he was pigeon-holed into existing research paths at his first university post. A brief stint with a biogenetics and biopharmaceutical company gave him helpful experience and brought him into contact with molecular virologists, bio-engineers, nanotechnology experts, and synthetic biologists. They gained use of a CRISPR VI. *This* would lead to the formation of a working research team at his second university position, where he became a full professor. That, in turn, allowed him to begin Project Pacem.

My mind wandered as he continued on about how the project grew and began to attract supports. I found myself curious—both in the subject and at how the people here allowed him to start with a personal history summation. Did any of this matter for what they wanted me for? I couldn't see how.

I was brought back into the moment when he paused and raised his hand into the air with a flair of the dramatic.

"And it was *then*, my dear Mr. Williamson, in the middle of Dr. Brighton's presentation, that I realized we had become so *enamored* with the possibilities of technology we had forgotten—what? What do you think we forgot?" He smiled, eyes bright and expectant. I felt like a student in that professor's class again.

"I would not presume to guess, doctor. Please enlighten me."

"Ah! The simplest answers are sometimes the most difficult to see, yes? Especially for academics! The experts! We are so myopic—yes?—that we do not see what a beginner might notice at the first! I had been railing against the narrowness of academics, and I was guilty myself! I had not stepped back far enough!"

I wondered if he would enlighten me or not. I had to pee.

"Nature!" He shouted. One woman farther down the table stifled a snicker. Others looked amused; others irritated.

"Nature?" I said.

"Yes, of course! Nature!" He leaned forward. "There we were, trying to invent it all from the beginning. Making a cake from scratch! But nature has been working on projects like this for millennia!"

I nodded, wishing I shared his enthusiasm. I didn't even know what he was talking about.

"So. We go back to the drawing board of the Project and think bigger. No, not bigger. Broader. What if we use *everything* at our disposal? All the sciences, all the technology, but also what nature has already done. Historical natural research. It was a light coming on for us. Within a year we had remapped the entire project—a wonderful interaction of many specialties and specialists and more and more—"

The man beside him touched his arm and whispered something in his ear. Dr. Androvich nodded and turned back to me. "But you want to know *to what end*? And what is your role?"

I nodded. Finally.

"Our goal—and we are so close—is to help humans become more healthy, make better decisions, be emotionally sound, free of terrible diseases. Supplements, vaccines, direct DNA modification, nanometer-level biological machines...well, the list goes on. The basic starting point to do all this is, ideally, the creation of a human embryo. A—"

"Not *creation*, Doctor." A firm but intense interjection from the silver-haired man at the end of the table.

The doctor waved his hand. "Yes, yes." I sensed this was an ongoing argument between the two. He looked at me and winked. "The administrators are so worried about terminology. But is there not a natural connection with this and birth the creation of a human? After all—"

"Doctor."

"Yes, yes, my apologies. Mr. Williamson, we are not creating a human. We begin with a male and female—just like God did, yes?—or Nature, if you prefer—choosing candidates that are exceptional in many of our desired characteristics. We work with them, making them even better with our advances. Nature has already produced some better than others in these areas. So we pick up and continue nature's work! Just like all academics do with previous research! A child produced by our subjects will have those exceptional characteristics. Then, we engage in *in vitro* engineering, using bio-bots, at the nano level, we alter musculature, organ tissue, DNA, and even synaptic connections. We can alter the diffusions of the neurotransmitters, edit myofibrils and myofilaments and how they connect with the motor end plates, we can—"

"Dr. Androvich, please. Mr. Williamson has a lot do to today. Can you sum up?" The silver-haired man again.

"Ah, yes, well, my apologies, Mr. Powell. Again."

These two men did not like each other. But I was shocked at what I was hearing. Rolf had said there was a *possibility* of *in vitro* fertilization. What Androvich just said not "a possibility." I'd be having a baby with a woman. Without intimacy, of course, but still. A child. Who would be genetically modified in the womb.

"They are asking me for the elevator speech, Mr. Williamson." He winked as if we shared a private joke. He adjusted his glasses. "I have practiced it, but it is quite difficult and far too inelegant and inaccurate." He took a deep breath. "Essentially, my theories—the result of decades of research and experiments—if proved sound, will produce technologies, medicines, and biotechnologies that will result in a significant leap in the fields of cognitive, physical, and psychological abilities. We can cure diseases and genetic errors, but also eradicate them, as well as increase the efficiency and durability of every characteristic of a human. This will benefit all humanity—help the First World become better, fairer, more efficient. But will also enable the Third World to do away with many of the things that hold them back. These advancements will not only make humans healthier and more durable, but also happier, more productive, and lead to a just and efficient world." He looked around the table, beaming. I wondered if he knew the purpose of punctuation.

Mr. Powell cleared his throat. "Thank you, doctor. Mr. Williamson, this theory is now being put into practice in our first tests. We require two select humans with specific cognitive, physical, and psychological characteristics, who will be subjected to a variety of procedures. Once completed, *in vitro* fertilization will produce a fetus that will also undergo innovative procedures. As it grows, further monitoring and procedures take place until it is viable. The technology allows us to bring it to term in a birthing tank. Our extensive research and investigation suggest you are one of those qualified individuals that may be perfect for our trials."

He waited. The whole table of people held their breath.

"Should you pass the rest of the tests," he added. "Do you have questions for us?"

I debated whether I should voice my concerns at this moment. I thought genetic engineering to produce a child was illegal. Wasn't there some international law passed a while back? But surely a university project would not be doing something illegal. The dollar signs dancing in my head were a deterrent to questioning their expertise, anyway. Rolf had walked out on me in a New York diner. I would not let that happen again.

I opted for sarcasm. "So I'm special?"

A woman across from Dr. Androvich spoke up. "Mr. Williamson, Dr. Androvich possesses that rapidly waning characteristics of humans—politeness. It slows him down." She nodded at the doctor as if they'd had this conversation before. "I do not suffer from that malady. There is nothing special about you that makes you any more valuable than any other human. You are exceptional in that you fit the criteria for our program. That's an accident of birth and is only valuable to our program as a collection of the characteristics. We have others who are also unique. In effect, you are not special. But you fit our needs at the moment."

I emitted a brief laugh. "That's what my last girlfriend said."

A few laughs from around the table, but not as many as I had hoped. These people need a vacation.

"All right, sorry. So what's next?" I had a lot of questions, mostly about the infant that would be born. To me. To some woman, I don't know. The legality was a curiosity, but I chalked it up to my lack of knowledge. A university would not fund and host a major project based on illegal work.

The woman continued. "If I may summarize for all the other departments as well as my own…" She glanced around the table to nods. "We'll begin the tests and processes today. Some are simple and traditional, some are complex and new and proprietary. A few require you to be under anesthesia. A battery of psychological tests will follow. We wait for results, based on later tests and the lab results."

"And then?"

"If the results are positive based on our models and needs, we move you to Phase Two."

"Which is?"

"Which is not your business until you have passed the first phase."

January 2019

The meeting broke up, and the Director motioned for me to follow her. "That wasn't too difficult, no?"

"It was fine."

"You did not ask any substantive questions. I am sure you have them."

"True. They don't really matter much to me, though. Just curiosity."

"Very well. You may ask me questions at any time. For now, the physical assessments begin, I will take you to your room, where you can disrobe privately and don a hospital gown. It will be your room for the duration, so you can leave your belongings there as well.'

"All of them?"

She frowned.

"A joke. What I am wearing is all I have."

"Ah. Yes. Apologies. I did not remember you were homeless." We stopped outside a large, metal door. She pushed a buzzer next to it and we waited. "You do not fit the model of most homeless people. Unfortunate circumstances."

"Perhaps, but also the result of me being so excited about a project that I ignored the warning signs."

"Yes." She looked down the corridor away from me and nodded. "Yes. That can happen."

The door opened into a small room containing a bed, dresser, desk, and chair, with a small bathroom and shower connected. There was a fingerprint lock which she helped me set. I washed my face, changed into the gown lying on the bed, and stepped back out.

The Director stayed with me throughout the rest of the afternoon, walking (and sometimes wheeling me) from room to room. The place reminded me of something from a science-fiction horror movie: clean, white, sterile, and everyone dressed in white. Gleaming instruments beeping and whirring. Monitors with streams of colorful data in copious form. The juxtaposition of a simple rubber mallet to test my reflexes (again) in the same room as a full-body scanning device that produced a complete 3D image of my internals.

"You encountered a violent physical altercation three to four days ago," a technician remarked.

"Yes. Your skill at observing bruises and stitches are astounding."

"I am not speaking of it. There are internal injuries—" he peered at a screen over my head "—Ja, Ja, by more than one person. Kicked by boots, perhaps, Ja, and maybe a heavy stick or rod."

"Baseball bat. You know baseball?"

He ignored me. "You have been treated professionally for the wounds. They missed a contusion above your liver that is bleeding a small amount. We'll fix that."

New York-Presbyterian was supposed to be one of the best, though perhaps their work with the homeless did not warrant their best effort. Still, I was impressed that this tech could determine that amount of detail.

The physical tests took two days. I slept for precisely eight hours each night—I think they were giving me some futurist medication to ensure it. The entire experience was painful, uncomfortable, and intrusive, but nothing that wasn't worth it. Even if I didn't pass, I told myself, I would have enough money to get started again. To get back where I was—only better.

It was the third day of psychological tests that bothered me. Five different psychologists interviewed me, each with a different specialty, I assumed. There were some standard tests for mental acuity, observational skills, intuition tests, and so on. It was the questions about parts of my life that got to me—I do not know how they could possibly have known some of the things they asked me about. Childhood events, conversations with friends in college, a family vacation to Michigan one year. And questions surrounding my parents' death. "How did you first learn your parents had been killed?" "What was the first thing you said after learning of their deaths?" "Did you see their bodies, and at what point?" "What did they look like?" And worse. I almost stormed out twice.

There were also questions about my startup, which I expected. This particular interviewer was a sharp-faced woman in a business suit who seemed to have no emotions whatsoever. Her questions were about how much I knew concerning the illegalities of the investors, and it felt more like a civil deposition than a psychological assessment. As she talked, I could not help but watch the mole on the side of her mouth, which never seemed to move as she spoke.

"You were served a subpoena concerning a lawsuit related to the investment company. *Peter Jackman, Hugh Laughlin, Karl Potter, Karolin Smirnoff, et al. v Lingo Franco Investments and Developments, GmBH.* Correct?"

The last word sounded more like "Korrekt" than "correct." I considered a pun to correct her, but I suspected she appreciated humor less than the rest of the people here. "Yes."

She nodded. "When was the last time you spoke with anyone at Lingo Franco?"

"Wait a minute. How did you know I received that subpoena? I got it four or five days ago in the hotel, and the name of the plaintiffs wasn't even on it, it just had John and Jane Does, and I—"

"Irrelevant. When was the last time you spoke with anyone at Lingo Franco?"

That was pretty much how it went. I kept from arguing by constantly reminding myself that soon I would go my merry way with plans and money to carry it out. The promise of control helped salve the invasion of the mental, emotional, and physical humiliation.

π

The attorney slid a packet of papers across the table at me. The top cover read:

Project Pacem
Subject Contract

I looked up at the Director, sitting beside the attorney. "Does this mean..."

"Yes." She did not smile.

I scanned it quickly, looking for the remuneration amount.

I was going to owe Rolf another hundred bucks. In a series of payments over a year, it was far more than the initial amount. Substantially more. Life-changingly more.

I'd read over the contract, which contained many more details than the previous. Still, it did not spell out everything that was going to result from this Project. There were gaps in information.

With this kind of money, not only could I get back to where I was, I could buy out all the people who did it to me. Or destroy *their* businesses. I could meet every dream I'd had. The sky was the limit.

I deserved this. I was going to be a rags to riches story. Doing what I wanted. With my own money this time. I looked up at the Director again, aware that the size of the smile on my face was almost embarrassing. "Aren't you going to say congratulations?"

"No." She stood up. "Come on. We have a lot to go over."

June 2032

The man pushed Salim into the middle seat and sat on the aisle seat, while the second man squeezed past to take a place by the window. Beaknose sat on the aisle.

His mother had always told him that, if a stranger ever tried to take him, he should make as much commotion as he could to get the attention of others. But Beaknose's mother perhaps had told him the same, for he opened his black jacket slightly to reveal the butt of a pistol tucked inside.

"We're not going to hurt you. Don't do anything. Just sit."

His mother had never offered advice on how to deal with a man with a gun. Salim had never even seen a gun, except on video.

Beaknose leaned back and faced forward. "I don't know what happened back there, but listen carefully: we are not going to hurt you as long as you behave. We are taking you to someone who wants to see you. He will not hurt you. But if you try to get away, we will hurt you. Verstehe?"

Without waiting for an answer, he looked at the other man. "Contact number four and tell him we have the target and to proceed to Baden-Baden. Continue attempts to contact number three, though I suspect he was a plant and the reason for the escape."

The man reached into his pocket and drew out a small tablet which he tapped and held to his ear. He repeated the actions. "No answer for either."

Beaknose drummed his fingers on the side of the plastic seat. He looked left then right. "Contact team two and have them meet us in Baden-Baden. I'll call team five and have them do an assessment of the Bahnhof."

While both were busy on their devices, Salim took stock of the train car, which was almost empty. An older man and woman sat about halfway up the car. Across and forward of them was a young man, dressed in a suit and tie. A woman sat near the front, in the seats that faced backward, somewhere around 45 or 50 years old. She was looking at Salim.

He looked away and back again. She was still staring. She mouthed the words, "Stay calm."

At least that was what Salim saw. 'Stay calm?' Had she been watching and sensed there was something wrong? Why 'stay calm'? Why not, 'are you alright?'

He nodded. The woman looked away. Blondish hair with streaks of brown. She was wearing a simple beige and black business suit. "Sensible" would be the word his mom would use to describe her. Her face was pleasant: a bit angular, perhaps, but light features. Salim thought she looked a bit weathered, though.

Both men were still on their devices, now speaking another language. It sounded Balkan.

He should have run home after his escape from the van. Maybe his mom was alive, and he could have gotten help for her. Same with his dad. What was he doing headed to Baden-Baden? Tears welled up in his eyes.

No! He'd been over this. That was emotion talking. He must remain focused. Time for regret and crying later.

The front door swooshed open followed by the clacking of the train wheels, muffled again as the door eased shut. The conductor entered to check tickets. This could present an opportunity.

He watched as the uniformed man, tablet in hand, made his way down the aisle, stopping first at the women, then the lone man on the left. He didn't have a ticket, so he purchased one from the conductor. The couple presented their tickets, before turning down the aisle toward Salim and his captors. Maybe there would be an opportunity.

"Tickets, Herren?"

Beaknose put his phone away and pulled out a wallet.

"Baden-Baden."

"Zwei Erwachsene und Ein Kind?"

"Ja."

"Siebenundfünfzig euro vierundvierzig, bitte."

The conductor held the tablet out, and Beaknose's tapped his money on its side. The conductor watched the screen, nodded, and left the car. Salim's heart sank. The men returned to their phones.

They said no one would hurt him. Maybe there was some logical explanation for this. Still, the scenes of violence and kidnapping did not suggest anything legal.

He looked up as the woman at the front of the car got up and approached. Her eyes fixed on Salim. She cocked her head to the side. "Are these men bothering you, dear?"

She doesn't know about the gun, Salim thought. Dangerous.

Both men put away their phones. Beaknose spoke. "We are fine, Frau. Move along, none of your business."

She turned an expressionless gaze on him. "Can the boy answer?" At that moment, the car door behind opened, and two men entered: the conductor and a fit-looking man of thirty or so, dressed casually. Salim took in his watch, his haircut, his demeanor, and his excellent physical condition. Train security.

"Is there a problem, Frau?" said the conductor.

The men said, "No."

"Yes, there is," said the woman. "I came on board at the same time as this young man, who appeared to be traveling alone. I saw these two men take him by the arms, speak harshly, and force him to sit between them, despite his desire to leave."   She held Salim with her eyes. "Isn't that true?"

Salim nodded, surprised and impressed.

"No!" Beaknose retorted. "I do not know what this woman rants about. This boy came on with us. He is our son. My son."

There was a moment of awkward silence as the conductor and officer looked first at Beaknose and then at Salim. Beaknose had the pale-skinned look of a typical Norman, thin and sharp. Salim was swarthy-skinned and had the thicker build of Middle-Eastern descent.

The conductor shook his head. "I saw him embark alone as I stood on the platform, Herr." The security guard remained silent and attentive.

"So you have lied once," the woman said, "and now you lie again. He is not your son. I believe we see your character."

Beaknose rose quickly, his face reddening. "He is adopted, Frau! How dare you!" The silent man beside the conductor, as fast as lightning, put his hand on Beaknose arm.

"Stay calm." The voice was quiet but laced with steel. His jacket, now open because of his outstretched arm, showed a holstered gun. The officer's other hand hovered nearby.

Beaknose stood still for a moment, perhaps considering his options, then slowly sat back down.

"Certainly," he said smoothly. "We can work this out. But this woman has nothing to do with this boy. She does not even know him."

"Yes, I do. I am his nanny."

"Then why," Beaknose said, with a triumphant air, "did you not get on the train with him?"

"Because, sir, I was not supposed to get on the train with him. I was sending him to visit his relatives in München. But I saw the two of you following him. So I got on the train at the last moment, behind you two, to make sure you did not have nefarious intentions. I told the conductor just that."

"This is utter—" began Beaknose.

The security guard put his hand out. "Excuse me." He leaned down to look in Salim's face. "Young man, do you wish to be with these two men? Or with your Nanny?"

Salim pointed to the woman.

"What is your name, young man?" The conductor asked.

"He is mute, sir," the woman said. "He cannot speak."

How did she know that?!

Everyone was looking at him. Salim signed his name.

Beaknose started. "Wait! If he was brought here with her, then why did I buy him a ticket? Where is *his* ticket?"

The woman turned to the conductor. "Why is *he* demanding answers? These two followed my charge onto the train, accosted him, and are holding him prisoner as we speak."

The conductor looked at the officer, who nodded. "The boy will go with the woman. You two will come with me."

The man on Salim's right began to raise, but Beaknose put out his hand. "Of course. Of course. My apologies, officers, I overreacted because of the accusations." He seemed distracted. "The truth is, we thought the boy was alone and were helping him to his destination. We were suspicious of this woman, which is why I said he was my son. Not knowing who she was." He looked at the woman. "Sorry for causing you concern. We meant well." Salim got up and squeezed into the aisle. "Have a nice trip," Beaknose said. His silky tone and kind demeanor were an impressive spot of acting.

The woman took Salim's hand and led him a short distance away.

Beaknose still speaking. "Truly sorry for the misunderstanding, sir. We won't cause any more problem, we'll just stay here."

The officer shook his head. "This need not take long. Come with me. At Baden-Baden we'll do a brief check and you can be on your way."

Beaknose sighed. "Very well." He rose along with his companion and followed the officer through the rear door of the car.

The conductor indicated the opposite direction to Salim and the woman. "Come with me to the first-class car. Our treat for the trouble."

"Thank you."

He led them forward, passing through three cars to arrive at the Erste Klasse car with compartments. The conductor opened the door to a "family" cubicle: a small compartment with facing seats that could seat four or six people. The woman thanked him again and slid the door shut as he left. Salim took a seat opposite.

"Are you okay?"

Salim signed an affirmative, and asked, *Who are you?*.

"I don't know much sign language, so we must go slow. Let's say I am just a Good Samaritan,."

Do you know me?

She hesitated. "No."

Thank you.

She smiled. "You're welcome." She turned serious. "Those men will not give up so easily. I suspect they won't allow themselves to be taken into the office at the station—the officer has no idea what he is up against. Listen carefully. As we approach the station, we'll move up to the first door of this car. The men will be with the officer in his compartment, where they will disembark about mid-train. I suspect they will incapacitate the officer just before we arrive, so they can disembark and watch for you. I will step onto the platform, then turn back, as if I am waiting for you and urging you to come on." She smiled. "But you won't be there."

No? he signed.

"No. You will have already made your way to the rear of the train, where you will disembark behind the men, cross the platform, and get on a train to Salzburg which I happen to know will be there. The men will be watching forward and not see you. I'll throw up my hands and walk away just before the train pulls out again. They will reboard the train, thinking you did not get off."

Salim smiled. *What if they see me going by the compartment?*

"They won't. The officer's compartment has no windows. It is his office that is also used as a holding cell."

Salim nodded.

"Also, take this…" she fumbled in her bag and took out a fifty-euro bill.

Salim hesitated.

"Take it." She pushed the bills into his hand, gently put her left hand over his and curled his fingers over the money.

Salim nodded, stuffing the money in his pocket.

"One other thing. Do not go home. You need to make your way to Colmar."

Colmar? Why? I don't know anyone there. Why can't I go home?

"Because it is dangerous. Colmar will be safe." She took his face in her hands. "I know this is confusing and frightening. It will become clear eventually—if you go to Colmar. But you have to be safe first. Salzburg."

Salim considered her words. He had followed the directions of a stranger before and it almost was a disaster. This woman saved him. For that reason, he was inclined to do as she said.

What about my parents?

She swallowed. "I will see if I can get in touch with them and let them know you are safe. What is your full name?"

So she didn't know everything about him. Still, she knew something about Beaknose and his companion. Was she a spy, associated with the man who allowed him to escape the van?

He told her his full name, but nothing more.

The rest of the trip, about fifteen minutes, was quiet. Salim tried to ask a few questions about who she was, but she declined to answer. As they approached the small, two-track station at Baden-Baden, they stood and moved to the aisle.

"Okay, make your way to the rear. Check each car before you enter to make sure the men haven't already escaped, though unlikely. They won't want to make their move until the last minute."

She placed her hand on his shoulder and squeezed. "Go quickly."

The plan went just as she described. Salim made his way to the last car. When the train arrived, he peeked out the exit door and looked up the platform. The two men stood near the first-class car with their backs to him. Beyond them, he could just make out the woman, standing on the platform facing into the train, gesturing to someone inside.

Across the platform was Car 4 of the EU230 bound for München and Salzburg, just as she said. He took a last glance at the men, jumped onto the platform and ran straight across and up into the second train, then turned to stand at the door, waiting. Soon, the alarm sounded and the doors closed. Ten seconds later, the train pulled out. Salim took a seat, almost laughing at the thought of the men's faces when the woman turned and left. If they got back on board the train, they'd search the whole thing and find no Salim.

He sat back and made himself comfortable for the forty-five-minute trip to München.

"Now we wait."

We were sitting in the cafeteria, eating dinner. I was surprised there were no dietary restrictions placed on me, so I took advantage. This was no ordinary hospital or research facility cafeteria. It was wrong to even call it a cafeteria. The food was incredible.

"When you finish eating, you return to your room until we meet for breakfast tomorrow." The Director had eaten every meal with me since I had been here.

"Then what?"

"In two or three days, we get results and the interpretation and analysis."

"Am I free until then? Can I go explore Vienna?"

She smiled. "It is a lovely city. One of my favorites. Especially if you love music. But, no. You cannot go."

"What?! I'm a prisoner?"

She shook her head. "You are not a prisoner. But you are under the guidelines of the program. Secrecy is crucial to its success. You signed a contract. Did you read it?"

"Yes, of course." I ate a scoop of crème brûlée—thin-crusted top, perfectly caramelized, with a creamy smooth body below. "But what if I don't pass and I leave? I can say whatever I want and do whatever I want."

"If you want to violate the NDA in the contract, yes."

I had read it a few times—I learned my lesson from before. I was just talking to gauge her reactions. "So much for the openness of the academy and shared knowledge, eh?"

"They will share it. Eventually. Except..."

"Except what? There are things about the project I don't know. Not only the Phase II stuff, but other things. Something is...there is a lot of paranoia here."

She shrugged. "It is not paranoia. In fact, I am surprised you haven't figured it out. To test Dr. Schlessinger's theories in practicum requires a lot of money and resources. A *lot* of money and—"

Why does everyone keep pointing that out?

"—there was no way that traditional academic benefactors and investors could or would provide what was needed. This meant wooing investors from the corporate world.

Government agency grants. And she traditional philanthropist organizations with deep pockets. Each one insists on requirements and safeguards in return, things that would not be required, were it a pure academic pursuit. And every group has its own set of restrictions."

I suspected, but was angling to see how much she would tell me. "Ah, yes. Philanthropy can only go so far in the pursuit of human goodness."

She looked at me and squinted her eyes. "Sometimes I cannot tell if you are sarcastic or serious. Perhaps a language problem."

"It's not a language problem. I would imagine the corporations expect to benefit by selling the procedures or drugs or whatever comes out of this."

"Of course. They stand to become fabulously wealthy. And governments stand to gain as well."

"Military?"

She shrugged. "Yes. Not exclusively. This is a world- and society-changing project. If it works as the models predict."

"And that worries you?"

She looked up sharply. "Global changes should worry even the most positive of us."

"Which you are not."

"Have you had enough to eat? It seems you are making up for the meager meals you had while homeless."

"Absolutely. Milking you all for everything I can." I noticed the change of subject but decided to let it go. I pushed the plates away from me. "Tell me. What are you the director *of*?"

"Pardon me?"

"You're called 'the Director.' I don't even know your name. What is your name?"

She pursed her lips. "That's one of the restrictions. Subjects cannot know the names of any of the staff."

"Dr. Androvich."

"Not the academics. They don't care about them, for some reason."

"Mr. Powell."

"Ah, yes." She smiled. "I told him that keeping secrets from the subjects on such a vast level would never work. Especially not when the subjects were required to possess highly developed observational skills. Keeping secrets from outsiders can even be difficult, but can be done. Secrecy from the people most involved is rarely successful. I argued that we could keep things from you all if we *tell* you they are secret, and why. But if we merely want to keep as much secret as possible, and pretend we aren't, and mislead, we will surely fail, and failure could have disastrous effects."

"You didn't answer my question. What are you Director of? At first I thought you were the Director of the entire program."

She laughed. "No. Not only am I not skilled and educated enough, but I also would never want the job."

"Okay. But you are the Director of something."

She sat back in her seat and fixed me with a gaze that made me want to look away. "What do you mean?"

I was getting frustrated. "Now *you* are being secretive and misleading. What is the department, building, area, subject matter that you direct?! What does it say on your business card under "Director.""

She held my gaze, then smiled. "I do not direct any of those things. You misunderstand the title." She leaned forward. "I am the director of you."

March–May 2019

"Who's the woman? The 'female subject' as you all call her. So endearing."

The Director shook her head. "Sorry, Pate. That's another piece of information you can't know. And I agree with it."

We were walking outside on the grounds of the Center. It was still cold, but it had finally stopped snowing a few days ago. It was one of those clear, crisp, blue-sky days that made the world look like it had been scrubbed clean.

"Why?"

"Any contact between subjects could compromise the project. That's SOP. Experiments with plants, animals, insects are always fraught with more variables than we would like. Human subjects even more so—especially when they interact with each other. Loyalties, blind spots, conflicts of interest, even—"

"What would any of that have to do with biology?"

"Please, Pate, you are smarter than that. Physiology is physiology. The Ancient Greek idea that matter and thought are separate has long been debunked. Go read some about quantum—"

"Okay okay, point taken."

"But I have another reason: you are both good people and have been through a lot in your lives. No need to complicate them any more."

"Well, I still disagree. After all, we're going to have a child together."

"You think *that* doesn't introduce a plethora of problematic issues?"

I couldn't argue with that.

The snow crunched under our feet. We had been together almost every day for the last two months. She didn't offend easily. She was a curious combination of compassion and steadfast logic. Unusual.

"Besides," she said, "There would be nothing to gain by meeting and a lot to lose."

"Well, I don't care. Just curious. I have plans for my life, and t doesn't include anyone else."

But we did meet.

π

It was an accident. Or perhaps it was destiny. God's plan. Though some would say it was the work of Satan, if anything.

As the weeks progressed, I had a lot of free time and almost no freedom. The library at the University was extensive, so I spent a lot of time reading up on biotechnology and gene modification, but it was slow going, as my background was all in technology unrelated to medicine or biology. I began practicing German and French, too. The Director, who spoke both, helped on occasion by holding parts of our discussions in those languages.

There were things I had to do for the Project daily—rather, things done to me. It was usually only a few hours. Bodily fluid tests, scans, MRIs, punctuated by "procedures." Some of these consisted of a regimen of medicinal doses—oral and injected. Others involved more invasive procedures with a local or a mild general anesthetic, but sometimes required being put under anesthesia. Every procedure was followed by days of tests. The doctors, researchers, and technicians were all patient with my questions, but their answers were often evasive or couched in so much jargon that it meant little to me. Part of the process was to edit a portion of my DNA they called a 'doubles gene.' The purpose, as near as I understood it, was to ensure that all of my *desired* genetic characteristics were passed on to my offspring. I had read of this sort of thing being performed successfully in animals and insects. It was how malaria had been eradicated in Africa.

I assumed they were doing the same to the 'female subject.' Once they had our DNA the way they wanted it, they would use my semen to inseminate one of her eggs to produce this child. At that point, my part would be finished, and I would be sent back to New York, significantly more wealthy than when I left.

They could not tell me how long the process would, as there was some trial-and-error. That's what the follow-up tests were for. But they seemed confident it would be about a year from the time I arrived.

I did not get much information about what happened after that. But by listening carefully, combined with all my reading, they would continue the editing and engineering both the female subject and the fetus. When the child was born, I assumed, the female subject would also be dismissed, joining me as one of the world's wealthy.

As for the child, they refused to answer any of my questions.

But it wasn't my concern and didn't matter. This was no different from donating to a sperm bank.

The first time I saw her was a mistake on the part of the staff, I am sure. I would guess that someone who oversaw scheduling was fired.

The Director was escorting me from one of the labs after a particularly lengthy session, some sort of concentrated radiation therapy. As we turned a corner outside the lab, I realized I'd left one of my books inside.

"Go get it," the Director said, with some irritation. "I'll wait. Hurry."

I retrieved the book and headed back down the hall. Voices behind me caused me to glance back, and I saw two people walked towards me from the far end of the hall. One was a man dressed in the white garb of the staff. The other was a woman, dressed in a gown like mine. Dark hair. Medium build. The man caught my eye and, in a smooth motion, took the woman's arm and herded her into a side room.

It had to be her. I said nothing to the Director, who was looking at her phone at the time.

π

After five or six weeks more weeks, I began to see the Director less often, and when I did, she was distracted. The project was demanding more of her time beyond her duties with me, and she got little sleep.

Every chance I had, I asked her and anyone who would listen if I could get permission to leave the Center grounds and explore Vienna—just for an hour or two. The answer had always been "no." I had a heated discussion with the Director about it, where I pointed out that keeping me confined was inhumane, my role was almost done, and surely they could find some way to feel safe about it—they were biotechnology experts.

One day in late March, she found me in the cafeteria.

"You can go out into the city if you'd like."

I looked up from my bowl of soup. "Just like that?"

She smiled, though had a bit of sadness in it. "Not 'just like that.' I had to argue and pester for weeks. You are right, it *is* inhumane. I finally convinced them that you could be trusted."

"Can I?"

Her eyes turned hard. "Pate, do not joke. I have stuck my neck out because *I* trust you. There are conditions, and if you screw up even a tiny bit, I will not only make you wish you were still homeless in New York, but I'll find a way to take your money away. Breach of contract. I'd have *no* trouble convincing them of that."

I had always suspected she could be a cast-iron bitch machine when needed, but I was taken aback. "Sorry. Sarcasm is my go-to. I do appreciate it, and I will not let you down. I just want some fresh air."

She nodded and softened a bit. "Very well."

Of course, there were conditions. I had to stay within the Ringstrasse, avoid train and bus stations, police stations, and don't draw any attention to myself. As a final step, they injected a GPS unit into my forearm.

I did not want to take advantage of the Directors' trust, so I went out only once or twice a week, for an hour or two. I made sure to thank her profusely when I saw her.

During the third week of my ersatz freedom, I walked down the Universitätsring and then the Schottenring, the two major streets that made a ring around the center of the old city. I had been ordered never to turn right on the Ring when leaving the University grounds. They wouldn't tell me why. But I could put up with their paranoia for fresh scenery and other faces.

I had planned to go to the River—someone said there was an excellent Indian restaurant on the Bank. But the day had turned cloudy, and without the sun, it was pretty cold, though it was the beginning of April. I went to Café Central instead—a closer walk. I had been to this beautiful café before—marble columns, arches, and excellent coffee and pastries. It was said that many poets and philosophers frequented the café in the past. I liked to think I was soaking up some of their lofty thoughts to counteract the overbearing science I was constantly subjected to.

I sat at a table near one side and ordered the *Italienisch* from the menu: a cappuccino and a croissant.

A man, dressed in drab casual clothes, entered and took a seat on the far side of the café. Close cropped hair, sunglasses. I had seen him behind me when I changed course and headed down Herrengasse. My shadow.

As I was spreading thick jam on my croissant, I heard someone speak English nearby. A woman, her back to me, was ordering. While most waiters—if not all—could speak enough English, this one was pretending to be without that skill. The woman was struggling. I got up and went over.

"May I help you order?"

She looked up. "Oh...thank you. Yes. I am trying to order *this*, I think, but I want turkey bacon if they have it." She pointed to an item on the menu.

Her wrist bore the mark as mine, in the same spot. An exact copy.

I looked up at the waiter, trying to hold my composure and frantically trying to figure a way to make my escape.

"Sir, Diese Frau möchte..." I looked down at the menu, I wasn't sure of the proper article to use, "Uh, Vitales Frühstück, Bitte. Aber mit Truthahnspeck?" I wasn't sure that was the right word. "Bitte."

"Ja, Herr. Frau. Einen Moment." He bowed his head and left.

"Thank you," she said. "I know a little German, but he was not willing to meet me halfway."

"Glad to help. Let me know if you need any more translation services."

She laughed—a melodious sound, appropriate here, in the city of music—and looked down coyishly at my arm, then jerked upright as a quiet "oh" escaped her lips. I thought I saw a slight sign of panic her eyes. "I should be fine now. Thank you." She nodded and turned back to the menu, as if perusing for more. Her self-control impressed me.

Under her breath, she said, "Eyes everywhere."

As I turned, I said, "Kunsthistorisches. Friday afternoon at 13:30."

As I stepped away, she whispered, "Odysseus and Irus exhibit. Bottom floor. Three exits."

She was good.

I returned to my table and positioned myself so that the man on the far side could not see my face.

I thought about her pretty brown eyes, rather almond-shaped, and long thick black hair. Her intelligence was apparent in the way she held herself, the way she spoke. Yet there was something else. Something drew me to her. Perhaps the connection of being chosen for the same secretive program. The two 'subjects.' Like prisoners of war in the same cell. It could also be that we shared a lot of the same characteristics physically, emotionally, mentally, and psychologically.

Or maybe I was just tired of being alone and would like to have some company.

I'm not sure why I suggested we meet at the museum and was even more surprised that she was in step with me so quickly. We could be risking our participation. And our money.

I smiled to myself. It was unlikely they would kick us out at this stage and start all over again just because of a couple of chance meetings. They needed us.

June 2032

Salim blinked and looked around. The car held about ten people at the moment. Most, if not all, seemed to be businessmen or women, perhaps headed home to München after a business trip, or to München for business tomorrow. Some were looking at papers. One was reading a novel. The rest seemed to be dozing.

The smooth ride of the train, the gentle whoosh of the air conditioner, and the steady clacking of the train wheels made it hard to stay awake. Twice he came to with a start. He was afraid to sleep.

He rose and walked through the entire line of train cars to keep himself alert. All the way up to the engine, then back to the last car. As he walked, he counted seats with one part of his mind, while exploring events of the previous twenty-four hours. Reviewing every sight, word, sound, expression, and activity, trying to find some sign that might lead to understanding. He knew that one innocuous clue sometimes opened other connections and insights which could lead to building theories that could be tested against the rest of the data.

Problems appeared in his mind like symbols, with pathways and curves and connecting devices. Like a three-dimensional maze or labyrinth, continually shifting in space and time as new connections and new data were considered. It was organic, like life, with a living structure. Some links and paths were dead ends or led off to unrelated or irrelevant parts. Sometimes, like a revelation, the right path (and the answer) would become readily apparent, a glowing, snaking path connecting events and objects. Yet the constant evolution of all the data meant that he couldn't just follow any path, however promising it might seem at the moment. He had to zoom out periodically to see the whole, with all its undulations and moving variations. Sometimes, the best one could hope for was a sound theory or two that could be scrutinized by adding more data. Other times—and these were the best—the truth became apparent, the answer solid, the theory proved. The sense of victory and insight was a thing of joy.

Salim did this sort of thing often—in his homework, school, and life. He thought everyone did it this way, but had learned that it was not usual. It came natural to him.

This was a different kind of problem, though. So many parts, so much ambiguity. He needed more information. If he could relax and organize what he *did* know, maybe it some keys would appear. He had been too reactive, and he spent a few moments berating himself for it. But it was time to put that aside and work the problem.

He took a seat in an empty compartment and unfolded the table between the seats. Using his finger as if it were a pen, he began to draw on the table. It was a technique he had used as far back as he could remember. He had a good memory, and he could remember everything he had drawn until he wiped it clean and it left his mind. If he didn't intentionally wipe it, the lists and diagrams stayed in his mind, filed away like registers and blocks on a memory chip.

He could still call to mind the simple problem he had worked out when he was two years old: how to get out of his playpen without tipping it over or hurting himself. There was no reason for him to keep that one, of course, except sentimentality.

He had sometimes wondered how complex the diagrams could be. Once, as an experiment, he explored his school environment: the buildings, furniture, where teachers and students were at different times, all the events and interactions he had witnessed in one day. It was not a problem, of course, but an analysis of a small society during one day. He began writing in one corner of his room and filled all four walls, then the ceiling, then used the open air for layers of invisible "boards." Finally, he used the floor. Standing in a corner, with no more room to write, he could see everything. He saw connections and found some high probabilities of things he had not realized. Frau Henckel and the principle were romantically involved but were attempting to keep it secret. Stefan and Pablo had had some sort of argument or fight over some girl that day, though they didn't talk about it. It appeared to be Leisl. He was pretty sure that Herr Schmeidel was either going to be fired or quit—not sure which yet. And there was one room in the main offices that had not been opened during the entire school year. He wondered why.

Once the table of the train compartment was full, he stood and used the windows, then the three walls of the compartment, and the ceiling. There was not a lot of room, so he erased some obviously irrelevant things.

An hour later, he sat back and gazed at his work. It moved as he watched, evolving into a kind of three-dimensional labyrinth. Much was faded, blurry, or blank—unknown or unclear elements. There were some clear paths to follow, but they ended prematurely without any connections. One of them had to be wrong—it was too disturbing and unlikely. He wiped it away.

The number of variables was overwhelming, but his lack of facts was the knife in the heart of the analysis. Were either or both of his parents dead? Why did the attack and kidnapping take place? Why that day? Where had third kidnapper run off to, and why did he help Salim escape? What were the three "teams" (and were there more than that, he was sure)? What action or scheme to kidnap a boy needed multiple teams? Who was the woman on the train, and why was she helping him?

The one thing that the diagram did make clear was that whatever was going on, the kidnapping was part of something much bigger. It was not about just him or his parents. Something big was lurking out there, something that would make sense of it. Without knowing more about what it might be, all the paths all led nowhere.

It did help him decide on his next course of action. He would not go on to Salzburg until he had more information. Instead, he would disembark at München and contact the Polizei. They would keep him safe, they could contact the Polizei in Heidelberg and find out what happened to his parents, and perhaps find out some information on his kidnappers.

Satisfied, he sat back to rest.

May–June 2019

The Odysseus und Irus exhibit at the Kunsthistorisches was a bronze relief housed in Room 34 on the lowest level. I arrived fifteen minutes early and waited in the upper galley at the top of the wide stairs, from which I could see the entrance. I pretended to read a brochure.

She came in, carrying her own brochure. She had rented an audio guide as well and walked straight through into the far gallery. Just before she passed through the archway, She glanced back, and then up at me.

It was not difficult for me to lose my shadow. This was not the same guy who was in the café—every time, it was someone different. He'd find me eventually because of the GPS embedded in my arm. But the GPS couldn't read elevation accurately on multiple floors in a concrete building, so he'd have to search all levels. The only stairs were in the center of the museum, with galleries on both sides.

I was sure she had lost her shadow as well.

She was standing at the exhibit as when I arrived. We stood side-by-side, looking at the mid-fifteenth century plaque.

I spoke first. "I estimate we have about thirteen minutes, tops. Should keep it to about seven to be safe,"

"Agreed."

"Is this a bad idea?"

"Yes. But I have become increasingly suspicious of the Project. They aren't telling me everything, and I suspect they are lying about some things. I want to know if it is the same for you."

"It is."

"Not surprised. There is a lot more going on than they let on. A *lot* more."

"How do you know that?"

"My...handler—my Director—has confided some things that should not have been told to me."

Of course, she had a Director, too. "I haven't been told much directly. But I can read between the lines, and the Director has let some things slip." I turned to her, and our eyes meet. My heart fluttered, in spite of the somber conversation. I had been lonely for a long time. "What do you think it is? Unethical activities? Violating international law on genetics? Bioweapon potentials, black market fears, the use of—"

"All that. Though I think they are finding ways to skirt the laws. But more, having to do with us. You and I. And... the baby."

"Baby?"

"Yes, the baby. What did they tell you?"

"*In vitro* fertilization."

"Well, they lied to you. I carry the child. To term."

"What?! They told me they'd bring it to term in a birthing tank." If they were going to do genome editing, it could be done in the birthing tank. From my reading, I had no clue what procedures would require a fetus be *in utero*. Unless—"

"Did they tell you that you would continue treatments after implantation?"

"Yes. And that's why I think—"

"They are doing more than editing the CRISPR genes. Doing additive—"

"I think so. With nanobots and organic machines. And they'll continue after the child is born as I nurse."

"They want you to nurse it?"

"He or she. Yes."

Both Rolf and the Director had been coy when I probed about the legal issues involving the child that would be produced by this project. I never asked outright if it was legal—I assumed had assumed it was. Surely they were not breaking the law—it could ruin the University. My questions were about the issues of legal guardianship, legal standing, and so on. I hadn't really cared; just curious. I was sure the child would be well-taken care of for its entire life. Still, it would be an experiment, a scientific toy. I was pretty sure I could not be legally responsible, though if there were serious crimes, and I knew about it—

But I don't. Or shouldn't. They are keeping it from us. Or trying to.

"Do you know anything about the legalities?

"No. But there's more—we are not the only subjects."

"We aren't? They told me we were..." I stopped. Did they actually tell me that? Or just lead me to assume it?

"We are right now. But there have been many before. When I ask, all I get is silence. The Director told me to never ask about it. I'm not supposed to know. Could jeopardize results. Which is bullshit. I wanted to know how far they got. I want to know what happened to the subjects, and the child, if there was one before."

I wasn't sure I agreed. If I could be implicated, and lose my money or worse, my freedom, then I'd prefer ignorance. "I don't know. Whatever happens to them, we can still live our lives. With the money. I would imagine you need it as badly as I do. They seemed to have chosen for that characteristic as well as—"

She whirled on me. "What's your name?"

"Pate."

"Nice to meet you, Pate." It no longer sounded like it. "I'm Eris." She paused, and I saw a bit of fire in her eyes.

"Pate, this is about far more than money. I need the money far worse than you do—"

"—I doubt that—"

"Quiet. We don't have much longer. This is about lives. Yours, mine, some engineered child—and perhaps the world. I don't want the money if it costs that."

"Don't be dramatic."

She held my eyes for a moment with a look that caused me to glance away.

"I'm not being dramatic. I know more than you do."

"I'm sorry," I said. I didn't want her to think badly of me. "It's disturbing. But it's out of our hands. These people have money and governmental and corporate power behind them. At most, if we think it is unpalatable to us, we could quit—and be in breach of contract. Then they'd find others and do it anyway. Maybe it's best not to know too much and just keep our heads down, take our money, and —"

Her nostrils flared. "Apparently they didn't screen for the self-centeredness gene. And you don't have to carry a baby to term and then live with that knowledge for the rest of your life."

I hung my head. "True. Sorry."

She shook her head. "I was hoping I could count on you. A two-headed investigation. I thought we'd have a lot in common, considering we were selected for similar reasons. Guess not." She turned away.

I grabbed her arm. "Wait."

"We need to get out of here, Pate. Our chaperones will show up soon and who knows what they will do."

"I'm sorry. I had a terrible last year. Not used to thinking about anything more than myself. Almost committed suicide by freezing to death,"

"Join the club. And get over yourself."

"Second chance?"

I could see the wheel turning in her head. What choice did she have, though? If she was going to get help, it was me or no one.

"Next Monday, the Hofburg, Alexander Apartments."

"Got it."

Without another word, she left. I dashed into the next room and examined the closest exhibit. After about fifteen seconds, a man entered alone and pretended to examine an exhibit on the other side of the room. My shadow.

It would be stupid to throw away a fortune over an infatuation.

π

Of course, they knew we had met even though they didn't catch us in the moment. The Director sat me down and threatened to terminate my contract, even suggesting they might try to recover expenses from us. She punctuated her threats with reminders that we were jeopardizing a billion-dollar project.

I was sure that Eris was getting the same treatment from her Director.

"I'm sorry, Director. It was a chance meeting, we had did not plan for it to happen—"

"Not the second time!"

"True. But once we'd met...well, anyway, the contract doesn't say subjects can't interact. I know, I just reread it last night. Besides, it means your chaperones didnt do their job."

She laughed without humor. "Yes, Mr. Powell made that quite clear to security. Apparently the one watching you and the one watching her had no idea the other existed." She pursed her lips. "You could still lose out on the rest of the money."

"And you'd lose out the progress so far and—"

"Shut up. You are about to meet with the Board right now. And they don't want me there. So my advice is that you be more contrite."

She dropped me off at the same conference room as my first meeting. This time it was only the suits in attendance—no researchers or medical staff, except for the head psychologist—the one I had met on the third day of my assessment. Not a surprise.

And Eris was sitting at the far end of the table.

I took my seat without looking at her. My peripheral vision told me that she was also studiously avoiding looking in my direction. Her head was down, as if in shame.

I knew it was an act. I followed suit.

Mr. Powell began speaking without introduction, and much the same as the Director: berating and threatening, though Mr. Powell was even more strident and intimidating.

He finally stopped. We waited. It was deadly quiet. Did everyone stop breathing?

"Well," Mr. Powell said, "What do you have to say?"

I held back and Eris spoke. "I am sorry, sir. It was by chance. We noticed each other's implants. After being so isolated for so long, it was just nice to have some human contact with someone who shared my situation. I knew we shouldn't, but it was in my mind that the purpose of this whole project is to make humans better, more capable, more well-adjusted." Nice. She might be onto something. "And I don't feel well-adjusted, and that helped. We did not share anything about the project." A lie. "But that is no excuse for doing something I was told not to do."

Mr. Powell looked at her for a moment with an expression I could not read. But it wasn't pure anger.

"Mr. Williamson?"

"I concur. It was irresponsible. It's the...loneliness, the isolation...it is difficult. But I agreed to the rules and knew what I was getting into. It was my responsibility to follow them, however difficult, and I apologize. It won't happen again."

The others at the table turned their heads away from me and towards him.

"Very well.' He looked off in the distance, drumming his fingers on the table. We all waited. Finally, he looked back and around the table. " I can imagine the difficulty—this is a unique project. But your actions have jeopardized it." He looked from Eris to me.

I opened my mouth to speak, then closed it.

"Yes, Mr. Williamson?

"I am just a subject here and have no understanding of the Project except my tiny part. But how are we jeopardizing it by simply spending a little time together?"

Despite Mr. Powell's force of presence, the people around the table exploded with comments contained words like "deniability" and "secrecy" and "uncountable and uncontrollable variables" and so on.

After a few moments, Mr. Powell held up his hand and brought the room to quiet.

"Everything they say is true. And for our investor's sake, we have a responsibility to keep a tight control on everything." He took a breath. "Those who do the real work here have often questioned whether we are too restrictive, too controlling. Yet the stakes are so high." He nodded to himself, proud of his insight, toughness, and capabilities. "So, here is my decision."

Here it comes. I was pretty sure they would not kick us out, though it was possible. I could make do with what I had already.

"Miss LaFleur's point is well-taken. The Project's overarching goal is about *humans* and humanity and not technology for lab results. That is exactly what your Director told me earlier today, Mr. Williamson. That we over-analyze and unnecessarily restrict our subjects. We have our reasons. But by doing so, she says, we have changed the environment, the well-being, and the mental state of the subjects—which all play a role in the efficacy of treatments and results. I believe the doctor can vouch for that assessment, as she is quite familiar with the subject on that aspect of research?" He nodded at the psychologist.

"Yes. It is common knowledge now that mental, emotional, and physical reactions to test procedures are negatively affected by contextual detrimental conditions affecting mood, emotions, and thinking patterns, real or imagined."

"Thank you, doctor. Moreover, Mr. Williamson and Miss LaFleur, I take your Director's advice seriously because of prior work in several significant industrial, corporate, and medical projects for the last fifteen years." *Hm. Mine was older than she looked.* "Her advice was that there would not be any detrimental effect in letting our subjects interact, like normal humans, *within reason.* She believes, in fact, it would increase the positive reactions of our tests. I am willing to entertain this concept. Opinions?"

I was shocked. For all the Director's dismissal of the importance of her role, she commanded respect from Powell.

The discussion went on for about twenty or thirty minutes. Some had genuine concerns, some were open to the idea, and some were almost apoplectic that it would even be considered. But the tide began to turn, mostly because no one could come up any *concrete* reason how it could be a problem. The psychologist spoke last.

"I suggest we find a middle road. The contracts contain detailed and specific NDA provisions with severe penalties that would, essentially, ruin their lives professionally and financially. Disclosure is where the real problems lies, and I have no doubts, based on my work with the subjects and the Director's input, they that they will both adhere to those provisions. The fact that we forbid them to contact, but they somehow ended up together in a city of two million, makes me wonder if it wasn't a coincidence and that

"You think someone planned their meeting? An inside job?" This was a small man with a large head and thick eyebrows.

"No, no, as you know, that's *not—*"

"The doctor and the Directors' interests in non-verifiable influences and activities are well known." Mr. Powell said. "You know what she means, John." He looked back at the doctor. "Continue."

"Yes, that is what I mean. Irrelevant in this discussion, I apologize. Since we have been allowing them limited freedom to explore the city, we might allow them to do so together. On occasion, as a test. They have GPSs and have Watchers." They call them *watchers*? "We can restrict their time for these outings and inside these facilities."

There was more discussion, but it was merely loose ends, with one man—John—stating his strong disapproval.

"Very well." Mr. Powell said. "I am inclined to adopt the doctor's suggestions. Let me be clear: this is a trial arrangement. IF there is the slightest problem or hint of a problem, I will shut it down and the discussion will be over. We'll work out the details. You are all dismissed. Miss LaFleur, please stay for a moment."

I was ushered out and left the restricted area. My escort led me to the cafeteria where the Director sat with a cup of coffee. I took the spot opposite.

"Thank you."

She nodded, pensive and unusually distant.

"Was what we did really that bad? Ten minutes at a museum?"

She stopped and looked at me. "And five minutes at the Café. I thought you were both smarter than that. What you did was bad from the Project perspective. Understand, I don't blame you for wanting to. This is...this is getting out of hand."

"What is?"

She looked away. "Nothing. I am just tired. This is has been quite stressful." She looked back up. "Your fault."

"I really didn't want to get you to get in trouble. You're the only person I like here."

"Except for Eris."

"I don't really know her."

"Don't be coy."

"Okay. True, she's interesting. But it could be captivity syndrome—bonding with another prisoner."

"Bad analogy. You know there cannot be a future with her."

I was taken aback. "Why not?" I didn't like being told what I could not do after my time here was done. At least beyond the NDA.

"You told me you just reread the contract."

"I did. Just not all of it."

She shook her head. "Don't do anything else stupid. I got you out of this one, and more. Above and beyond. So grow up. Toe the line."

"I will. I promise. And I do appreciate it. Those ten minutes made me feel like a human rather than a splotch in a Petri dish."

She nodded and she glanced down as her tablet bleeped. "I have been summoned to a meeting with Mr. Powell to discuss the specifics. She turned to leave.

"Wait, one question, Director. Some short guy in there said something about your 'interest in non-verifiable influences.' What was he talking about?"

She actually laughed. "Paul. Yeah. He does not believe that there is anything more to life than just what we see, measure, and catalog. I believe life and the universe are more complex than that."

"What? Magic? God? Pantheism?"

"None of your business."

"Well, for what it's worth, I prefer controlling my destiny."

"And how has that worked out for you so far?" With that, she turned and left.

π

She laughed, twirling away from me, her hair spinning out from under her hat, making a beautiful halo around her head.

I laughed too. "Come on, I am serious."

She stopped her spinning and looked back at me, laughing again. She looked so perfect in her hat, her coat, her mittens. Her cheeks and nose were red from the cool breeze, and her thick, gray scarf had come loose from the spinning.

"But look where we are," she sighed, holding her arms out. "Isn't it great? Not the place for serious talk. It is a place for mindless romance." I looked past her, across the castle rampart, out and down below to the verdant valley of farms and roads. Far beyond, the Alps rose up in majesty, looking closer than they were in all their massiveness. Gray and black rock, with green patches at the bottom, reaching up powerfully to the cloud-covered sky, as if they were shaking a fist at the heavens. Crowned at the top with gleaming snow.

She was right. This was a place of unplanned romance, not plotting and designing. Still...what we had discovered so far about the Project was disturbing. Harvesting of DNA from other subjects. Prior *in vitro* engineering and even tank births—we still didn't know what happened to those subjects and the babies. And a suspicion—only a suspicion at the moment—that some of this Project was funded by international black market operatives and shadowy military projects out of China and Russia. All the talk about "helping all humanity" could be taking a sinister turn.

Still, we could be wrong. Secrecy and seclusion breeds paranoia. We both knew that and tried to check each other.

But she was right. It was hard to care about any of that here. After all, we were pawns. Well-paid pawns. With new lives waiting for us, wherever we wanted. Far away from these people.

That was why I had asked if she would marry me once we were away from here. She laughed and made light of it, until she saw my hurt.

"I'm sorry, Pate. I can't think about that. Do I want a reminder of this place in my life every day?" She put her hand to my face and stroked my cheek. "You are wonderful. In another situation…"

I dropped my head, realizing that I had fallen in love with her.

"Oh, my dear. I have hurt you. Please understand it is not personal; I have come to care about you so much. But this Project—and my prior life…" She embraced me. "I'm not saying no. Just can't talk about it now."

She wanted to enjoy our time here. After all, it was the first time they allowed us to take a trip outside of Vienna— a surprise that was presented to us as an award for following the rules so stringently. So we *should* enjoy it. Hard to argue about that.

I forced a laugh. "Some people are set up by their friends. We were set up by a corporate-government-academic project. Does that give you pause?"

"Not here!" she shouted to the sky. "Not in Salzburg!" She used the German name with an exaggerated accent.

I laughed again. "Even with our babysitter?" I nodded towards the other end of the parapet.

"Even more so! Even all the money and planning and experts could not outwit romance!"

I pulled her to me. "I love you, Eris."

She lay her head on my chest. "I love you, Pate."

She got quiet. I heard a sniffle and pushed her way, holding her shoulders, looking in her face.

"Are you crying?"

She wiped her eyes. "A little."

"Happiness? Or sadness?"

"Both. More sad than happy."

It was cold. Not freezing cold, not dead-of-winter cold—but still biting. We stood on a stone parapet, facing the long valley before us, stone and rock behind and in front. Far below, a slow stream of water flowed through an artificial stream bed. It had originally been a natural intermittent stream, but human engineers had intruded, thinking to improve on nature.

I heard another sniffle and turned to look at her. "What is it?"

She sighed. "I'm pregnant."

June–September 2019

"You're going home."

"What?"

"You've served your purpose, and it's time to go."

"Did I do something wrong? Were the results not good?"

"To the contrary. The results have exceeded our best hopes. You played your part well, and now it is time to exit the stage."

"I don't want to leave."

"You don't want to leave *Eris*."

"Or Vienna. On the other hand, I could do without you."

She nodded. "I know. I'm sorry."

"I didn't mean that. Bad joke. Truth is, you've been a bright spot in this ordeal. The one person who seems... human."

She nodded again, but still seemed sad.

"What is it?"

She pulled her hand away and looked at me. Firm. Cold. "When you leave here, you can never see her again."

"The hell I can't. I can do whatever I want, at least when she leaves. I *did* go back and read the entire contract. Carefully. There is no restriction on that issue."

She leaned forward. "No legal restriction."

"What does that mean?"

She answered by picking up half of her sandwich and taking a bite. She chewed with care. I waited, not taking my eyes off her.

Finally, she swallowed and put the sandwich down. "Pate, I care about you. That is why I will say something that I should not. You do not know what the results of this project portend because they haven't told you. It will change the world if it goes their way. What they are doing is so important to them that they will do almost anything to keep it to themselves. And there are others who want it so bad that they would do even worse."

I felt a cold hard lump in my throat. "What are you saying?"

"Take your money, get on that plane tomorrow, and—"

"Tomorrow?!"

"—take your money, get on that plane tomorrow, and go far away. Not anywhere you have ever been before. Become a recluse. Never think of the Project again."

I sat, shaking in anger. "No way. I wanted this money for a reason. I'm going to start the company I wanted to start —but with *my* money this time. Do it the right way. They aren't going to tell me what I can do for the rest of my life!"

"They are not telling you that. *I* am telling you that. For your own good."

"This is not right. It's not fair."

She laughed without mirth. "For such an intelligent man, where did you get the idea that fairness is readily available in the world?"

"Because we strive for it, as humans."

"No, we don't. We strive for control of our lives and the world around us."

I stared at her. "I thought *I'd* become a pessimist. And I thought you were the one who believes there is something more than just the scientifically verifiable?"

"I do believe that." She stacked her dishes on her tray. "But I don't have control over much. And neither do you." She stood and picked up her tray. "Rolf will take you to the airport tomorrow morning. Be ready at 7:30."

"Can I say goodbye to her?"

"No."

I stood up. "No?!"

She sighed again and sat her tray down, leaning on the table with both arms. "I tried, Pate. I tried. I have gone to bat too many times. They were adamant. It was unconditionally 'no.'"

"They can't stop me from coming back to Vienna if I want to."

"You're going to make me say it?" She straightened up. "If you come back to this city, and try to see her, you will find yourself deported and your passport revoked. Or you might end up in jail."

"For what?!"

"For anything they can make up!" She lowered her voice and looked around the empty cafeteria. "They have money, power, and connections. It may not be 'fair,' Pate, but that's what will happen. Grow up and face reality!"

She left without another word, leaving her tray behind.

π

New York, New York. So nice they named it twice.

I didn't need to work. I didn't need to do anything, except eat and sleep, and I didn't much feel like doing either of those.

A large sum of money had been deposited into twenty different bank accounts, set up for me by the Project. Most were regular checking accounts, some were high interest-bearing with restrictions, one was a money market, one a CD, and another a retirement account. That had all been worked out ahead of time as part of the contract.

I'd had plans, ideas, schemes. I'd worked on a lot of it during my hours in the library in Vienna.

None of it held any interest for me.

I ignored the Director's advice to go far to somewhere I had never been. Instead, I had checked into a residence suite at the Langham on Fifth Avenue, because I could. I ordered room service twice a day; left the TV on continuously without watching it, and stared out at the city skyline and the Empire State building.

I knew that I could not go on like this forever. I'd have to pick myself up and move on. Do *something*. But for now, I was going to wait until I felt like it.

I could afford to wallow in misery, and that's what I was going to do.

π

The doorbell chimed. I frowned and got up, pulling on a robe. I had not ordered a meal yet. I opened the door to one of the stewards who usually brought me my meals.

"Good morning, Mr. Williamson. Sorry to disturb you, but this package came for you, and the deliverer said it was urgent."

"I didn't order anything."

"It has your name and room on it. It came for you via courier from Lisbon."

"Lisbon?" I craned my neck to look at the package he held out.

Pate Williamson
The Langham
400 Fifth Avenue
New York, NY, 10018
United States of America

Who would have my address? I don't know anyone in Lisbon. The return label read:

Jouer-Le-Rôle
R. Rosa Araújo 8, 1250-195
Lisboa, Portugal

The name was a phrase, not a person. "Playing the Role." A store, perhaps?

"We scan all packages, sir, as you know. It is safe—standard electronics.

"Electronics?"

"Yes. Consumer electronics. A computer or tablet, perhaps."

"Very well. Thank you. Hang on." I stepped back and grabbed a $50 from the entry table. "Here." I took the package and shut the door on him as he was thanking me.

It was a tablet in an original box, with an envelope taped to it. I inspected the box. Factory sealed. I open the envelope and pulled out a single sheet of paper. No letterhead, no signature.

VPN: https://rollensecuritiedesystems.fr
FOLLOW INSTRUCTIONS ON HOME PAGE.
REBOOT. LOGIN
  Login: Human213fleur935
PW: FriedenInUnsererZeuit4592104
  pop: mail.rollensecuritiedesystems.fr
Port: 453
Encryption method: SSL
username: Paolo-029584-pepper.
PW: /EW!qb/z$uRmaV]K%s,]W6M5:Hg

I turned on the tablet, and it took me through an automated setup. After connecting to the hotel WIFI network, I signed on to the website. It had me download an app, run it, then restart and sign in again. Once online, I opened the mail app and began setting it up as instructed.

My curiosity had gotten the best of me, and I was more interested by this than anything in months. I forced myself to go slow with the ridiculously long password. Finished, I clicked "Check Mail."

One item appeared in the inbox. From "Joer." No subject. I opened it.

Delete immediately after reading. Empty trash securely.
Schloss Heidelberg. Across from gift center, large tree with scaffolding. Monday next. Just after sundown.
Leave no trail. Travel incognito.

π

With enough money, it is easy to get a false passport and a plane ticket. I had not cut my hair since I had left Vienna, so I called in a stylist to trim it and to color it. I bought some plain, inexpensive, casual clothes—a style I would never have purchased or worn.

I didn't know who sent the tablet and letter, but it could only be one of two people, I figured. The return address was a mystery, though.

I sat in Coach for the eight-hour flight to the Berlin Tegel Airport, had a brief layover, and then another 90-minute leg to the Karlsruhe/Baden-Baden Airport. I didn't give much thought to the accommodations I *could* have had, because of what I hoped was going to happen when I arrived. Hell, I'd have ridden over in the hold of a tanker and walked across Europe.

If I was right.

Heidelberg had been one of my favorite cities when I had tromped around Europe in between my sophomore and junior years. Touristy without being touristy. A great castle. Good summer weather.

I took a taxi from the airport to Heidelberg, having the driver drop me off at the castle. I gave him a hundred euros and jumped out near the Visitor's Center.

She was standing sideways, by the tree. I could see the slight, rounded protrusion of her belly.

π

We stood at a huge portico beside the castle, looking out over the city and the river. Fireworks exploded over the water, lighting up the banks on both sides. Each flash illuminated the people packed tightly together at the river's edge and up here around us. A little boy nearby was shouting, "Feuer! Feuer!"

She turned and looked up into my eyes. A look that made my heart hurt.

"What is it?" I said.

She pursed her lips, accentuating the wrinkles there. Sadness in her eyes. Regret. Perhaps some fear. "This is wonderful. And we'll do it again. But in six months it will be over. You know that."

I refuse to accept it. "No. They can't tell us what to do."

Tears filled her eyes. "They can do anything they want, Pate. And we are powerless."

"I refuse to believe that. There must be *some* option. Some way. It isn't fair." I reached up and brushed away a tear that had appeared below her left eye. "We belong together. I'll figure something out."

She came into my arms. I held her tight for a moment, then she pulled back and looked at me. Fireworks lit up the side of her face. The castle tower loomed behind. In this dim light, it looked strong, for all its nine hundred years. But dawn would show that it was merely a ruin.

"No, Pate. I won't spend the rest of my life looking over my shoulder. In fear. My early life was..." She shook her head. "I won't do it."

"Eris, please..."

"I have to go back now. You know they won't be fooled for long by our body doubles in the city. I don't know when the next time will be."

"Body doubles? She is good?"

She smiled. "I told her you would know who was behind it."

"You talked to her? My Director?"

She gave me a funny look. "What?"

"Well, I figured it was her who did this. Was it your Director, not mine?"

"Pate, there aren't two Directors. It's the same person."

June 2032

The train pulled into the tidy and high-tech München train station. It was almost empty at this late hour. This was a terminal station—all the trains came straight in and the tracks ended. If he had decided to go to Salzburg, he'd have to buy a ticket and switch trains.

He was struck by silence inside the station. A few trains sat silent and dark, waiting for the morning route, he supposed. Other tracks were empty. The large platform was lit by a series of low-power LED lamps, bathing the platform in a dim, yellow light.

Only a few people were in evidence, walking with heads down: all singles or couples. He surveyed the shops, restaurants, and ticket offices lined up facing the tracks. All were dark under their screen signage, still glowing. He scanned the area for Polizei, and saw no one in uniform.

The ticket office was dark, but he checked the door anyway. Locked. Nearby was an enclosed waiting room: a plain room with glass walls and aluminum struts that faced the tracks. Inside were seats, benches, and a wall-mounted screen showing some old German sitcom. The lone occupant was a man sleeping on a bench.

The information booth down the platform was also dark and empty. There must be no more trains until morning.

He spotted two uniformed DeutcheBahn employees coming from his train, a male and female. He approached.

Hello. Do you know sign language?

The woman spoke. "I don't know sign. Are you supposed to meet someone?"

Salim shook his head.

"Waiting for another train? The next one is not until 0515."

He shook his head again, and then pantomimed a badge on his lapel and a flashing light over his head.

"Ah," the man said, "Polizei?"

Salim nodded.

"Usually there is a security officer there—" he pointed to one of the dark shops facing the trains, "—but perhaps he is out attending to business or taking a break. There is a regular Polizei station out the north exit, to the right, about two miles down."

Salim signed his thanks and went the north exit, pushing open the heavy glass door. Tall, dark buildings lined the streets. It looked like the financial center. A few cars flew by, all self-driving taxis. In both directions, the street was a deep, black canyon, punctuated here and there by glowing blobs of blue, red, yellow, and white: signs, door lights, street light, cars.

Recent events had made him paranoid. He turned and went back inside. Maybe the security guard would be back soon. He felt ashamed. Salim knew that German cities— even big ones—were safe for adults and even children traveling alone. It had a low rate of violent crime, and burglaries and robberies were rare, mostly related to touristry and tourists.

But he was on the wrong side of statistics today.

He sat down beside the door of the security office with his back to the wall.

December 2019 – March 2020

I met Eris two more times over the next three months, and after the second, I moved to London to make my flights shorter. There was a Langham in London, which was tempting, but I wanted a change—and I figured that unpredictability was a good idea. So I took a suite at The Goring.

I thought back over the many conversations I'd had with the Director. She subtly but intentionally made me believe that Eris had a different Director. It wasn't the deception that bothered me as much as its pointless nature. Just another in a stack of deceptions—and I was sure there were more.

Nevertheless, I was indebted to her for arranging these brief meetings. After I moved, we met three more times, once a month. Only for a few hours. Once, in Paris, it was a whole day and night. We stood, arm in arm, looking at the ruined Notre Dame Cathedral. Then Berlin, where we spent time in the crowded Ku' damm. And once in London, where we walked Covent Gardens for two hours. Eris told me that she thought another meeting would occur in January in Lyon.

I was surprised at the capabilities the Director had and got away with it—she must have a network of people working with her—mostly security and surveillance experts, I guessed, since it was a sure bet the Project didn't know what she was doing. It made me reconsider her role and abilities. She had to be more than a functionary or mere administrator.

The bigger question was 'why?' Why would she risk so much for Eris and I? What did she get out of it? At the moment, I didn't care.

But March was coming.

π

The phone beeped. I blinked hard; it was still dark. Rolling over, I focused on the clock: 3:37 AM. I waved my arm over the bedside.

"Hello?"

"Pate?"

"Yes? Who is this, and why the—"

'This is the Director."

I bolted upright. "Isn't this some breach of—"

"No. Sanctioned. You need to come to Vienna now."

"What? Why? Oh! The birth?"

"No..." Her voice broke. Fear gripped my bowels. "Yes, but no. It was...a difficult birth. The baby didn't make it. Eris is dying."

"What?!"

"Medical complications. Maybe due to the treatments. We don't know at the moment. If you want to see her... well, you better get here."

"That's the most advanced medical facility in the world! They can save her!"

"We can argue about it or you can get your ass on a plane. I had to threaten to resign before they agreed to let me call and invite you."

"Wait! Is—"

The line went dead.

March 2020

It was quiet except for the gentle beeping of a machine. The antiseptic smell, mixed with other scents I didn't want to think about, completed the offensive olfactory montage.

She was in an induced coma. Keeping her alive until I could get here. Uncharacteristic grace from the cold heart of the Project. What had it cost the Director?

They backed off some of the medication to allow her to wake. I watched as her face changed from smoothness and serenity to grimaces and confusion. The machine's beeping increased in frequency. I squeezed her hand, and she opened her eyes. The lids were sticky, and as she licked her lips, I saw a white substance on them.

I looked up at the Director.

"I'll give you some privacy," she said. "Ten minutes. Her pain will increase." The door swooshed gently as she left.

"Eris. I love you."

She smiled and nodded. But did not speak.

"Don't leave me."

She frowned and looked away, then back at me, pain in her eyes.

"I'm sorry," I said. "What I want to say is that I am so thankful I met you. For all the wrongness of this Project, and as much as I hate it, I am grateful to it because it led me to you. A year of you in my life is worth everything."

She smiled and closed her eyes. Her hand squeezed mine and went limp. I leaned over and kissed her lips, and I could barely discern any returning kiss. She opened her mouth to speak, but it was only a wheezing croak. I put my ear to her mouth, and she whispered. "I love you." She said something else, but I could not make it out. I asked her to repeat it, but she lay silent with her eyes closed.

I talked for the next eight minutes. I spoke of my favorite times, places, and foods we shared. I told her about my parents. Tears came to my eyes as I talked, and when I looked down, she had matching tears. After a while, I could tell she was in severe pain. The beeping became angrier. I wanted to squeeze every second out of this time, but I didn't want her to suffer, either.

She let out a moan. A nurse came. "I'm sorry, I need to increase her dose."

Soon, Eris' face became smooth. The beeping became steady and slow, with long, painful spaces between. A gentle reminder that there was still a life within that motionless body. A soul that could feel. A heart that beat, however weakly. I look at the nurse.

"Not much longer now." She was trying to be kind. I wanted to punch her in the face. To mar that pretty visage with bruises and blood. "She's not feeling any pain."

π

"They'd like to run a few tests on you since you are here," the Director said.

"No way. I'm done with all of you." I had been crying, but now I was mad. She was escorting me out of the hospital rooms, and I realized we were headed in the direction of the labs.

"I understand your anger. I'm angry, too. Just let them do this, and you can go away forever. After all, they've lost a lot."

"Why do I care? Besides, my contract is up. I owe you nothing."

She sighed. "I'm sorry, Pate, but that is not true. The contract allows them to perform periodic checkups up to two years after you exit the program."

"You're all a bunch of heartless bastards." I was on the edge of exploding.

She nodded without looking at me. "Yes. We are."

"At least let me speak to Dr. Androvich. This Project was his passion, and he's not a bureaucrat or a corporate shill."

"He's not here. He left the Project and returned to Edinburgh."

"What?! The man who created the Project? It's *his* brainchild."

"Yes, well, after this last failure..." She stopped. "Come on, one more test and—"

"After this last failure *what?!*"

She looked away and appeared to be struggling. She looked away. "He and Perry began arguing more and more. He decided he wanted nothing more to do with the Project."

"That makes no sense. It was his *life's work*."

She stood. "Come on. Get this over with, and then you can leave and try to have a decent life. At least you have money to do whatever you want."

I stood my ground, fuming.

"You don't really have a choice."

I relented, and neither of us spoke until we reached the door of the lab.

"Goodbye, Pate. God be with you."

I turned to her. "You're not going in?"

"No."

"And that's it? 'God be with you?'"

"Yes. That's it." She turned away. I watched her back until she turned the far corner. She never looked back.

The room I remembered all too well. Two technicians directed me behind a partition to disrobe and don on a hospital gown. I sat in the chair and they strapped me in.

'What the—"

"Sorry, Mr. Williamson, just a precaution. This procedure might cause some involuntary muscle spasms, and we don't want you to hurt yourself." That had happened before, but those were pretty intrusive procedures.

"Procedure? No one said anything about a procedure."

She stepped back. "I'm sorry. I should have explained. It's merely a series of tests that will take about an hour. You might have a reaction, you might not. You might need to rest for a few hours after and eat something, but that depends on how you feel. Would you like me to call a doctor and the Director? They can explain in more detail."

I just wanted out of this place. I knew from experience it could take hours to get a doctor. "No. Go ahead and let's finish this."

π

Beep.

Beep.

Where am I?

I opened my eyes to blurry vision. I felt drugged. As the room resolved into details, memories flooded back. My room. The Project. Tests today? The Director should be—

Eris is dead.

I sat bolt upright as a nurse came in.

"Mr. Williamson—"

"What the *hell* is going on?" I swung my legs over the side of the bed and tried to stand up, but almost passed out. I sat back down with her help.

"The doctor is on is the way. You had a reaction to the procedure, but you'll be okay."

"I wanted to leave right after —"

"Yes, yes, you can leave as soon as you're feeling better, the doctor is—"

The door opened and a doctor came in—a doctor I had never met. "Mr. Williamson, my deepest apologies. Your vitals are returning to normal, and you may leave as soon as you feel up to it. Perhaps an hour or less if we get some orange juice and food in you. I just signed the release papers. You had an unusual reaction to the medication, and we felt the need to keep you—"

"Who are you?"

"I'm Dr. Sterling, the—"

"I've never seen you before."

He flinched. "Well, I, ah, have been here for—"

"It doesn't matter. Why don't I remember anything since the lab?"

He sighed. "We gave you the same pre-test medication you had before, so we do not know what happened. If you *are* willing to stay, we'd like to do more tests to find out—"

"Absolutely not! I'm starting to think you are a bunch of hacks. I'm leaving."

He nodded. "Perfectly fine, as is your right. We gave you a sedative once we realized the reaction, enough to sleep it off. We checked your vitals half-hourly, and they have been returning to normal. I'll have someone bring your clothes and belongings immediately. Ah, here's some food."

A nurse entered with a tray and set it down in front of me. I gulped the orange juice as if I had scurvy. "Good. Where is the Director? I want to talk to her before I leave."

"I...I can check if she's available."

"Do that." I looked at the nurse as he left and smiled. I enjoyed ordering a Project doctor around for once. "Well," I said. "That was fun. Do you think this is as outrageous as I do?"

She opened her mouth, then closed it. "I...I'm sorry, sir. I am just a nurse. I just do my job."

I held her gaze for a while, then realized she was right. She was a small cog in a mighty wheel. I nodded and took a bite of a peeled, hard-boiled egg.

We remained silent until the doctor returned. "She is occupied. Your clothes and belongings are on their way. Once you are ready, the nurse here will accompany you to the exit."

"Tell me what—"

He turned and left, ignoring me, and within a minute, an orderly came in to drop off my belongings. I was feeling much better—the egg and orange juice were probably enhanced for just that purpose. The nurse stepped out while I dressed. Everything was there, including my cash, watch, and other valuables. I examined my wallet carefully to see if it had been rifled through. I always put cards, credit cards, and cash in a particular order in a particle orientation. Everything was as I left it.

Eris is dead.

I stepped out the door, and the nurse led me through the labyrinthine corridors to the lobby. As we neared the receptionist desk, I veered toward it.

"Where are you going?" Shouted the nurse. "You have to leave!"

"Just here." She followed me.

"I'd like to leave a message for someone, please?" I said to the woman behind the desk.

"Certainly, sir." She picked up the phone. "Who is the party?"

"The Director."

She frowned. "I need a name."

I didn't know her name. Strange, in over a year, I had never heard it. I looked at the nurse. She went around the desk and punched a few buttons. I frowned. Is her name a secret, too? The receptionist held the phone to her ear, listened for a moment, frowned, then punched a few more buttons. I waited.

"Hello. Yes, this is reception. I am trying to leave a message at extension 45863, but I get the non-active tone... yes...I'll hold." She stared at the desk.

"What's the Director's name?" I asked the nurse. She shook her head.

"Ah, well...okay, thank you." The receptionist hung up. "That individual no longer works here."

π

I was unceremoniously and physically removed from the building. The nurse had called security, and they had no interest in my arguments to the contrary.

Without Rolf to return me to the airport, I hailed a taxi and ordered the AI to take me to the best hotel in town. I was not leaving the city. I was simmering with fury and pretty sure there was nothing I could do. I could go back to London or New York and resume my solitary life of opulent misery, but I wasn't ready to accept that.

I went to the desk and asked for a room. As I filled out the paperwork, I saw the clerk had written "19 März" in the date field. I looked up.

"Entschuldigung, bitte? Was ist heutiges Datum? In English?"

"It is the nineteenth of March, sir."

I pulled out my airline ticket stub and read

17 March 2019

I had left London early Tuesday morning on the 17th and arrived at the hospital in the early afternoon. I saw Eris, then went for the tests in the late afternoon. Even if I was unconscious all night, it should only be Wednesday the 18th.

I had lost two days.

June 2032

"Wake up! Wake up!"

Salim blinked and jumped to his feet. Two men stood in front of him.

"Are you Salim?" The man reached out and took his arm.

He came fully awake with a start and tried to pull away.

"It's okay. We are Polizei." Salim now saw the uniform and badge. Behind him was another man in a Deutsche-Bahn uniform—the security guard he had been waiting for.

"Are you Salim?"

How does he know my name? Salim nodded.

The man seemed relieved. "Ach so. The Polizei have been looking for you! Stuttgart called when you did not get off the train. Your parents are quite worried!"

A warm wave of joy and relief spread through him, and he began to sign rapidly. *My parents? Are they okay? Where are they? How did you find me?*

The man laughed. "Stop! I do not speak sign language." His eyes twinkled. "We go to the station and sort it out."

The security guard, thinner and younger, nodded. As they walked out of the north entrance and turned right, Salim noted that the sky was beginning to lighten. He must have slept for two or three hours.

The police station appeared to have only a skeleton crew working at this time of the morning. Many of the offices were dark. The man led Salim to a conference room, indicated a seat, and left. A few moments later, a female Polizei brought him a cup of tea. Salim picked up the mug and blew on it, then took a long draught. It was so delicious and warming. Soon he would be back with his parents. He had been so sure they were dead. Now, they would explain what happened, and this nightmare would be over. He sighed and took another sip.

The woman returned. "Come with me." She had a blanket draped over one arm. He followed her into the next room, which appeared to be a waiting room with a large couch and a few chairs.

"You can wait here. No one will disturb you. Your parents will be here in an hour or so. Sleep if you can. Wouldn't want you to get sick after being in that station all night!"

He signed *thank you* and sat down on the couch.

How nice. But he had never been sick. Not even the sniffles. Mom said it was because they were a healthy family, though his mom and dad were sick sometimes.

He lay down and pulled the blanket over him and was asleep before the officer left the room.

June 2020

It took me three months to find out where they had buried her. After a few calls to the University and the medical center, and trying to get someone to talk to me without success, I changed tactics. I hired both private detectives and researchers who took what I knew and, after a short time, delivered a list of names, phone numbers, emails, and addresses. Using internet and fake phones, I began contacting one after one. Even when they did not know who I was, they feigned ignorance about the entire project. "You must have the wrong number."

Frustrated with my contracted hires, I berated them for the cost. They pointed out that I hired them to find names and contact information, not find out what they knew. "However, Mr. Williamson, we have associates for hire that could find out what they know."

I pretended I didn't know what he meant and told them to hire their associates.

Within weeks, I received the address of a graveyard in Calne, near Avebury in the UK. I didn't know if that was Eris hometown. She and I never talked much about our childhoods, though I was aware she had lived in England.

I rented a car at Heathrow and drove out to Calne. It was a small, ancient town on the banks of a narrow river.

Quaint, beautiful, sleepy. And beautiful. The graveyard was a mile or so outside the town, connected to an ancient church.

I crunched up the gravel walkway and walked methodically down every row of gravestones. It was a large burial site, dating back many centuries, and I was prepared to walk for days. But it was easy to find the newer graves by inspecting the grounds and the condition.

Thirty minutes after I arrived, I stood before a simple stone slab, unadorned except for some plain engraving.

> *Eris LaFleur*
> *31 July 1997 – 18 March 2020*

I had not even known her birthday until now.

The freshly dug turf had been placed back on top of the grave, and the grass was only just starting to grow back.

She had told me that she had no living family—like me. I wondered if that was one characteristic the project sought. Why would that be important?

The day was gray, and a heavy mist lay close to the ground. The long grass below my feet was matted from the weight of the dew. It sounded as if the air was filled with cotton.

I surprised myself by my own screaming, "Why, *why?!*" and looked around self-consciously. I was alone in this forgotten part of the world.

I had done everything asked of me. I tried to be responsible and fair. And my investors and my college roommate and friend took advantage of me. I thought the Project was a way to recover—to start again. Then Eris, and for the first time, I wanted more than just a career and to make a difference in the world. And the same project that I thought could save me took that from me, leaving me with the money to follow my dreams that I didn't care about any longer.

Eris—she was perfect. For me, anyway. What kind of God must exist to allow innocent people to die! Job had cursed God as uncaring and silent. Jeremiah cursed him as deceitful. I'm with those guys.

I began crying, and as I let go, it came in huge sobs. I fell to my knees. For my loss. For the death of youthful innocence. For the end of my naïve, stupid dreams.

The moisture seeped through the knees of my trousers as the thick, wet air pressed in around me as if trying to suffocate my sobs. The death of love.

Part of me wanted revenge. But I was too tired, too sad. *Just kill me too.*

I heard voices, far away. Turning, I saw three nuns walking down one of the dirt paths through the graveyard. They didn't see me, or, if they did, they paid no attention. Three copies of the same person, with subtle distinctions in size, gait, and posture. They walked, side by side, hands folded in front. The Three Graces. Faith, Hope, and Love.

All three have abandoned me.

What might these three servants of the Lord say to me? Would they have answers? I doubted it. What did they know of suffering, cloistered away in their stone cells?

The intellectual side of me took exception to. They might know a lot about suffering. They might be nuns *because* of their suffering. What did *I* know? It's not all about me.

I stood.

"It's not all about me," I said aloud.

I had been mourning my losses. My bad fortune. What had been done to me. I felt powerless.

But I am not powerless. The Project had given me two gifts. One, they told me how unique my mind, body, and genetics were. And two, they gave me a boatload of money. When I needed a task performed, and was at a dead-end, I used that money to hire people who found Eris' grave within weeks.

What else could that money do? It could start a new business. Major capital. I was confident enough that it would be a success this time. I had learned.

Or, I could use my abilities and money to do something else.

Lady Faith and Lady Love may have abandoned me, but Lady Hope was still visible in the distance.

I took a deep breath. Before I take any other steps, I needed to confront someone. That conversation would determine my next move.

June 2020

It didn't take long for my newly hired resources to track him down. I enjoyed the montage of emotions on his face when he opened the door to me: confusion, recognition, surprise, and then fear.

Interesting.

He tried to shut the door in my face, so I stuck my foot between it and the frame. Funny, in a world of high technology, that old trick still works.

"You have to talk to me, Doctor."

"No, no. I cannot! Please go!" The joyful and enthusiastic researcher was gone, replaced with a panicked old academic who was afraid of something. Very afraid.

"I won't leave. I'll make a scene."

"No, my dear boy. Please. I will call the police."

"Do it." I was pretty sure he would not.

Silence. Sigh. Resignation. "Okay. Briefly. Not here. Meet me outside the Whiski Bar on High Street. 10pm. Do not let anyone see you."

I nodded and left. What was he so afraid of? I was never told I couldn't make contact with staff people, though perhaps they didn't consider I would ever want to. But what difference did it make if he talked to me? He had an NDA just like I did.

Still, he'd always been kind to me, and I felt terrible about forcing him. But I needed answers. I bought a hoodie from a local tourist shop and a hat as an attempt to make myself inconspicuous on his behalf.

The Whiski Bar was a small pub wedged between a Ladbroke's and the entrance to a close. It was the kind of place that locals would frequent, and tourists wouldn't likely notice it unless they were directed to it. A glass and wood storefront, with three tables out front—just planks of wood nailed to whisky barrels. The day had been warm, but it was cooling down quickly. Still, in June, it wouldn't get much below 11.

I went directly to the menu posted beside the door, pretending to examine it as I scanned the outside tables. Four locals sat at one: three young men and a woman, laughing. The middle table was empty. A lone man sat at the far table wearing a large, heavy coat, a scarf, and a ratty old tam. He was staring at a glass of whisky in front of him. I walked over. "Doctor?"

He looked up. Disheveled and looking much older than the quick look I had earlier. "Sit."

I sat. He looked back down at his glass as I searched his face. Sad. Disheartened. Such a contrast to his former self.

Motion to my left. "May I get you something, mate? Would you like a menu?"

"Whisky."

"We have quite a selection; I'll fetch you the list." He turned.

"No, no. What is your favorite?"

"Och, that would be the Auchentoshan 18. It's a local whisky from the Lowlands, and only 227 bottles are—"

"That's fine. Bring the bottle."

"Oh! Well, mate, the price is—"

"I don't care."

His speech became more proper. "Very well, sir. I shall return."

I looked back at the Doctor. He had not moved.

"Doctor Androvich?"

"I'm sorry, my boy."

I frowned. "For?"

He sighed, picked up his glass and took a slow sip, placing it back down with care, as if it might explode. "That you got involved in this...this disaster."

"Disaster?"

"For you, yes?"

We sat, having agreed on at least that much. The waiter returned with the bottle and a glass. I waved him away as he started to open it. I tore off the cap cover and pulled the cork, filling my glass with a generous pour.

His glass was empty, and he did not protest as I filled it. "And you, doctor? Also a disaster?"

"Yes." He took a sip. "Yes. Quite."

"So much secrecy. More than would be warranted for a medical breakthrough. Crucial details that might have changed my decisions were kept from me."

He sighed again. I was getting a little tired of the poor-me act, but I reminded myself that he had lost his life's work.

He shook his head. "Even I didn't know for a long time. Then I suspected. But I didn't want to know. It was my dream come true—unlimited funds and staff to pursue my theories and dreams of a better world. So I ignored the shadows. The rumors. Just like my ancestors did...in..." He downed the dram, and, without asking, took the bottle and poured himself another. "Your pain. Your loss. It is all my fault." He sat back, staring behind me. I followed his gaze to the sprawling castle at the pinnacle of the mountain. The ancient walls, at the edge of the precipice, had stood for almost a millennia, and would probably stand for another. Attacked, damaged, rebuilt, expanded, modernized—it had stood the test of time. Impregnable except by subterfuge from the inside.

"I played God, though that was not my intention. I...I thought to work *with* God...to improve." He shook his head. "But maybe..." He looked at me now, turning those old eyes on mine, now brimming with tears. "...maybe that is my sin...to assume I could improve upon God's work..."

I felt a pang of sympathy despite myself. Why can't I be allowed righteous anger? I laid my head on the table. "It was not you. It was them."

"Yes...but I presented them the opportunity...and ignored the abuses...a thing that they wanted so badly that they would kill."

I raised up. "Kill? Who'd they kill?"

He jerked and looked to both sides. "I mean Eris. Her death. Not—no one killed her, of course. But she died all the same." His eyes flicked to mine, to the side, and then back to his glass.

I took a long draft. "Doctor—Vlad, if I may—tell me. Tell me how we got here. Tell me who is responsible."

He gave me a small smile. "Oh. How nice it would be to unburden...to enter the confessional...and..."

I waited.

"What the hell." He downed the glass, poured another, and began talking. He took me to the University of St. Petersburg, where he first worked with genetic engineering and biotechnologies. CRISPR was not even a glimmer in Doudna and Charpentier's minds at that point. But he found things—thought of things—that no one else had. It was as if he was born for it. To help humanity. He perceived techniques that were so ground-breaking that the technology did not exist to do what he proposed. He studied other disciplines and worked with experts in those fields, pushing some of the more genius mechanical and electronic engineers to invent the technology he needed. Biomathematics, sequencing, AI experts, medical geneticists, and a variety of pathologists, psychologists, occupational therapists, physiotherapists—

He went on for so long naming research and practical fields and skills that I lost track. Many I had never heard of, and could not even guess what they were. But while academic research tends to the insular, Androvich's scope was impressively broad.

Hired by the University of Vienna as a researcher, grants began to pour in. He assembled a team to devise experiments to test the viability of his theories. The success was promising, and as he and others published, major grants began to appear. From philanthropists and philanthropic organizations, but soon, corporations and governments began to approach the project.

"Pate, I was stunned at the amount of money. I was in my 50s by then, and I had never heard of a program being financed to that degree. By an order of magnitude."

"Did it make you suspicious?"

"No. I was convinced of my own brilliance, and no one around me was dissuading me or offering words of caution. I *knew* what I could do, and I just assumed others had the same vision. Of course people wanted to fund it—I had seen things no one else had. I was way ahead of the curve."

He stared up at the castle once more, lost in some thought of the past. I waited.

"I assumed that everyone was excited for the same reason I was: the advancement of a field, changing the history of science, the betterment of humanity, and so on. I knew, of course, that some of the results could be used in ways that would make other people a lot of money. Procedures to eradicate diseases, to create more efficient workers, better soldiers, and so on. I even knew some might want to use it for designer babies—it had been tried even after it was outlawed. But I trusted in the community to prevent unethical use, and I thought since it was my project, my staff and I would control how it would be used. I never dreamed the university itself would be so blinded by the money coming in as to compromise their integrity and standing."

Poor man. He had little understanding of just how much the quest for money and power can strip people of their humanity. Being a university makes no difference except in flowery words on brochures about "the pursuit of knowledge" and "academic integrity."

"So what happened? When did you begin to..." I wasn't sure how to phrase it without insulting him.

"We were close to testing some of the procedures on human subjects. Just small, independent, tests at first. But they were pushing to begin earlier than I wanted to. They played on my vanity, told me I was too modest in interpreting the results. Even the university was pushing me. Once again, we had remarkable success. They began pushing for the full theory to be tested *in vitro* on human subjects. I hadn't even thought that was legal yet, at least not without first presenting all the data and procedures to the academic community. But I had been working almost non-stop for three years. I had quit attending conferences, I read nothing but the literature related to my work. I didn't even know my country had a new Prime Minister for a year! The lawyers assured me that it was fine. I argued that we still weren't ready, and I'd need to check with the academic community myself. They pushed harder. I told them I would quit."

"But you didn't." This was all sounding a bit too familiar to me, in a different field, many years ago.

"No. Their response was just short of threatening, and, frankly, I was still hoping..."

I refilled both of our glasses.

"So we went ahead. I knew it was too early. While the full procedure was successful in so many ways, it always ended in stillborns, or death soon thereafter. Twice we lost the female subject, too."

I bolted upright. "What?! There were other subjects before us? Subjects who died?"

He looked surprised. "You didn't know? Of course there were. Twenty-six over the last six years. They didn't tell you?"

"No, Doctor Androvich, they *didn't* tell me! And neither did you!" I wanted to punch him.

He put his head in his hands. "I should have known. Of course they didn't tell you."

"What happened?"

He began discussing the issues with his immediate staff, finding they were all as uncomfortable as he was. But all attempts to pull back, even by the whole head medical staff, came to no avail. They were ignored or threatened.

"So I proposed another stage in the project. I told them it had been the goal all along. I told them that the goal all along was to find subjects that already had the genetic characteristics we wanted. And to perform the procedures on them, which would be far more effective, because we wouldn't need to perform such drastic engineering."

He shook his head. "I lied to them, Pate. That was never part of my project. I told them that because I thought that finding the perfect subjects would take so long that I'd have time to do something. *Anything.*"

He took a deep breath and looked into my eyes. "I underestimated how much money they were willing to spend. I am not sure everything they did to find you was legal. Access to records—"

"Yes," I said, refilling our glasses. "They knew some things about me I don't think they could have known otherwise."

"When they found you and Eris, I panicked. In the meeting where they told us we had you both, I lost control. I told them everything I thought. And I was shocked that they agreed. They said we would continue, but slow the pace and be much more precise with this new stage."

I snorted. "And you believed them? They had a sudden change of heart, did they?"

He looked up and grimaced as he continued to describe how his closest and most tenured partners began disappearing. One day, they didn't show up to work, and when he inquired, he was told that they did not fit well and they had decided to leave on their own and didn't want to make a big fuss.

"They left without saying anything to me. Some had been my colleagues and friends for decades. They would not have done that unless forced."

"Did you try to contact them?"

He looked offended. "Of course I did. That's what I'm telling you. They were *gone.* Old telly numbers, addresses, email, everything. When I inquired further, they told me they heard they went to some distant place, that they were well-compensated with a severance package, and probably went away to rest and get away from it all—this was high pressure, long hours, years-long job, they reminded me." He shook his head. "Maybe so. But no call? No email?"

"Surely you don't think they were killed?! Is that what you meant earlier?"

"Maybe they were telling me the truth. Maybe they were just angry at me for allowing this tragedy of research to go on for so long."

I didn't believe he really thought that, and now I was getting angry. And scared. I took a few deep breaths.

"I am getting the feeling, doctor, that something more sinister is going on here than just breaking academic rules and regulations."

He looked at me again, his jaw working. "I will not try to dissuade you of that opinion."

I divided the last of the Auchentoshan between us. "Why did you leave? Why quit your beloved project?"

Tears filled his eyes again. "It was no longer my beloved project. I had allowed it to be hijacked. When I found out what—"

He broke down. Sobbing quietly.

I didn't care. "Found out *what*?"

He composed himself. "I cannot tell you. I will *not* tell you."

I fumed. "Yes, you will."

"I wish I could. I know it sounds trite—but it is for your own good. I am protecting you.

"Sounds like protecting your own arse, doctor."

"Maybe, in part. But I will no longer allow people to be hurt because of my actions. Even indirectly. And telling you would—"

"They *are* hurt, you old bastard!" I threw the glass against the wall. People turned to look, then looked away. "This is all your fault. I deserve to know *everything*!"

He dropped his head and began weeping. I felt a momentary blip of sympathy again. What did they do to this guy?

I shook my head. No matter. He had information I needed.

"Fine, Doctor. But I *will* find out. I will harass you and make your life miserable until you do."

He looked up, his eyes wide and wet. "*Please*, Pate. I am doing this for you. My life is already ruined. I have nothing left except to protect those I hurt. You—"

"Is everything okay, gentleman?" The waiter.

"Yes, thank you," I said. "My friend and I have had a rough week, and neither of us is handling it well. Apologies. We'll calm down." I took my seat.

The man looked at Androvich. "Sir? Are you okay?"

"I am fine. My friend is correct. We'll be quiet."

He nodded. "Another outburst and I will ask you to leave, I'm afraid."

"One more thing." I leaned over the table and put both hands down. "I want her money."

"What?"

"The money that she was owed. I want it."

"I...I don't—"

"That money belongs to me. We had a baby. We were a couple. It's mine, and I want it."

I looked away, back up High Street, past Giles Cathedral, to the fortress.

"It isn't yours, Pate. It's hers."

"She's dead, you bastard."

"There was no contractual provision about payment in the event of death, except to direct family. And neither of you had any."

"Convenient. There was nothing in the contract warning me about the dangers and the prior deaths either. Maybe I should take it to an attorney. You know you won't remain unscathed."

He sat upright for the first time and began to talk rapidly, repeating himself. "You were not married. Not direct family. The money would have gone to her family, in the event of her death, but—"

"—I am *the only family she has left* in any sense, and the money is mine. It's the least you can do."

He sat. His face seemed to be contorting. "It's not—it's not in my control—"

"Tell you what. You find a way to get me that money, and you will never hear from me again. I'll find out the secret you're keeping another way."

He sat silent, looking at the table. Our waiter approached and I held up my hand. He backed away.

"I will see what I can do."

June 2020

The Goring hotel became my base of operations. I set up a team of freelance detectives, researchers, and the best freelance technology experts and hackers to find out everything they could about Eris, Androvich, Mr. Perry, and anyone else that seemed important concerning the operation of the Project. I made it a priority for them to find the Director. A tall task, considering I didn't know her name, age, or country of origin, though I could make a guess at the latter two. But we knew where she lived during the year I was in the project, and with a general guess at her age and being from a French-speaking region or country, they went to work.

Meanwhile, I changed my financial advisors and investors and moved most of it to Switzerland. We set up shell accounts and front organizations. I did not think the professor would have any luck getting me Eris' money, especially since he was no longer part of the project. I was not even sure why I threatened him for that. I had a lot of money, of course, but it would not be enough to do what I wanted. At least not and let me be able to live afterward. So I needed to make the money grow.

I took some time to investigate the fringes of legal covert operations and stealth technique experts, locating a man named Tasta, one of the best freelancers in Europe. Governments and corporations both used his services, and, I suspected, private citizens engaged in less-than-savory pursuits.

I didn't want to engage in illegalities, but I was not beyond exploiting loopholes and bending rules, if necessary. Tasta understood that, and seemed to take a liking to me and my project. And perhaps my money.

Tasta was also willing to help me learn covert techniques. I need to be hard to find, because when I started to cause problems, they would come after me. Maybe Androvich was exaggerating, maybe they wouldn't really murder to protect their investment. But I would take no chances. I even considered plastic surgery, but my experts convinced me that these extremes were unnecessary. Instead, they took me in and taught me multiple techniques—things as simple as a hair cut and uncharacteristic style, subtle hair coloring or graying, and growing a beard or mustache. Couple that with things like learning how to stand and walk differently, adopting unnatural mannerisms. For instance, I had never noticed that Europeans, when standing still, stood upright, but Americans tend to cock the hips and bend a knee. These things were difficult, but I had good teachers, and they assured me that, once mastered, I could walk through a train station unnoticed by my own mother. If I had one.

The weeks went by with no leads concerning the Director. My teams turned up a lot of contact information, along with some surprising things about the Project itself. For example, the most substantial grants came from the Russian military (how was that even possible?).

I told them to search for some trail in Lisbon, of course, but they turned up nothing and said she had never been there. They knew that she had left Vienna the day before I did (during my missing two days) with a suitcase and boxes. She had taken a taxi to the Vienna Central Train Station, and CCTV showed she boarded a train for Berlin but was never caught on camera exiting the train at any stop.

I was frustrated. I spent hours on the phone and in briefings, sometimes yelling, though I knew that browbeating my hires did no good.

Then, one day, a break came, which had nothing to do with all the activity I had set into motion.

I had left my rooms—a rare occasion—at the advice of Tasta to get out and get some air and something other than hotel food. With my jacket and cap pulled low, I practiced my new gait. I went to the Bowery Meat Company, sitting at a table off to the side near a window. I was practicing some of my new skills by focusing on the input of all five senses—being "situationally aware," as my trainer put it. A woman with a baby in a stroller sat at the table close behind me. Her mannerisms, the way she sat, how she moved a chair around to be close behind mine, told me something was not right. Perhaps nothing of importance— I had learned that just because something was out-of-place or seemed suspicious, didn't mean it meant nothing important. Maybe she had a fight with her husband that morning. Maybe she was dying of cancer.

I focused as she played with the baby, making cooing noises. I looked out the window and could see her reflection.

She looked up at my reflection. "Pate? Don't let on."

I was taken aback, despite my observations.

"You don't leave the hotel much."

She was still looking at the object in her hand. A phone. She kept tapping the screen. I turned back to my meal and took a bite.

"No. Maybe this is why." I picked up a spoon and took a sip of French onion soup. Hot. Too sweet.

"The Director sends her greetings."

I smiled.

"She knows you are looking for her and says stop immediately. You need to focus on other things."

"How do I know you are from her?"

"She said you'd ask. She said to say, 'I just don't know if I have a role to play'— 'jouer le-rôle.'"

"Good enough. So what should I be focusing on?"

"The baby is not dead."

September 2020

"All assets in place. I'll say again: it's a bad idea for you to go in."

"I'm not going in. I'm waiting outside."

"You know what I mean. Let my people bring him in; you wait at the safe house."

"No, Tasta. We've been over this."

"Yes, and I am pleading one last time. Extraction is our expertise. Let us do what we do best."

I sighed and leaned back. "Look, you are the best. Your team is the best. But it's my child and my link to Eris. Once your men get him out, I'm taking him. I vowed I would never entrust anyone else to ensure the safety of those I love."

"You don't trust me."

"I do. I just have to do this."

It was his turn to sigh. "It's not mission-wise."

"Your people are ready with the decoys?"

"Yes. Four, as we discussed. With you, they'll have five targets to monitor. The primary variable is the same as before: we don't know how many they have inside. We'll get him out. I just don't know if they have enough people to give chase to all five decoys. If they do, they'll be hunting you, too."

"I have my exit ready."

"I know, and I wish you had let my team handle that, too."

"Cell strategy keeps everyone safer and less chance of breaches."

"And keeps you from having to trust anyone."

"Shut up and do your job."

He turned to watch his screens and spoke a few brief checks into his mic. "Okay, we're go. Waiting for you."

"Do it." I stood up and adjusted my jacket.

He tapped a code into the screen before him. Red lights came on, and the screens showed jerky movement—body cams as the assets moved into position. He watched for a moment, then barked. "Go. Godspeed."

I adjusted my earpiece, opened the truck door, and jumped out into the streets of Istanbul.

I sprinted through the crowd, clutching the infant to my chest. I could feel my long, dark hair bobbing this way and that as I weaved my way through the market. Scanning ten and twenty feet ahead, twisting to the left and the right to avoid collisions. Every few moments, I glanced back. Tasta's variable was in play—they had enough to chase all five of us. Two were still chasing me and didn't care if they bowled people over. I hoped they would not shoot into the crowd.

The crowd became dense and I had to slow down. Despite my best attempts, I brushed or banged into people. I was only dimly aware of the shouts behind me.

The crowd would be just as thick outside the Grand Bazaar, but I'd have more room to move and options to the river. This was one of the busiest places in all Istanbul, along with the Blue Mosque and the Hagia Sophia, especially on Holy Days. That's why we chose today.

I hadn't expected them to be on my trail so quickly. Tasta's Team One had led the team into the building. It was a former bank, still looking like an operating bank. Nice touch. But something had gone wrong: Tasta wasn't answering my comms.

The figure in my arms was still and made no sound despite the jostling ride. He was about six months old. His tiny eyes were shut tight. His small hands clutched at my jacket forcefully enough to cause little white patches to appear on his dark, smooth skin.

I didn't have time to ponder the overwhelming emotions lying beneath the surface. Escape first.

I took a quick right into one of the many narrow alleyways that made the vast, covered marketplace of the massive labyrinth. Row upon row of stalls flew past, filled with garments and goods. Brief glimpses of faces as I ran: Arabic, Asian, European, American. Expressions frozen at the moment I flashed by, from blank looks to outrage. Arab men yelled at me. Arab men yelled all the time at everything. They let out their emotions, never keeping them bottled up—rage, sadness, happiness. Yelling, keening, laughing. The Asians said nothing, just gasped or emitted a short, quick squeak, like little birds. Europeans offered brief exclamations, "Merde!" "Scheisse!" Americans said little, offering only irritated glances. Americans didn't know how to show emotion unless they were mad. Then they exploded, out of control, embarrassing themselves and everyone. The British were more reserved. Usually.

I reached up and tapped my earpiece. "Tasta, Tasta!"
Nothing.
I briefly considered the effects of national origin on emotional expression and noted how odd it was that I

would ponder the subject while in flight from men trying to kill me.

If I remembered aright, there were two more major aisleways, then a quick right to the southwestern exit fifty feet away. From there, I would head downhill to the river, using side streets and parallels, if necessary, to reach the boat. Pietro would be waiting for me, engines idling. Powerful engines.

I shifted my hold on the child and glanced back. I had gained some ground, racing between the stalls of spices and herbs. Piled high on either side, in wooden bins and display cases, an astonishing variety of roots, powders, grasses, and minerals. For the first time, I noticed the buzz of the crowd.

The entrance was ahead—a large, arched opening with sunlight pouring in like a rent in Heaven. I twisted to avoid a particularly fat man, regained my balance, and sprinted the last ten meters.

Too late, I spotted a man coming from behind one pillar. I careened off him, still on my feet, falling-running. As I spun, I glimpsed the man crashing to the ground—a seller of Turkish tops. His collection exploded from the box, scattering and spinning across the ground, a dance troupe of Christmas-ornament-shaped instruments with red, green, and yellow pull-lines snaking behind. I almost dropped the child. I bent over, trying to maintain my balance. As I regained my footing, a car appeared, moving slowly, perpendicular to my path. Too late to stop, I took the impact on my right side, protecting the child. Pain. Perhaps broken ribs. Now in the clear, I sprinted again down the street, the driver behind me cursing in Arabic.

Still no answer from Tasta. This was bad. I would not let them recapture him.

I glanced back. They were just leaving the entrance of the Bazaar. My collisions had slowed me down, but the traffic allowed me to gain back some distance. Darting between cars, I turned down a narrow alley, ran for a block, then turned onto a downhill street.

On the straightaway, they began to gain on me—they were not carrying a child. The street was too open, too steep, with too many cars and too many people. Normal for Istanbul, but a problem for me today.

We weren't going to make it to the boat.

I crossed the street, darted between two cars, then up and between two others and headed toward the sidewalk. Glancing back, I saw I was blocked from their view by the traffic which included two busses. I turned down an alley—the map in my mind read "Asthma Kandil"—then back down a street to the river.

I was running out of time and had too far to go.

One block ahead was an SUV, parked on the sidewalk with the back door open and stroller beside the car. A woman stood at the back of the vehicle with the hatch open, rummaging inside. I tried Tasta one more time to no avail. A truck lumbered uphill just beside her, beginning to turn into a lane.

I reached the stroller and stuttered to a halt. Inside was an infant; perhaps younger than mine, but not much. Looking back, I saw the truck was blocking the view of my pursuers.

I laid my child in the stroller and picked up the other, hardly pausing to get a grip.

I crossed the street again, accompanied by the honking of moving cars and the shouts of frustrated drivers. Down another alley, then turning back down. Once more, I reached up and tapped my earpiece.

"Tasta?! Switched out target with another in a stroller on...on...Bali Paşa. Tasta?!"

All I could do was hope he heard me even though I was getting nothing. The baby in my arms was crying. I glanced down. Close enough—dark-skinned, around the same size. If Tasta's men could get to the real child—

If he heard me.

I glanced back. The men crossing the street, passing the car and stroller without hesitation. Excellent.

Ahead, a bus was stopped in the middle of a cross street. Beyond it, the road was reasonably clear. I could see the deep blue of the Bosphorus three or four blocks away. Just this side was a ribbon of concrete and metal: the river road. I wasn't going to make it but had to give it a good show. I shot out between the corner and the back of the bus.

I never saw the car coming.

π

The driver of the car was standing at the edge of my periphery, talking and gesticulating, explaining his innocence to anyone who cared to listen.

A man knelt down beside me, imploring the crowd to back up and give him room. "I am a doctor!" he yelled in Arabic. I doubted it. It was one of the men chasing me.

I lay on my back, arms outstretched. The "doctor" leaned over me and looking in my face. He smiled. "Stupid American boy."

He reached down and took my head in his hand, then brought it away to show me his fingers covered with blood. He turned and yelled at the crowd to back up again. I looked around, frantic, but could see nothing but faces, both repulsed and attracted.

"Someone call an ambulance!" yelled the "doctor." Another man knelt down, taking off his turban, holding it again the side of my head. The "doctor" pretended to examine my arms and legs.

In the crowd, I saw a man in a black jacket holding the baby: silent but alive. I tried to yell, but no sound came out.

"Just relax," the second man said. "Help will be here soon." He stood, and the first man bent down close to my face.

He squinted, peering with close-set eyes. His long, beak-like nose turned this way and that, as if he were trying to pick up a scent. Pale skin was almost white below his knit cap.

He curled his lips in a tight smile that might have been mistaken for a grimace. "Exitus acta probat."

I passed out.

π

"This is outrageous! You *assured* me he was safe. You *assured* me he could not be found."

"Sir, we cannot account for everything. They only have to be correct once, we have to plan for *everything*." The Director of Security held Powell's gaze for so long the man wondered if they were in a blinking contest. Powell sat back abruptly and steepled his hands in front of him.

"Very well. Tell me, Jonathan. Tell me."

"It was a well-organized incursion, with multiple teams —"

"I don't care *how*. I care where he is and who it was."

"It was Pate."

"Excuse me?! The *subject*? The previously *homeless* kid outwitted you?"

This was too much. "He's not a kid. And it was *your* project that sought for someone with characteristics that happen to be well-suited to espionage and execution of complex plans. He may have been homeless, but now, *thanks to you*, he is wealthy—wealthy enough to hire a crack team to track us and launch a successful incursion and abduction." Jonathan sat back and caught his breath, wondering if he had gone too far.

Powell showed no sign offense. "Very well. All true. Where is he now?"

"This is where it gets interesting—"

"People say that when they don't have an answer."

"—because Pate's people lost him, too."

"Explain."

"We were in chase, we caught up, we retrieved the baby—but it was the wrong one. At first, we thought Pate's people had made a switch somewhere, but our surveillance showed they were searching just like us."

"A decoy. Playacting."

"That was my first thought. But the people they were using, the methods—it was no decoy. And they are still looking, just as we are."

"Then who took him?"

"No idea. No leads. Even our mole with the police has found nothing. Oh—" he paused a moment. "As a side note, the police's work may lead them to demand a meeting with them."

"I don't care." He sat back and stroked his chin. "This is someone with a lot of resources, pre-planning, and power."

"Yes."

"Russians?"

"Unlikely, considering they are looking, too."

"Another corporate entity?"

"Perhaps. But our surveillance of all the players makes it unlikely. Not an iota of unusual activity."

"Black markets?"

Jonathan shrugged. "Possibly. Not the ones we know of and monitor."

"And Pate?"

"We lost him. He had a severe head injury. His people got him out and went underground. He could be dead."

They sat for a moment, Powell lost in thought. After a time, he slapped the table and stood. "All resources into the search. Everything. Worldwide. Stop the search for more subjects and—"

"No more subjects?!"

"For now. Continue with the ones already in the pipeline. Also, don't expend resources on finding Pate, just monitor whatever is needed in case he pops up."

"Yes, sir. We'll find the baby."

June 2032

Salim woke to the sound of voices in the next room.

Raised voices. Not in anger, but in frustration. He sat up and listened.

"I am sorry, sir, I have my orders. From *Berlin*."

"This is not the agreement we made!"

Salim threw the blanket off and jumped up from the couch.

"I don't know anything about any agreement. I only know what I was told."

"I am taking him."

"No, sir, you are not. And if you cause problems, I will have you arrested."

Silence. "Fine. But this isn't the end of it."

It was his father's voice.

September 2020

I awake to the smell of coffee. Light through my eyelids. I open them and see sunlight streaming through a large plate glass window. Clear and bright. Almost white.

Next to the window is a door. A knock sounds, and before I can answer, the door opens to admit a *femme de chambre* carrying a tray. I am lying on a bed. I can't move. I watch her with one eye. She is tiny and delicate, with dark hair and a small mouth. Pretty. Round, white eyes, with a dollop of chocolate for pupils.

"Crème, monsieur?" Her voice is a well-tuned instrument, smooth and soft.

I try to say, "Oui, et sucre, s'il vous plait," but my throat will not open and only a squeak escapes. My mouth is dry. My tongue is stuck.

π

Turkish men yell. Europeans shout short, single words. Asians squeak. Americans are silent until they explode.

Exitus acta probat.

"Where did you get the idea that fairness is readily available in the world?"

"Because we strive for it, as humans."

"No, we don't. We strive for control of our lives and the world around us."

"Tasta?! Tasta?!" I wonder if he got him.

Jouer le rôle, mon ami.

"I thought you were the one who believes there is something more than just the scientifically verifiable?"

"I do believe that. But I don't have control over much. And neither do you."

Auchentoshan 18 year. Finest in the land. Only 227 bottles this year. My favorite.

π

"Pate? Can you hear me?"

Can't open eyes.

Beeping. Motion. Odors.

"Pate? It's Tasta."

Tasta. Tasta. "Did you..." Only a whisper. So much effort. "Did you get him?"

Hand on arm. "No, Pate. We heard your message, but when we got there, we found only a wailing, frantic woman and an empty stroller."

π

"Vitales Frühstück, Bitte."

You're still an accomplice if you don't ask the right questions.

"You were beat up three or four days ago."

Big man. Dressed in jeans, a black t-shirt, and a thick leather jacket. Hands me an envelope. I took it, then was immediately sorry.

"Thank you."

Stupid.

"Can I buy you breakfast? There is an excellent diner down the street. I have an offer you can't refuse."

π

"They didn't get him, Pate."

"The Project?"

"Yes, but it is more complicated than that. The Project was working with a third party to hide the child."

"So who was chasing me?"

"Both? One or the other? I don't know. I told you. We were monitoring everything. Every person that came out. Every line of communication. We knew where you were the whole time, even though you couldn't hear me. We were on our way."

"You wouldn't have made it in time."

"No, we wouldn't have."

"So I did the right thing?"

"Aside from wanting to do it yourself? Yes. *They don't have him.* I can promise you that."

"Then who?"

Tasta sat back in the chair. "We don't know."

I had been in this hospital for almost two weeks. Broken ribs, concussion, internal bleeding, ruptured spleen, severed humerus ball in my left arm. And nothing to show for it. "Well, at least the Project and their allies don't have him. That's good."

"Let's hope it's not someone worse."

I frowned. "What could be worse?"

"How about black marketeers? Or that fanatical religious group that's been protesting every genetic engineering project and has no problem killing in the name of God. But I don't think anyone like that got him. We got to the SUV three minutes after you. Pram was empty. Woman was screaming. I sent one team down to get you while three other teams fanned out in a search pattern. It's like he disappeared into the streets. We tracked the Istanbul police—are still tracking—as they search for the woman's baby. They don't know there were two, of course."

"Could it be the Soviets?"

"Don't say 'Soviets' like some spy novel. The group chasing you was a black ops organization—we think they are under Russian military control, called the Sekretnye Sledovat. Also known to work with a black market group out of the Balkans."

"And they were working with the Project?!"

"It looks that way. The police are not searching for our target, they are searching for the woman's baby—who is being held by the Sekretnye Sledovat, thinking it was the target. We have a good idea where they are holding that kid. Why they haven't dumped him off somewhere, I don't know. We've been feeding the police clues, but so far the incompetents haven't figured it out. Hopefully soon. Then we can watch what the Sekretnye does. They will want to find you."

"If you are sure neither they nor the project got him, then who does?"

"I told you, no idea. It's like he disappeared."

"How is that possible?"

"Someone with a lot of connections, money, and hired professionals who had been surveilling the same as us. They must have had some idea we were going to do this. That's what bothers me the most."

"A mole inside?"

He gave me a dirty look. "No way. I know my people."

"Then how? Once you eliminate the impossible, whatever remains, no matter how improbable, must be the truth."

"Sherlock Holmes? Really? Nope. I have multiple checks in place. Essential in my line of work. No. This is someone else. Something new. Some new player, maybe, either government or corporate."

I was sure he was wrong.

π

I learned I was in a medical facility reserved for vulnerable UK military and intelligence personnel. How Tasta and his team gained access to it, I had no idea. I just wanted to get out.

When they finally agreed I was recovered enough to leave, Tasta insisted that I enlist two bodyguards. I argued, but he refused to keep working for me unless I agreed.

I packed up my belongings, and we headed back to London to regroup.

As I dumped my bags into my room, the doorman appeared with a package.

"Mr. Williamson, a messenger delivered this envelope via armed courier last week. They insisted you be notified immediately, but we had no idea of your location, and you did not return calls."

"That's ok. What is it?"

"Our scans show just plain paper."

I took the package from him, handed him a stack of bills, and ushered him out.

I ripped the top off the transport package, and it fell open to reveal a plain envelope with my name and a return address.

The University of Edinburgh.

Inside was a single handwritten note and a card with a bank account number and transfer access codes.

I hope this helps. Perhaps this is part of my redemption.
Vlad.

I pulled out my tablet, tapped into one of my accounts, entered the information on the card, and initiated the transfer. A confirmation box popped up in front of me.

Confirm transfer of 127 million GBP from Androvich, Vladimir, to your CI Account # 0309095409ue09235 ?
Cancel | Confirm

October 2020 – July 2021

"Androvich is dead, Pate."

"What? How? I mean, he looked bad when I last saw him in Edinburgh four months ago, but—"

"An explosion in his personal lab."

I frowned. "An explosion in a *genetics* lab?"

"Police report says it was likely a gas leak in the old basement. Gasses built up because the lab was sealed, making quite an explosion. The report did not determine the source of ignition, though."

"Body?"

"ID'd by DNA records."

"That bad?" I stared off into space. I had no love lost for the doctor, but he was always kind to me. And he got me Eris's money.

I sat up. "What about his files? Records, computers? Backups?"

"The building was a total loss."

"Get your people there. Find out everything you can."

"You suspect something?"

"'I'd bet on it."

π

"Well?" Tasta said, sitting across from me at my desk.

I set down the report. Not a scrap of evidence that the explosion was anything other than an accident. No visitors at the lab that day. The professor had followed his routine.

What remained of his body showed no signs of trauma beyond the explosion, though the state of the remains made it impossible to know for sure. Which proved nothing. There was just nothing to see here.

Until page four.

They found no computers in the wreckage. No electronic devices of any kind. No paper records either—which was unusual because, even all but the worst conflagrations, *some* paper evidence survived in metal or concrete protection pockets. Even as ash. But the crucial piece of data was in Section 34.

Every offsite data backup had been wiped.

Every copy of everything Dr. Androvich had written, noted, entered, assigned, procured, and preserved was gone. At least from his home, lab, and tech services.

"Everything? Everywhere?" I said.

"No. If you read the footnotes—"

"I don't read footnotes. If it matters, put it in the main text."

"Nevertheless, no. What is missing is all of his groundwork. Every bit of research, theories, models, that *he* did, has vanished. The heart and core of the Project."

"So someone—"

"No. Listen. Our tech forensics are the best. It wasn't copied and then wiped. It was not transferred out. It was destroyed. Not only did someone want it *gone*, but they also wanted anyone who investigated to know it was gone for good."

I stared out the window. "I should have seen this coming."

"Pate, if someone killed him and then wiped every—well, it makes no sense. We're missing something. Everyone *wants* that data—"

"Except for the Sword of God."

"True, but they are a fringe religious group without resources to pull off a murder and a data wipe like this. It wasn't them. We're missing something.

"I know who did it."

Tasta looked dubious. "Excuse me?"

"No one killed him, Tasta."

"Well, someone did, because...oh. I see."

We sat in silence, the wheels turning in both our minds. Finally, Tasta spoke into the somber silence.

"Okay, I see why you might think that. But *he* has even less a reason to kill himself" He stopped. "Oh."

"Exactly. Your mind is running a little behind mine."

"To be fair, you knew him. I only know him through records."

"They used him and abused him and his work, refused to listen to him, took his Project away from him, and shut him out of the results. He made sure that it would be tough to replicate."

"But it was his life's work."

"Right. Which might keep most people from destroying it. But he also felt tremendous guilt about what he had wrought. It's the only conclusion that makes sense of the data."

"Except for one thing."

"What's that?"

"He didn't have the skills to pull it off either. He might have been able to wipe all the data. But to set off an explosion so to destroy what you wanted, but no more, and to wipe the data but leave the evidence he did, well, he was a brilliant man—but that's not his area.."

"No. But he had the money to hire someone to help him."

"So someone helped him, and we're back where we started."

"I don't think so. Who would he hire?"

Tasta pondered the question. "Unlikely he'd go to black-market operatives like you did. Can't be government or corporate, not their style."

"Correct."

Tasta frowned. "You think it's the same people who kidnapped the baby in Istanbul."

"I do."

"So we are right back where we started. Oh, by the way, since you don't read footnotes, you didn't see the one in the appendix under 'Issues Unrelated to Explosion'?"

"No. If it's important, it—"

"Yeah, yeah, yeah. The money he sent you? It didn't come from the Project."

"What?!"

"Well, it did come from the Project, but it was not what was owed to Eris. It was from Androvich's severance. He gave you his own money before he killed himself."

π

The French real estate agent was thin and muscular. She had blondish/brown hair, pulled back tight. I was sure that she went to a gym every morning wearing a severe expression, ate vegetarian lunches, and drove a smart car. She wore an expensive business suit with a white blouse—tight enough to show she was female, but the style said she was a woman not to be messed with. Unless she wanted to be. Her French was High French, and her English was impeccable with only a slight trace of an accent. Enough to give it an exotic tone. Intentionally, I assumed.

"Here, Monsieur, is a fine suite, as you can see. The furniture is all Louis XIV originals. The accoutrements are all modern."

"Le Roi-Soliel himself could not ask for more finely-appointed chambre, madame. C'est magnifique. The view?"

She strode to the window and threw open the curtains. "Le Champ de Mar, the Tower, and the Seine." She flung open the heavy drapes on the other side. "There...Mont Martre. The Arc de Triomphe is behind the Tower, but you can see its lights at night."

I nodded. "It is a bit large for one person."

She inclined her head five degrees. "It may be Monsieur, depending on your needs. The room on Île Saint Louis is smaller and just as finely decorated. It lacks the view—if it is important to Monsieur."

She was beautiful, in her own sharp and defined way. Much like—my heart caught in my throat.

"You may take your time, Monsieur. I will hold all three apartments for two days. We can revisit each if you like."

"No—non. Il n'est pas nécessaire. I will take this one." It had the grandeur I was looking for. Anyone I met with would be suitably impressed and intimidated. "I will pay for a year in advance, oui?"

She showed emotion for the first time all day. "Monsieur? It is three months that is necessary, then month to month—a year is not necessary—"

"One year, madame. Make the arrangements." I tried to sound firm, decisive and used to being obeyed. With a touch of eccentricity. It did not matter here, but it was good practice for me. Part of the plan. And I was pretty sure that someday, someone would come snooping and ask questions of this real estate agent.

She bowed. "Tres bien, Monsieur. It shall be so. Merci."

"One more thing. You came highly recommended, and I was told you had a contact in the UK. Discrete."

"Oui. One of the best in Europe and the UK. Many of my well-placed clients use—"

"Can he handle substantial land purchases? Out-of-the-way places?"

"Naturellement, monsieur."

"Excellent. I need you to put him in touch with one of my assistants."

π

"Of *course* it's possible. It isn't even technically illegal, but it's questionable. Could bring trouble." He pushed his glasses up on his nose, his limp, long blond hair falling down over his face. "Sir," he added.

I could tell he was impressed. By the room, by my presence behind the huge desk I had purchased and had delivered. He was not, however, intimidated at all by all the electronics Tasta has set up. That was his wheelhouse, though I suspected his tech was located in messy rooms with half-empty cans of Red Bull, or Jolt, or whatever these techies drank today. His clothes, poorly chosen and mismatched, were nevertheless expensive. Tasta said he was one of the best, and he had used him in the past with great satisfaction. I was going to compensate him enough to keep him from other clients, because I needed his full attention. And I didn't want a mole.

"But you can do it?"

His mouth opened and then closed. "I can do it. But the risk—"

I held up a hand, then turned the paper towards him and allowed him to read the contract. It was short and to the point. I eschewed legalese, and only by berating my attorneys could I get them to write so anyone could understand it.

He scanned it, reached the bottom, and saw the number,

"Ack." He stared. "Ah...yes...that is quite..."

I held his gaze without expression. He gathered himself and spoke.

"Yes. My team can do this. Will do this. Shall I—"

"Good," I said, trying to sound gruff and distracted, as if I had larger things on my mind. Which I did. "Make arrangements and give me a report before you begin. Method, team members, any tech you need. All Benelux countries. Turkey, all of the UK including the Commonwealths, Northern Ireland, as well as the US and all its territories.

He blinked. "The States, too? That's...a lot of—"

"If it's too much for you, can you suggest someone else?" I kept my voice emotionless.

"Oh, no, sir, no, we can do it. I was simply talking of the complexity of the searches. The time needed. So many organizations and databases, plus the networks of social and government tiers of—"

I waved my hand to stop him. "I don't care about the details. Do what you need to do to get my results."

"Yes, sir. One more thing."

"What is it?" I affected irritation.

He took a breath, as if bracing himself. "If you really want a thorough search...well. It would require hacking systems that the authorities *would* deem illegal. They would never pursue it...through legal channels...because they would not want it known those systems exist. So..."

"So you are afraid of what they'll do if you get caught?"

"Frankly, yes. If any of us were caught."

"Are you going to get caught?"

He seemed offended. "No. We're the best."

"Then it's moot isn't it?" A little incentive to be extra careful. "But if you need to take unusual precautions, let me know and we'll deal with it."

He smiled for the first time. "We'll get to work right away, sir."

June 2032

Salim ran to the door and threw it open, causing the two men inside to jump. They looked at each other and back at Salim. Salim skidded to a halt. Something wasn't right.

His dad smiled, stood, and walked over. "Salim, so good to find you!" He embraced him.

Salim pulled away and signed to him. *Mom?*

"Yes, she is fine. Nasty bump on the head. She is resting at home. That...that's why she's not here."

What happened to you? They said you were dead.

"Who?"

The kidnappers.

"Oh. No, it was—"

"Why don't you both sit down? It has been quite a night," the other man said, whom Salim did not recognize. He wore a suit and tie, and looked quite neat and fit, as if the suit had become part of him, like a second skin. He had dark, short-cropped hair, and a square face. It gave him a military look.

Salim and his father sat down next to each other on a couch. His dad was not demonstrative, but he was sensitive and caring when Salim was troubled. But he did not touch him or look at him. Was it this man's presence?

The other man spoke. "Salim, are you well? Did they care for you effectively?"

A strange way of speaking. His pronunciation was perfect. Too perfect. German was not his native language.

Salim signed that he was fine and that they had taken good care of him. Salim's dad translated.

"Good, good. I am Detektiv Hasel, and I will be examining this case. But first, we are glad to find you."

What is happening? Why did those men attack us and take me? Where is—

"Hold, hold," Hasel said. Salim detected that he was hiding some irritation. Or impatience. "I don't know sign language, and we have much to investigate. I have many reasons to ask you."

Salim looked at his father, who looked back and nodded, then glanced back at Hasel and nodded.

"Very well, first, we must go. We have to get you both home. We shall talk along the way. I have a car outside."

"Oh, uh..." Salim's dad said. "I thought we'd take the train home...can't we continue this later? He has been through a lot..." He seemed more nervous than Salim had ever seen him. He was always so self-assured. "The boy is very tired."

Hasel looked at him without expression, as if the man was trying to communicate something to his dad without speaking.

After a moment, Hasel's gaze softened.

"No, I am so sorry. As you know, kidnaps are not usual here. We want to get all information while is fresh."

His dad sighed with a funny expression, as if he had been asked to taste something unpleasant.

"Good. Let us exit now." He stood. Salim and his dad followed Hasel out the door into a hallway, and out into the lobby of the police station. The officer who had brought Salim from the trains approached.

"Herr Hasel, may I be of any further assistance?" He had adopted the demeanor of a servant, deferring to Hasel as if he were a superior in the chain of command.

"You have been more than helpful. I will report your efficiency and skills to the main office."

The officer colored slightly. "I shall call ahead and let them know you are on your way."

Hasel took two steps forward, bringing him close to the official. His face was only a hands' length away from the other man's face. "No, my good man, we need as few people speaking of this as possible while we investigate. I will call once we are on our road, on the secure line, since I must make report finally."

"Very well, sir."

With a curt nod, Hasel motioned Salim and his father to a side door which deposited them into a narrow alley. A silver, late-model Mercedes sedan sat idling. Hasel opened the back door, and, once Salim and his dad climbed in, shut it with a solid clunk. Another man sat in the driver's seat. Salim noted that the self-driving AI was off. The man was operating it himself.

Hasel got into the passenger seat. "Go. Fast, but not reckless." The man drove down the alley, easing the car onto a street at the end. There was not much traffic at this time of the morning. When the man turned, Salim saw he was wearing a priest's collar.

Hasel turned his head part way to the back seat. "This is Father Gerhardt. He is assisting in our investigation."

Salim looked at his father, who registered no expression. Salim touched his arm. *A priest?*

Hasel saw. "What did he say?"

His father stirred as if coming out of a dream. "He is wondering why a priest would help with a kidnapping investigation."

"Ah, yes, it is a good question. He is the one who brought us information of the men who kidnaps. I had him come with me to interview along while we drove. Save time."

If that were so, Salim thought, *why was the priest driving? Shouldn't he be a passenger?*

The priest spoke. "Guten Morgen, gentlemen. I hope you enjoy the ride. I am happy you are reunited."

Salim looked out the tinted window. Soon, they entered the Autobahn and picked up speed. It must be about seven or eight in the morning now.

When they were on the expressway, Salim noted they were headed south, not north.

His dad did not seem to notice.

September 2020

He paused before the double doors to examine the carvings on either side. Heavy oak. Fine craftsmanship. Gold leaf trim. The ornate sign—also gold—beside the door, in fancy script, read: "Le Suite D'Imperiale."

He sneered and wiped his large, beaked nose, then raised his finger to the bell. He paused, imagining the man inside, wearing a fancy Italian robe that cost more than most people make in a lifetime. Sitting behind his ornate desk, with a fountain pen that cost more than most people's cars. Drinking something expensive: Louis XIII or perhaps Clasa Azul Ultra. The hotel suite would be decorated as if it were his own home. Did the man even *have* a home? Every time he'd met with him it was in an exorbitant hotel suite like this one.

The man behind the desk was also democratically insufferable: he insulted and ridiculed the small and large, the rich and poor, the powerful and weak. His deameanor was rude and demanding to everyone he met, from the Prime Minister to the bar-back. It did not matter whether it was a trifle or a multi-million dollar matter. The type of mug in which his coffee came held the potential for tears and even a firing.

He lowered his finger from the bell and scowled at the door, considering that hatred for the man was only overcome by the amount of money he was paid to work for him. Was it worth being debased and humiliated?

Yes. Yes, indeed.

He wiped his brow and examined the moisture on the white dappled skin of his fingers. Taking his black jacket off, he folded it over his left arm, took a deep breath, and pressed the button.

A gruff voice bellowed—unintelligible through the thick wooden doors. He hesitated. Come in or go away? He made the decision and turned the brass door lever and pushed. It was unlocked, and it took a bit of force, but once moving, it swung open on well-oiled heavy-duty hinges. He allowed the door to open just enough for him to squeeze through, pushing it shut as quietly as he could behind him. The man inside often said he hated timidity, but his temper showed he also hated boldness if it caught him at the wrong time.

The room spread out like a Versailles reception room. Opulent touches everywhere. Overstuffed furniture in fine cloth and leather. Thick, heavy drapes. An oak floor with deep pile carpets. Gold and silver trim everywhere. But it was the wall on the far side of the room that captured his attention. Made entirely of high-quality glass, so clean that it appeared it was no barrier at all. Being this high, it gave him vertigo. The whole city was laid out below like a miniature model: the Left Bank, the Eiffel Tower, the Seine. He imagined a mighty wind blowing, sweeping him and all the room's furnishings out over the city, to float down among the old and new, the rich and poor, the clean and filthy.

"Don't stand gawking! Sit down!"

He sat behind a gigantic desk on an enormous chair, like a monarch on the throne. Dressed in a black suit, the sheen of the fine, expensive cloth was apparent from across the room. The suit was large, for he was a large man —not so much fat as substantial. His chest was barrel-strong, and the shirt underneath the suit, though perfectly tailored, made one wonder if a deep breath would send the buttons flying. His large hands were folded on the desk in front of him, shiny diamond cuff links glinting at his wrists. It was as if body contained too much person to be contained by clothing made by lesser humans.

A shock of black and silver above the glowering visage. Blue steel eyes. The stereotype of a powerful mob boss, a ruthless corporate mogul, or a wealthy politician over-stuffed with countless bribes and perks.

Yet he was none of those things. Many of his assignments were illegal, and yet some of the work was legitimate work for governments and corporations.

No matter. He did what he was told and was paid well.

The desk was bare except for a tablet with a single scanned page on the screen. In front of the desk sat a lone chair, plain and out of place. The seat for minions. He sat down.

The eyes fixed him in place like a bolt arrow. "Well?!"

He shook his head. "Nothing, so far, sir. We had him. Had the baby and then it was the wrong one. Montrey thought it was an elaborate and multi-layered ruse. But our investigations shows it was not. Williamson was really trying to escape from us. He did switch the child, but it was not part of his plan. It was desperation because the project people were about to catch him. Someone else took the child."

"'Someone' is vague and you know I hate vague. *Who?!*"

"Yes, sir." This was difficult. Sometimes the man before him wanted every single detail. At other times, he wanted the bottom line. If you miscalculate either way, he'd be angry at your incompetence. If you ask which he wants, he becomes furious at your incompetence. *Ah well*, he thought. *Audaces fortuna iuvat*. That wasn't really true, but so be it. "We are pursuing a number of leads. Our working theory is that there was a third party, watching for the right moment. Which means they knew of Williamson's plan." He paused, waiting.

"An idiot could surmise that without doing any research."

"Yes, sir, but in my opinion—"

"Not interested in your opinion, seeing as it's useless. Facts."

"Yes, sir. We don't know who the third party is, but it is a group with a lot of resources and skill. I have ordered most of my assets to assess, monitor, and investigate along those lines."

"And?"

"Nothing so far. We have ruled out the American and UK governments. Russia is still a possibility, but some of the data contravenes that. Obviously not the Project, they do not have the resources or sophistication to pull off a ruse if that was the purpose."

"*And?!*"

"A corporate entity or another dark organization."

He slammed his hand on the table. "So it could be *anyone*?! Do I pay you to find out the obvious?!" He sneered. "Okay, try this, *fils de pute*! Did it occur to you that it matters less *who* than *where?*"

He cringed. He'd been avoiding that subject because he had even less intelligence on it. "No leads. He just disappeared into..."

The man stood up, seeming to fill every corner with his presence. He would swear the room got darker and air seemed to spark. "You've told me nothing I couldn't have figured out myself. Get out! I want a complete report in five days—who, where, and how. Williamson and his people caught the Project and you by surprise—and he is a guy who has *never* done this sort of thing before. Five days, then I fire your ass and ruin your life. At best. Now get out and get me some real intelligence."

"Yes, sir." He stood and backed up, catching the back of his calf on the chair leg and almost falling. He turned, trying not to shake, as the man bellowed again.

"One more thing. I want all of that Doctor's information."

He stopped and turned. "Androvich?"

"Yes. Everything. I want his computers, his written notes, his utility bills, *everything*. And I don't care what you have to do to get it."

September 2020

"You need to tell me what going on. You are obviously keeping things from us, and we cannot do our job if we don't have all the information available." The BMLVS officer sat at the head of the table, with two others—from the EISIC and the BKA—on either side. The University and Project staff filled out the rest of the conference table. At least those who had been summoned.

Dr. Harrington sighed. "As I have told you, this is a significantly well-funded research project involving DNA research and biogenetics, using voluntary human subjects and, in a few cases, *in utero* fertilization. A baby that was born here was kidnapped."

"You've said that in various permutations, and I've told you that it tells me nothing about why and who. That's a pretty essential element in solving crimes. Let's try again. Why in God's name did you call us about a missing child case which turned into a child-swapping case that is somehow connected to a wealthy high-tech research program? Why would a *courier* show up with one of the children—a courier who can tell us nothing, including who paid him? Meanwhile, the other child is missing, a child for which there is *no official record* of ever being born, no one reported him missing, and you won't even tell me his name. With that little to go on, I'd say we have illegal genetic research and child trafficking issue here. Tell me more and convince me otherwise."

Dr. Harrington blanched and someone around the table emitted a small squeak. "I...I assure you we have done nothing of the sort. Our research follows all the international guidelines as put forth by the NHGRI, the NHLBI, and all pertinent WHO guidelines. The research requires confidentiality, and unless you have a warrant, I cannot divulge personal information by law."

"Well, that's convenient. I'll tell you what—"

The door flew open and a man burst in wearing a tailored suit and carrying a briefcase.

"Excuse me, sir," the BMLVS officer said, "but we are holding a private interview—"

"And without an attorney present. I am that attorney, and I am telling you now this interview is over."

"We are investigating a crime of a missing child, sir."

"The missing child was returned to the police station and reunited with its mother this morning."

"*One* child was. But there is another child, one that was swapped with the missing child, who is missing."

"And who reported that crime?"

"No one, we—"

"Then how do you know there was a crime?"

The officer stood abruptly. "Don't play games, counsel."

"I'm not playing games, I am keeping you from overstepping your authority. You are harassing these people because you *think* there was a kidnapped child—a child for who you have no name, no records, and no one who reported it missing."

The officer stood for a moment, his jaw working. Dr. Harrington held his breath. He did not want to cross a European security official.

The officer sighed and turned to pick up his papers. "Very well, counsel. Have it your way." He looked at his colleagues. "Let's go."

They gathered their notebooks. As they walked past the attorney, the officer said, "We'll be back. With a warrant."

"Good luck with that," the attorney replied.

August 2021 – January 2022

I paused in the doorway of the dark smokiness of the pub in the Quartierre Latin. I had never been to this part of Paris, and I didn't like it. The Metro took me all the way past the Grande Arche, to the Conflans Fin d'Oise stop. Five cross streets later, I had arrived at this dingy hell-hole. The room smelled of smoke, body odor, and urine. This was not a pub for tourists.

I knew this because my team had spent two months trying to locate the man I was about to meet.

It was filled with the noise of thirty people talking and watching a raucous rugby match on the television mounted in a corner. An occasional laugh, yell, or shout punched through the din on occasion.

My conscience pricked at me, and I pushed it away. I'd insist on no killings, but I was not naïve considering the people I was dealing with. Both the people I was after, and the one I was to meet here.

I ordered a whisky from the bar and went to sit at a booth in the corner, under a banner that said "Celtic—Get Jinky With It." The table, like the pub, was old, worn, and stained.

A figure appeared out of the gloom like a phantom, shrouded in black. He took the seat across from me.

He rivaled the pub in disgustingness. I took a sip of my whisky. He stared into my eyes, I looked into his. Finally, he spoke.

"Vous-êtes l'homme d'Ecosse?"

"Oui."

"English, then. I found the man. Works for major trafficker based in Paris. Name is Pierce. Robbery, kidnapping, carefully planned mayhem, and so on."

"And you are sure he's the one?"

He harrumphed. "Yes, of course. Long history of criminal activity. Placed in Istanbul same time as you. CCTV show him carrying bundle from the scene. In touch with police. Left Istanbul. No sign of man for many years, but we locate in Paris now.

I nodded. "And your people can track him in real-time? And keep him from getting the boy?"

"Not *my* team. I work for the team."

"Yes, I understand that. Answer the question."

"Oui."

"And you understand I do not want anyone killed?"

He laughed. "Yes, it was said you say it. We do not kill any—what is word—any time, anywhere—"

"Indiscriminately."

"—any way. Yes, 'indiscriminately.' We ensure safety. We cannot say same if we become in danger. Do you want successful job or do you want to keep your morals intact?"

"I want the job done, with an assurance that there will be no killing unless necessary to keep us safe."

"It is also that you do not want us to obtain the boy for you?"

"Correct."

He leaned over the side of the chair, held one nostril closed with a finger, and blew his nose on the floor. He smiled at me. His yellowed, crooked teeth peered out like a lighthouse in a nasty storm.

"Eh bien, eh bien—but my people are the best. Better than MI6, better than CIA. Much best to avoid the merde of regulations, ça va?"

"That's why I am having you do everything except get him. I have a team for that. You are the security detail, bouncers, and diversionary elements. As discussed."

He shook his head. "We are best. But well. I am instructed to make the agreement with you. You have the money?"

"Yes. Half will be deposited tonight, the rest after. And you assure me the team is trustworthy?" Not that I was sure his word was trustworthy.

He looked angry. "Of course! We demand no less than perfections for our clients." He leaned back. "It is why we are so much money. As you know already."

"Trustworthiness, competence, and success is what I require. For that, money is no object." I leaned forward, hoping to appear intimidating. "I demand it. Less than that makes me angry."

He laughed. "Putain, oui, mon ami!" He leaned in, as if he understood me and we were co-conspirators. We were not. He was a tool I needed. "You are new to this, oui? As I was told." I tried to keep my expression unchanged and hoped the darkness kept him from seeing my flushed face.

"New *here*, yes."

He nodded. "Ça va, ça va. So we have the agreement?"

"Yes."

He took a tablet out of his pocket and tapped on it for a moment.

"It is done."

"Good, You will hear from my people as soon as I return to London."

"C'est bien. Stay safe, American. These men you are dealing with do not have your morals."

π

After a year and a half of preparations, everything was in place. I spent the first eight months, with Tasta's help, educating myself in intelligence and surveillance, both in the public and private sector. I learned a lot. How to find people. How to stay hidden. How to work with and around laws and authorities to avoid becoming a target.

I had failed once by being too anxious and too impatient. Not this time. I had an extensive team, and we would cover every possibility. They had taken her away from me, but I *was* going to get part of her back. Tasta kept telling me it could be years before even a single lead surfaced. I told him if it took a lifetime, I was fine with it.

Until we located him, though, there was not much to do. I had one loose end to tie up. I went to my desk and opened a secure channel from my screen.

"Hello, Powers and Bilton. How may I help you.?"

"Mr. Powers, please."

"I'm sorry, sir, he is in a meeting. May I ask who is calling and take a message?"

"Tell him it's Pate."

"Oh, yes, sir. I will put you right through."

"Pate! Good to hear from you. I assume you're ready to proceed?"

"Yes. I'll have a courier bring you the cash."

"I'll say again, that really makes me uncomfortable. It's a ridiculous amount of money to carry around."

"Well, you're not going to be carrying it around. My representative is trained in handling large amounts of cash and assets. He'll meet you, and both of you will go to your bank to deposit it. The paper trail will show it as the sale of your deceased parent's estate."

"As discussed. Which one did you decide on?"

"The northernmost island."

"Nice choice. Quite remote. Will serve you nicely." He had no idea. "But you don't want to fly out and see it first?"

"Not necessary. It has the requisite characteristics."

"Very well. I'll contact you when all the papers are signed and it's out of escrow."

"Thank you. Remember, any slip-up, and it could mean your reputation."

"Please, Pate. I have been doing this work for people like you for a long time. No one has ever regretted placing that task in my hands. I have told you all this."

"I know. And since you have dealt with so many, you probably also know how paranoid we are."

He laughed. "It is true that I must repeat this speech often. Do not worry, mate, you will be satisfied with my services."

We hung up, and I sent a message to Tasta about the location and to start setting up security and technology. That'll be another load of money.

All worth it—once the plan succeeds. However long it takes.

7 June 2032

Breakfast the next day was the usual. As it had been for years. I had begun to lose hope, yet every time Tasta told me it was time to give up, some new piece of information came up. Nothing to lead us to him, but another piece of the puzzle.

For whatever reason, though, I felt renewed today. The information that came in my morning briefing gave me more hope the anything in almost ten years. This time, I was ready.

It had been my fault for trying to conserve resources for the Istanbul operation. Bringing in more people was dangerous, of course. The larger an organization, the more likely a breach or a spy. I had been scrupulous about secrecy, my desire for no one to be hurt, and that laws not be broken.

Yet being so careful caused me to lose him twice. Now that the endgame was near, I needed to step up it up. Focus the mind on facts, logic, and asking key questions: "what *can* I control?" "What is the *goal*?" "What *matters at this moment*?" Cultivating a calculating view of the events would lead to success, I was sure.

Now, with the plan on the verge of implementation, the only thing that mattered was getting him back and honoring the memory of Eris. I found myself caring less who got hurt, but I avoided feelings of revenge. Revenge was an emotional need, and therefore irrelevant.

I spent the morning reviewing the pertinent intelligence that Tasta had sent, looking over my finances, transferring and selling some assets, and analyzing the contingency plans that the extraction team had produced, and finishing the paperwork on my land purchase up north.

I got up, washed my face, donned a suit, and left for my lunch meeting. After, I'd spend time at Le Physical Therapse de Cologne, then a brief dinner with Tasta and Renner. Another productive day. This was how we do it bit-by-bit, hour-by-hour, day-by-day, week-by-week. The most massive undertaking could be accomplished in this manner without anxiety or fear. And would bring success.

My tablet beeped a notification, and the text appeared in the air above: "München negative. Following up on two leads—perhaps at counter purpose to each other."

π

The phone beeped. I was already awake thinking about how I wish I could sleep for another hour.

I waved my hand toward the telecom. "Tasta calling," it said.

"What's up, Tasta?"

"Found him."

I bolted upright. "Go on!"

"Heidelberg. Living with a family, apparently has been there for almost the whole time. Husband and wife, with no records before them having a child until about ten years ago. Witness protection, perhaps. Underground re-identity, more likely."

"Who?"

"No leads. My suspicion is the same group who took him in Istanbul."

"I don't pay you to determine the obvious."

"Working on it, boss."

"All right. I'll be on my way in fifteen minutes."

"Slow down. The reason we located him is that he was kidnapped."

"What?!"

"Yeah. A private organization. Perhaps someone hired by Medezin Research or some other big corporation Or maybe Russia or China, though it doesn't look governmental."

"They found him before you?!"

"Matter of days. Maybe hours. We were close. Anyway—"

"Are you tracking?!"

"*Anyway*, it appears they were going to take him via train somewhere, but he got away and—"

"He escaped?! Where?"

"Pate! Please allow me to present all the intelligence, and then you can criticize and ask questions."

I took a deep breath and sat down, trying to slow my pounding heart. Emotion was the enemy. "Yes. Apologies."

"CCTV shows him getting on a train alone, after he escaped the kidnappers, but the kidnappers followed him and boarded the same train. The kidnappers disembarked at München, without the boy, then re-embarked the same train at the last moment. Interviews tell us there was a woman with the boy, but she also disembarked alone München. Train went on to Salzburg, but the boy was not seen to disembark at any stop. We're working the München scene for any clues. I suggest you go to the airport and stand by."

"Okay. On my way."

"Pate?"

"Yes?"

"Be prepared. He got on the train and did not get off. That does not bode well."

"You're wrong. Everyone wants him alive."

"Not everyone."

TARGETING

7 June 2032

The phone rang. The elderly man frowned and turned away from the symbols hovering over his desk, which he had been staring at for some time. His desk was covered with papers, tablets, open and closed books, and scraps of notes. After moving and rearranging some materials, he uncovered the phone. It was an old, black plastic, phone, with many buttons and no screen. Classic. Well-worn. His colleagues made fun of him for keeping it; the head of technology services was exasperated with him for having to customize it to access the wires network. But it had worked without fail for decades, and did not have any patience for software glitches and no need for updates.

He picked up the receiver, attached by a cord, and started to put it to his ear, but stopped and removed his glasses first. "Yes?"

"Herr Doktor Schlessinger? A Herr Schmidt is on the phone. From Berlin."

"Berlin? Herr Schmidt? I do not know—"

"With the *Polizei.*"

The wheels in his mind spun, and his heart jumped a bit. "I will speak with him, Frau Mauser."

He waited.

"Herr Doktor Schlessinger? This is Otto Schmidt from the Sekurite Deutsche in Berlin. Do you recall?"

"Of course I remember you, Herr Schmidt. I am not senile yet, no matter what my students might whisper."

Schmidt laughed. "I would not dare accuse you, of all people, of being senile. But it has been ten years."

"Indeed. But our paths crossed over substantial events. Not easily forgotten."

"Ja, ja. How is the work going? Since...then."

"Considerably more difficult, thanks to you and others, as you know. Minor strides. Nothing like where we were. What a loss."

"I agree. A tragedy that Herr Doktor Androvich died so early."

A sore subject, and one that Schlessinger did not want to broach with this man. "I suspect you did not call to reminisce."

"Yes. I have some news that might interest you, and you will want my help."

More likely you want my help, Schlessinger thought. But his anticipation of what this call might mean, coming from this man, had the best of him. "Yes, please enlighten me."

"Pacem."

The Doctor sat bolt upright. "No?! The real thing? No mere tidbit, like the last time we spoke."

"No. We found him." Schlessinger could hear the joy Schmidt had from drawing the story out.

"Alive?"

"Very much so. We've never had reason to think otherwise. We just didn't know where he was."

"That's not what you told everyone else."

"Official story. To wit—a murder and a kidnapping event popped up last night. Not all that unusual, until the locals started to investigate. They contacted us because they could find no full history of the victims or relatives. We began to search, and found some curious things."

The doctor relaxed. "Such as? What's the connection to the Pace Project?"

"No background on the victim or husband until about ten years ago. Private re-identification—and extensive. *And* expensive. Their boy was kidnapped, his profile, including age, fits. While not conclusive, the data points to him, and none negates the conclusion. It's him."

"If true, this is of momentous importance. For a lot of people. And also dangerous for him. What do you know about the individuals involved?"

"I am not at liberty to discuss our intelligence at the moment."

"Herr Schmidt, need I remind you that anything related to Pacem belongs to us, here, at the University?"

"We are dealing with crimes, or potential crimes, and that is *my* purview."

Schlessinger sighed. It was an old debate, and one he was too weary to rehash. As much as he had argued that the project had always been about science, biology, and philanthropy, he could not deny that it came to involve politics, intrigue, secrecy—and some illegality.

Schmidt spoke again, in a softer voice. "You know what is at stake, and the danger if others find this same information. *When* they hear it, because they will."

Schlessinger felt an old sinking feeling, just as he had so many times over a decade ago. "What do you want from me?"

"I'd like to meet with you—in person—to review what I have and see what you can give me on the subject of Pacem. Might help us locate him before anyone else."

"You said he was kidnapped."

"I did not say that. I said there was a murder and a kidnapping."

"Obtuse. In any case, I have no additional information beyond what you already have."

"It's been ten years. Time, new perspectives, and this new knowledge may bring something to light."

"I am not sure I have anything to offer."

"I'll be the judge of that. Besides, I know you want to know more. How about we meet?"

That was true, as much as he might not want it to be. Painful memories could resurface. The same old frustrations. And the questions about what they had really been doing.

But there was always a chance that they could recover what they had begun. To return to the purity of the research and experimentation. To regain what belonged to the project, and start anew to finish Androvich's dream. *His* dream, not the selfish machinations of governments and biotech companies and others.

After all this time, he had resigned himself to minor advances and the writing of theoretical articles. Nothing groundbreaking. He was not Doctor Androvich. No one was. But now...

"Doctor Schlessinger?"

The doctor took a deep breath. "Very well. Where shall we meet?"

"Meet me at the cloister of St. Stephan's Church in thirty minutes?"

"You're in Vienna?"

"Yes."

"Come to my office and—"

"No. Please indulge me."

Schlessinger shook his head in exasperation. Here we go again with the intrigue. But the academic in him would not let him walk away.

"Very well. Thirty minutes."

He jumped out of his chair, lifting his coat from the floor where it had fallen, and rushed out into the common departmental office. Frau Maucher was typing furiously on her keypad, her stubby fingers engaged in a flying dance. "I will be out for an hour or so, Frau." She nodded without looking up.

He went down the hall to an office door and knocked and stepped in without waiting. The room was small, neat, modern, and well-organized. A contrast in every way to Schlessinger's office. A young blond man sat in a chair beside his desk, reading a book. He looked up.

"Come with me, Tom." Schlessinger said, "We are going to church."

Tom laughed. "Excuse me?"

"Yes. For enlightenment. And perhaps some fine blessings."

"Okay..." The young American professor was used to the quirks of his senior colleague. "I have already been to church this week." He stood and lifted his coat off a rack.

"I promise this will be like no ecclesiastical experience you have ever had. And, along the way, I will reveal mysteries kept long hidden."

"Really?" Tom said as he pulled on his coat. "Have you discovered the meaning of life?"

"Perhaps. We are going too meet someone who may open up a whole new phase of our research. Along the way, I am going to tell you the truth about Pace Projectus."

7 June 2032

Dr. Schlessinger and Tom Aster walked the Schottengasse towards MichaelerPlatz, the cobbled streets of old Vienna beneath their feet. Since it was November, the roads and pedestrian walkways were not too busy. The snows had not started yet, so the sky was clear, though it was quite cold. To Tom's credit, he waited as Schlessinger seemed deep in thought.

After Androvich's death, Schlessinger had gone over every single report and note that had not been destroyed. Papers that had been published. Unpublished papers that had been placed in the University repository. He went back to Vlad's grad school and requested any notes, papers, project summaries—anything the brilliant man had left behind.

It hinted at what he had done later. It laid the groundwork for the Pace Project. But none of it contained enough for Schlessinger to recreate the project or core procedures. It was like trying to reconstruct a Van Gogh from the paint, brushes, size of the canvas, and early sketches. It gave you just enough to get an idea of the final form, without being able to recreate it.

Schmidt had refused to allow Schlessinger to see the sealed police reports, but one of the investigators had a soft heart gave him an hour's access one day. Something about a beloved grandfather she'd lost recently. Schlessinger was glad that he appeared to be a kindly old man.

The report didn't say it wasn't an accident, of course. It was an old boiler that had exploded—an old man, removed from his own project, denied visitation rights for his own brainchild, absent-mindedly forgetting to shut off the gas. An errant spark from...something.

Yet the underlying data painted another possibility. All off-site backups—gone. Every email he had sent since he had left Vienna—gone. Every text message and phone call, logged with the provider, was gone. As if he never had a phone in Edinburgh. Schlessinger was a well-known Luddite when it came to technology, but even he knew that was unlikely and had nothing to do with a boiler explosion. Besides, he'd asked Dr. Rodney in the IT Department. Rodney said that there were copies on back-ups, copies with the provider—so many, in fact, that a complete wipe could only be done with a tremendous amount of money and a lot of exceptional hackers or inside jobs. And it would take a lot of money. Dr. Rodney declared such a scenario impossible.

"No one could pull it off. Not in this day and age. Why do you ask? Planning a coup?" He laughed.

Yet someone had pulled it off.

After Schlessinger saw the sealed report, he went back to Vienna and cowered like a terrified animal.

He was terrified. Anyone who could do that could do anything. To anyone.

His colleagues and the administration thought he was just in grief after losing his friend and the pertinent data from his research project.

It took two years before the University convinced him to restart the project.

He had a lot to work with. He could make advances in the field. Extraction of DNA, PCR, and the advances in the

CRISPR technology provided some stunning new possibilities. But IVF was out of the question. Not only would Schlessinger refuse to perform it because he didn't have the data or ability, but the University would not allow it. Not again. The administrators who had were long gone.

"It had been so promising, Tom. You don't know this from our current research, or what you've seen of our past work, but Vlad proved his theory sound! Yes, there were problems early on with dominant expressions duplicating, dropping out, and it all led nowhere. We conducted hundreds of experiments, varying the methods and specificities each time. Nothing. The theory was so promising; the reality was that it could not be done. He was quite frustrated. Then—"

"But, wait. Why was none of this in the historical reports? It would have been so helpful! Surely he was not covering up his failures. Such a brilliant man did not seem to care about—"

"Oh, no. He did not see them as failures; merely as eliminating the methods that did not work. Each time, he felt he was drawing closer."

Tom nodded. "But he died before he could produce a successful experiment?"

"No. This is the dirty secret, my friend. He succeeded. Beyond expectations. He had a revelation."

"Revelation?"

"Yes. He realized that the experiment did not need to take place from start to finish in the lab. There was a better way."

Tom laughed. "Better ways than in a controlled environment where you can measure and calibrate everything?"

"Ja, indeed. One that is biologically sound."

Tom was mystified. What method of experimentation did not involve the lab, computers, experiments, measurements, control—

If none of this was in the notes and papers, then it must be because it was necessary to keep it secret. Why? Funding restrictions? Danger of rival researchers? Illegalities? Surely not. Not here, at one of the premier cyto-research schools in Europe. And beyond. What could it be? That did not primarily involve a lab?

They had already passed into MichaelerPlatz and turned left onto Kohlmarkt. They walked in silence for the next block, Schlessinger smiling and waiting for Tom to process the new information. As they turned right onto Graben, Tom drew up short and gasped.

Tom stopped dead in his tracks. "Oh, no, you don't mean…"

Schlessinger, having halted as well, turned to face his friend, still smiling. "Yes?"

"Direct manipulation and selection in a human? A…a… natural biological lab?" he whispered, as if someone might overhear and question them.

"Yes, indeed. More or less. It was quite complicated and quite ingenious."

"But, Dr. Schlessinger, how is that possible?" Despite knowing him for three years, he still called the doctor by his formal title. This was not America, where familiarity came days or even hours. Tom liked to joke that America was a young country, so its people had to hurry to catch up with all the ancient countries; therefore, they had no time for formalities. "If he got that far and succeeded—and I can't even begin to conceive of how—why isn't it in the reports and notes."

Dr. Schlessinger motioned ahead of them. "Let's keep walking." The huge plaza of Grabenstrasse narrowed down as they approached Stephensplatz and the Stephanskirche.

"Vlad's work turned on using the concept of cancer cells, designing, manipulating, and coercing them—"

"Cancer cells?!" Tom exclaimed. "In utero? How in the world is that possible? Dangers involved to both subjects, I would expect multiple miscarriages, the necessity of abortions—or the birth of monsters, take your poison—and—"

"Tom, Tom, slow down. We can discuss the science and the ethical ramifications later. Suffice to say that Vlad was more brilliant than even his reputation. But, here we are at the church, and our meeting with the Polizei."

"Polizei?"

"The rest can wait. What you need to know is this: when Vlad's work produced a successful specimen, word got out far more quickly than we expected, in spite of all of our precautions. Suddenly, there were governments, military organizations, multi-nationals, and every legitimate and illegitimate bio firm. Black marketeers. They offered us money, they threatened us, and they declared they had legal authority over such a discovery. Needless to say, we were overwhelmed and unprepared. We were scientists doing theoretical and practical research, overseen by a gaggle of university administrators and businessmen. We knew the response would be strong—we had no idea it would be violent."

"Violent? They tried to steal the data?"

They stopped in the square before the Stephenskloster, its ancient door resplendent before them; the multi-colored roof, stained with black from rain and soot, towering above.

"You misunderstand. People were killed. There were outright threats of violence, theft, and kidnapping."

"What? Well, surely the University contacted the authorities?!"

"It was the government—governments—and military authorities who were threatening us. Police matters, they said. Military secrets, they told us. Vital national security."

Tom frowned. "Over a genetic experiment?!"

"You fail to understand what this means to them, just as we failed to think ahead. To us, it was an experiment in genetics, the human genome, health, prophylactic medicine, and so forth. But to them, it was the fountain of youth, the elixir of life. To be able to live with no disease, no sickness, a body that heals itself, protects itself from all negative antibodies, germs, weaknesses, viruses, etc. Increased mental capacity to synthesize massive amounts of information. There are even good chances that it slowed the breakdown of mitochondria in the bodies cells—everywhere."

Tom's eyebrows went up. "Really? Wow...that would be—"

"A panacea? Yes. So everyone wanted it."

Tom was silent for a moment. Then, "So...what happened?"

"Someone—and I only found out all of this later—organized a deception. Both subjects died. The baby died. The Project was completely reorganized, and all the staff and researchers were let go—with substantial parachutes and iron-clan NDAs. Including Vlad."

"Including Vlad?!"

"Yes. He was inconsolable. He moved back to Edinburgh. There was some indication that he was continuing to work, but he was largely unresponsive to any contact. Even from me."

"And then he killed himself?"

"No one knows for sure. There are indications the explosion was not an accident. And all of his data disappeared."

"Couldn't he have decided to destroy it all to keep it from being misused?"

"Possible, Ja. Unlikely in my opinion. He would have needed help to wipe all the data from all the places it disappeared. Also, a major cash withdrawal was made by him just weeks before. Almost all the money he had been given as severance."

"Where did the money go?"

"No one knows. To this day."

Tom was silent again, processing the information. "So, doctor, what about the subjects? You said there was a deception?"

"Yes. We had all been told the baby had died in childbirth, but reports later said that he had lived. And that he had been kidnapped. Some strange rumors about him being in Istanbul. I could not find anyone who could—or would—confirm anything. And there has been no sign or word of the subject in over ten years. Nor have there been any public use of the procedures or theories. So most people think the subject died or was killed—perhaps inadvertently in the battle among warring factions."

"I was told that Androvich kept everything in his head, and that was why we were still trying to reconstruct the theory. And working on side-projects as a result of the work that survived."

"Yes, well, that is the official story—and so it died with him. When most of his research, procedures, lab results, experimental results, and test subjects vanished, what else could we do? We tried to reconstruct how Vlad arrived at the point where the experiment was viable. We met dead end after dead end."

"But we have produced some incredible advances."

Schlessinger nodded. "True. We are part of the advancing field. But nothing close to Vlad's work."

The old professor turned to the American. "I have wanted to bring you into the cabal of those of us who know the full story—and now I have. And I have done so now because of this meeting. But you know only the basics. I ask you to remain silent, but listen close and carefully. I will depend on your recollections and insights later."

They entered the grand and ancient church through the massive doors, swung open during the day for tourists and supplicants. The inside was almost empty of people this time of year. Their footsteps echoed in the vast space. The darkness was lit only by candles and the winter sunlight streaming in through the large stained glass windows which lined the vaulted nave.

"We are meeting a Deutsche security officer, the one who originally contacted us about our experiments and worked with us throughout the crisis. Ostensibly to protect us, but they had their own agenda, of course."

"But why was the German government involved? Here in Austria?"

"We were told it had something to do with an agreement with the Austrian government because they were responsible for a lot of our grant money."

They turned down the right-hand transept, and the older man led Tom to a side door which led out into the small cloister.

"That's a bit unusual, isn't it?"

"Yes," Schlessinger replied.

Two men were sitting on one of the many stone benches near the entrance to the cloister, dressed in business suits. They had the look of paramilitary, Tom thought. Small, compact, serious, with short dark hair. They looked quite fit. The older of the two rose as they approached.

"Dr. Schlessinger, how good it is to see you again. Thank you for meeting me." The two men shook hands. "I assumed you would be coming alone."

"Ah, yes, well, Herr Schmidt, this is Dr. Aster, a colleague, and fellow researcher. He knows all about our project and its history—"

Schmidt interrupted. "—all of it?"

Dr. Schlessinger cocked his head. "Yes. He is a tenured member of the research team at the University."

"I see. Well, he will have to be vetted before he can be part of our conversation."

Schlessinger banked on Schmidt needing him. "I vouch for him, sir, and that should be quite enough. Though I respect you, and you always treated me fairly in spite of what we went through, I still feel the need for a witness to be present with me. You understand why." Schlessinger held Schmidt in a gaze usually reserved for errant students. "Otherwise, we leave."

The two men held each other's gaze.

Schmidt nodded. "Very well. For now, I will trust you— you have never given me any reason to doubt you."

Schmidt introduced the other man as Herr Weiss, his deputy on the case. They shook hands all around and sat down on the opposing benches: academics on one side, the officers on the other.

"On this case?" said Dr. Schlessinger. "What case?"

Schmidt sighed and leaned forward. "We found him."

"Found him? Found who? No!"

"Yes."

Schlessinger stood. "What? How? When? How is his health? Where is he?"

Schmidt stood and took Schlessingers' arm. "Slow down. Doctor. I knew this would be a shock after so many years, and so much fruitless investigation. It is why I wanted to meet you in person. Now...please sit."

Tom noticed that Schlessinger was trembling. "Yes. Yes. Oh, my...yes..." Both men returned to their seats.

"Someone—not us—located him. They kidnapped him—but these were amateurs, and we are not sure who they were working for. Some of the events, people, and details of the case triggered certain procedures put in place by myself just in case the subject surfaced. We had had some false positives three or four times in the last half-decade. But this turned out to be the real thing."

"Kidnapped? Again? Where was he? Who was it?"

"Doctor, please. Allow me to relate the facts to you, and then you can ask questions."

Dr. Schlessinger wiped his face with his hands. "Yes, yes. I apologize. Continue."

"The subject escaped. He may have had help because an anonymous tip led us to München. The subject ended up at the München police station on his own. We instructed them to hold the subject, and I sent a team to collect him. They should be there momentarily. We will meet them back in Berlin." Schmidt paused.

Schlessinger raised his eyebrows. "Yes? I want to be there."

Schmidt shook his head. "No. This is an investigation."

"He's my—our—subject!"

"I'm not saying you can't see him—just not yet."

"He belongs to the project! He's been missing for ten years! He is—"

"Doctor! I would not be here if I didn't think you could help us. But we're going to follow our procedures. We're not going to lose him again, like last time."

A tablet buzzed, and Herr Weiss moved off down the side of the colonnaded cloister to view the message.

Schlessinger shook his head. "I do not trust this. Your people do not have a history of great competence."

Schmidt pursed his lips. He sighed. "True. But we have had ten years to learn from our mistake and prepare. Besides, I have always been fair to you, have I not?"

Schlessinger sighed. "Yes, Herr Schmidt, you have. Unlike many others in that whole mess."

"As I said, we have had ten years to plan for this—"

Weiss strode up and interrupted. "Sir, you need to see this."

Schmidt frowned in annoyance and looked at the tablet Weiss held out. A look of confusion crossed his face, then anger. He stood and shoved the tablet away. "Sheiss!! Street Polizei! A wonder they make it through the day alive. Ach! We have to go, Weiss. Get our men out there searching the net, Interpol, and so forth: you know the drill. Alles klar?"

"What's going on?" Schlessinger asked.

"It appears," he said, "that we have lost him."

Schlessinger snorted in a most unacademic manner.

7 June 2032

They drove for hours, stopping about every ninety minutes to switch cars. This was some operation.

After the first switch, Salim touched his father's arm and asked him where they were going, getting only a frown and a shake of the head. His father then turned back to staring out the window.

Salim pictured a map of Germany. There were no major cities or towns south of München. His mind began to reel with questions, and he did not seem to be able to focus on problem-solving. It was like a computer virus that caused random data to spew forth without purpose or connection. What was the meaning of conversation between his dad and the police officer at the station? Hasel and Gerhardt were clearly not from the Berlin police or security. Why were they headed south? Did changing cars mean they were afraid of being pursued? They said his mom would be at the station, but his father said she was recovering. Why was his father so out of character?

Despite the overflow of questions, the last twenty-four hours had taken quite a toll on Salim, and he eventually fell asleep. When he awoke, it was late afternoon. He sat up straight and rubbed the sleep from his eyes. Tall, gray mountains loomed in the distance, snow-capped and imposing. The Swiss Alps? More likely the Bavarian Alps, or maybe even the Italian Alps.

Hasel was fiddling with a tablet. Gerhardt was asleep, his head lolling to the side, having set the car on automatic mode. The steady droning of the engine and the unchanging scenery caused Salim to doze again.

He awoke again when the automobile stopped. They hustled him and his father out of the vehicle and into another at a small petrol station on the edge of a little town. Hasel was walking across the concrete from the station with a brown paper sack. As they all took their seats, he handed out sandwiches and bottled water.

"We have a long way to go yet, Meine Freunde. You eat. Many hours."

Salim began asking questions, but Hasel and Father Gerhardt merely smiled and said, "We don't understand sign language. But everything will be okay."

He tried to talk to his father again, urging him to ask them where they were going. "Not now, Salim. What is, will be."

π

The communications screen lit up, and Officer Johansson tapped his earpiece to answer. A crisp voice said, "This is Headquarters Berlin. Commander Nuenhoff here. Detektiv Hasel should arrive around noon. Has the father arrived yet?"

"Yes, sir, he is here. Hasel arrived at six."

"Excuse me? This is impossible. He did not leave *here* until six"

"Well, he arrived at the same time as his father. They all just left to return to HQ."

"Mein Gott, idiot! You say he left with the father and boy?"

"Ja...ten minutes ago."

The line went dead.

π

The War Room buzzed with noise: people talked on phones, talked with each other, feeds from screens and HUDs spewed a steady stream of narration or background noise along with video. Groups of two and three people huddled together around consoles or tablet screens, talking and gesticulating. A huge screen covered one wall, divided into twenty different feeds playing news reports, mug shots, real-time satellite images, and CCTV feeds.

Ian Walker stood to one side of the room, waiting.

They'd rung him at 3:00 am and called him to come here. A secure location away from the main offices of MI6. Foregoing his usual walk to the Tube and the trip to British Genetics, he called a car to deliver him ASAP.

He sipped at the cardboard cup of coffee that he'd been given by a large, blonde woman, who said nothing. Other than the security guard who scanned his face, fingerprints, and retinas and brought him here, no one had spoken to him.

His corporate department rarely had dealings with government agencies, though he knew many senior administrators and the attorneys did so often. Once, when one of their Dover labs was burglurized, and the thieves stole some toxic and infectious (not to mention IP-protected) cultures, the police and intelligence were quite interested. For a while, Ian was sure *he* was a suspect! It turned out to be a competitor, and though the thief was caught, no one else was ever indicted. After Ian had been cleared, the authorities used him as a bio consultant to help them handle the recovery of the samples, which led to other work.

He knew of no current biohazard events, but that meant little. He was a lab rat, even though he oversaw an entire project for BG. So until they elected to tell him why he was here, he would stand by and wait.

He did recognized a few people. Sir William Hampton, the CEO of BG, stood talking quietly with a Scotland Yard official—quite senior, by the looks of his uniform accoutrements.

"There! There!" yelled a man sitting at a console where two others leaned over watching. A tall, dark-haired woman, dressed to the nines, walked over and peered at the display hovering above the man's station.

"That one?" She pointed. "You think that's the car?"

"Yes. Look—model, make, color, and you can just make out the last three numbers on the plate in this screenshot: 587."

One of the others spoke up, an older, balding man. "Could be 567. And it looks like there are only three people in the car, not four."

"If you squint it looks like an 8. And the kid could be laying down."

The woman spoke again. "Affirmative. We go with this unless and until evidence says otherwise. Find the next cam down the line and get it up. What's the road?"

"That's the E35, headed south towards Florence, just as Gelbert suspected."

"Doesn't mean they will *stop* in Florence."

"Not if they are who we think they are."

"We don't know yet. Stay with what we know. Could be someone wanting us to *think* they are the Sword of God."

"Enough second-guessing," the woman said. "Get our people on the ground in Florence. If they pass through, we alert our teams in Rome and move the Florence team to the rear. Let Metro know when you have something."

The people scattered to other stations and began typing, swiping, and tapping furiously. Ian watched the woman make her way over to a glass-walled office, stopping at the door to speak to a distinguished-looking elderly man standing just inside.

Another man made his way over to Ian's boss, interrupting the conversation.

"Sir Hampton, I'm Lieutenant Dover, I have good intelligence that the first group is a previously unknown participant. I haven't been able to track names to any known corporations, institutions, governmental groups, or fringe groups. We have a hypothesis that it may be a group out of France that one of our stations has been monitoring for terrorist activity. Minor data flag connections. The second group is a Deutsche security and intelligence team. The third is a pure unknown at the moment. Still running checks, but we need more data. We've got all profiles maxed."

Strange, Ian thought. They're tracking people through a lot of intelligence networks, but he'd heard no indication of a connection with biogenetic research. Why had they called him?

Sir Hampton scanned the room and spotted Ian, beckoning to him. "Sorry to keep you standing around, Ian. This is Lieutenant Dover, Scotland Yard's head of the biogenetic terrorism task force."

Ian shook Lieutenant's hand. Biogenetic terrorism?

"Thank you for coming so quickly, Dr. Walker. We need your help, or at least I hope we will soon."

"Glad to be of service. What can I do?"

He glanced at Sir Hampton. "Perhaps we should fill you in first. The conference room?"

Once seated in a glass-enclosed cubicle, with a long glass-top desk, a holo-screen, and a full view of the War Room, Sir Hampton began. "There is a lot to this operation, so I will have to be brief, and in doing so, far too general. I assume your expertise will allow you to fill in the gaps. But this may be difficult for you to digest."

Ian said nothing. People often thought academic researchers were soft.

"First, I need you to call your wife and tell her that you will not be home for a few weeks, and will be incommunicado."

"Excuse me?"

"By being here, you are in danger, and you are now under the secure protection of Scotland Yard and the MI6, and you must keep out of sight.

The table, the room around him, and the War Room receded from his vision. Everything became dreamlike. Sounds became muffled. Sir Hampton leaned forward

"I am sorry that it has come to this. I am not being overly dramatic, I assure you."

"But...I'm just a scientist."

"Indeed you are, and one of the best in your field. It is why I hired you."

"Thank you, sir, but—"

"Let me finish. We did extensive investigation into your background, personal and private. But we didn't find everything, did we?" He glanced over at the officer.

"I…I am not sure what you mean, sir? I haven't—

""I'm not blaming you, doctor. I understand why you didn't tell us."

A knot began to grow in Ian"s stomach. He felt beads of sweat on his forehead.

"Over ten years ago, you worked with Dr. Vladimir Androvich at the University of Vienna, on a secret project that ended with the number of kidnappings, murders, and suicides. Am I correct?"

Ian opened his mouth, then closed it. How could this be happening? The project had been a failure and had ended abruptly. He'd been required to sign a comprehensive NDA, and told things that were almost threats. He'd heard that the project's failure had ruined some of the staff's lives, and a few had even committed suicide. There were other rumors, but that was normal when something as substantial as Project Pacem happened. Kooky conspiracy theories. He'd been given a generous exit package, especially for an IVF doctor.

"You were told that the baby died, and the project ended in failure, and funding was cut off."

They knew about the baby? "Y—yes."

"Did you know that wasn't true? The child has been found, and everyone is going nuts. And I mean everyone. You can guess why."

Ian looked from Sir Hampton to the Lieutenant in sheer panic and fainted.

π

"Idiot!" He slammed his fist on the arm of his plush chair. "If you don't get after him, he's gonna find the open man!"

Over the cheering of the crowd, loud through speakers in the ceiling, he heard a phone beep in the other part of the house. He ignored it, intent on hearing the announcers extol the skills and intelligence of the opposing team's quarterback. He rolled his eyes.

"Jo?" his wife said, standing in the doorway.

"What?" he said, without looking back.

"It's Blanchard, he insists on speaking to you."

"Tell him to screw himself. The Redskins are playing."

"I told him. He said to say it concerns 'Project Paysome.'"

He turned to his wife. "What the hell is that?"

"I don't know. He said *you'd* know."

"Means nothing to me." He worked hard at Langley, and he only asked that on Sundays—"

He sat bolt upright, swiping the air above him to pause the live feed. "Pacem? Did he say *Pacem*?"

His wife recoiled at the force of his voice. "Uh, maybe. paysom, pace 'em, I don't know—"

"Get out, now."

She blinked and left the room as her husband tapped into the secure line to his office on the display floating in front of him.

π

The car decelerated. It was almost evening, and they sped down a four-lane road leading into a modern city. Or maybe the outskirts of an older town, contemporary accretions to an ancient town, crusting to the old bergs like new barnacles on a reef. The road and building signs were in Italian. Salim had not learned Italian except for a little he picked up from videos. He remembered the gelato stands that appeared every spring in his home town along the Haupstrasse. His mouth watered and his heart hurt. What was his mom doing right now? What were his schoolmates doing?

He turned to see his father dozing. He poked him awake and pointed. His father watched for a moment, then nodded then lay his head back against the seat and closed his eyes.

It was as if someone else's personality had been transplanted into his father. Or like a button was tapped and a new program began running. Stress and drama could bring out different facets of a personality, but he had seen his dad in crises before, and it was not like this. When Salim's grandmother died, when the neighbor's house caught fire, when his mom's brother was killed gruesomely in that train wreck near Mannheim. During those times, his father had been serious and focused—he took charge and showed compassion.

It was nothing like this.

7 June 2032

"They call themselves The Sword of God, Pate. Some crazy fringe group. Base is in Italy, but they have people all over Europe and the UK."

"With a lot of money and good resources."

"To some degree, but they are amateurs," Tasta said. "Anyway, back to the topic at hand. Parents are British origin but German citizens for over a decade. Father works as a technician in a local doctor's office. The mother is—was —a low-level worker at a large media and print company. Nothing on their previous life so far—someone did a relocation and identity program for them, and it's as good as my guys could do. We can probably suss it out with more time—"

I cut him off. "Irrelevant. I don't care who they are or were. You're certain of the identification?"

He nodded. "Yes, sir. Past leads were based on sightings or single data points. Here, almost every piece of intelligence suggests a match. The one anomaly is how he got there, who these Brits are, and why—"

"Probability?"

"My experts say 92%."

That was better than I hoped. This could really be him.

"Alright. Let's initiate the plan with the new exigencies. And you have those guys working on real-time planning now?

"Yes, *those guys* are working. Locked in a room analyzing everything we get and working up models and probabilities and contingencies. Everything is in place and we'll get him."

"That's what you told me last time. And you were wrong, and people died, and I ended up in the hospital, and he went missing for over a decade."

Tasta didn't respond. I didn't know if he was waiting for me or monitoring something off-screen.

"Apologies, Tasta, those memories are still fresh. I know we are up against some highly capable people and organizations. One of which is a mystery."

"All true. But we are highly capable, too. We know the rest of the players, and we've been studying their tendencies for many years. We have a better hand than they do, by all accounts."

His tendency to overstate abilities and outcomes bothered me. "And you said *that* last time. So how do you assess this unknown group?"

"The variable last time was that we did not even know the unknown party existed. We still don't know much about them, but we know they are out there. My hunch is that they are the ones that secreted him away. And that they prefer to work behind the scenes, hidden, unlike the rest of the groups."

"So you're not worried?"

"I didn't say that. I worry about them more than all the rest."

This was a curious statement, because it was the others who had caused all my problems in the first place.

"Because this group doesn't seem to care about *doing* anything with him except hiding him. That makes it hard to assess motives and goals. Who would do that for twelve years? *Just* to keep him away from everyone else."

"That's not dissimilar to my goal."

"True."

I stood up. The HUD rotated up to follow me. "I wonder..."

"What?"

"I don't want to use him. Or exploit him. Or even get him to cooperate. I want to keep him away from everyone who does. Who else would have that same agenda?"

"They are not an ally, whoever they are, Pate. We don't know *what* they were doing with him, covertly, all these years."

"Covertly?"

"Without him knowing. With the cooperation of the parents. My guess is that they *have* been using him, without his knowledge in a safe environment."

I tapped the tabletop. "Maybe. I've changed my mind: send me all the intelligence you have on these Brits and the mystery party, keep investigating and send everything new that comes in."

"Yes, sir." He spoke off-screen, and his device masked his voice. He turned back. "Done."

"Okay, enough of that. They are in Firenze, you say?"

"Yes, that's where the trail ended. Three of the biotech companies are on their trail, as is a joint force of the Brits and the Americans. At least one black market operation is trailing."

I sat and pondered. This was more complicated than the first operation. Which was saying something.

"Okay. Let's move, Tasta."

He stood. "Yes, sir. We'll be ready within hours. Are you coming?"

"Of course."

"I'll make arrangements. But, sir, if I may, with all due respect—"

I held up a hand. "No, I will not insist on taking on roles that are not my skill set. No repeat of last time. But I want to be part of the team. I have skills, too, you know.

"Absolutely you do, sir." He smiled. "As part of my team, I urge you to stick with those and only those. "To be honest, your training in the last ten years is nothing short of amazing. I didn't think you were capable of it. It usually takes—"

"Stop. And thanks. But I learned my lesson last time. Control the chaotic and know the variables, and everything is in our grasp. See you soon."

I wiped the air in front of me to clear the display.

Game on.

7 June 2032

About thirty minutes later, they entered a large city. Salim watched for anything that might tell him where they were. He saw nothing familiar.

His dad was still sleeping. The car smelled of stale food, sweat, and a slight musty odor from the air conditioner. The two men had alternated driving: one slept while the other drove. It appeared they wanted to get there quickly.

As the car passed under a bridge, Salim craned his neck to look out the back window at a large sign on the bridge. Though he didn't know Italian, he saw "Firenze." Florence? Why Florence? Why Italy?

Salim slumped back. He wanted to see his mother. His dad had implied that her injuries were not that bad, but it had looked terrible. His dad was acting like a different person. Gerhardt and Hasel said they were associated with the German Police, but surely were not. And now he was in Italy.

He could make no sense of any of it.

They exited the freeway, and Salim caught a glance of the road sign: Viale Fratelli something. They passed through a modern industrial section into older parts of the city. Structures of steel, glass, and concrete gave way to buildings of wood and cut stone. Smoothly paved streets gave way to cobbled roads. One-way streets and pedestrian-only roads. Statues. Fountains. Ornate carvings, worn and blackened with age. The car slowed. The crowds increased.

They turned and crept into a narrow alley, just wide enough for the vehicle. Hasel set it back to self-driving mode and let the AI do the maneuvering. Sometimes it slowed almost to a stop to pass an occasional trash can or motorcycle without touching it. Brick and stone walls rose impossibly high on either side. No one spoke. The car was noiseless. Salim imagined they were in a submarine, crawling along the bottom of an ocean trench, silent running.

They came to a stop in front of an old wooden garage door. Gerhardt got out and unlocked the door and swung it up. Hasel took control and maneuvered the vehicle into a dark cavern, watching Gerhardt until he held up a hand for Hasel to stop. Gerhardt went back and swung the old door shut with a bang.

As Salim's eyes adjusted, he saw the room was lit by a bare bulb somewhere above. The space around the car was cluttered with boxes, garbage cans, old paint cans—the detritus of a long-lived-in building.

Hasel spoke. "Okay, we arrive. We go in and we stay for long time. Come."

Salim scooted over by his dad and got out. Hasel led the way through a narrow door with Gerhardt following up behind. Despite the relative friendliness of the two men, it was clear that he and his dad were closely guarded prisoners.

Salim breathed in the musty, woody smell of old buildings that was so common in these ancient towns. They were in a long hallway, lit from above by cheap-looking fake-crystal lights, added to the building long after it was built. The walls were made of stone covered with plaster; the floor was paved with dingy tiles. Plaster was chipped and missing in many places, dirt and bits of crumbled plaster and stone littered the hallway.

At the end of the hall was a set of wooden stairs. The center of each step had been worn to a shallow concave dip by the feet of people walking up and down for generations. At the top was another hallway, paneled in cheap wood. Instead of tile, the floor was made of wood, which creaked as they walked.

Salim catalogued every detail, working to organize the information into a complete picture of the interior. Partly for future reference, but also to take his mind off their predicament. This building was not as old as some, he was sure, but it had not been kept up or renovated with any degree of care. It did not feel abandoned so much as ignored.

Hasel stopped by a framed door of thick wood, much heavier than the others they had passed. He swung it open with a creak and groan and motioned Salim and his dad inside.

His dad did not move. "Hasel—or whatever your real name is—I protest. The police will be searching for us—have been, I am sure, once they discovered your ruse. I ask, I beg, let us at least have a phone call. To put friends and family at ease."

Hasel smiled a tight smile. "Ah, well, yes, you are such a detective. Still, you have no idea of us. We are not to harm you."

"I know who you are. Let the boy go, at least. I have valuable information that can help you."

The man formerly known as Hasel laughed with great heartiness. "Well, if you know who we are, then you know we cannot let the boy leave."

His dad knew these people? Salim thought with a shock. *Had he known they were not the police all along?*

"So we are prisoners?" His father's voice was more strident now, Salim noted with satisfaction. Perhaps his real father was returning. "Which makes *you* kidnappers. Across borders." He nodded. "I am sure you know the penalty."

Hasel became serious. "No, my friend, no. We are your saviors. Isn't that right, Father?"

Salim looked back at Gerhardt, who was smiling, though he was not looking at Hasel or the other two. He was staring down the hallway. "In a manner of speaking, though it sounds blasphemous to use that word. I prefer 'ambassadors'. Or guardians, perhaps. Yet we are saving the world from certain destruction." Salim followed Gerhardt's gaze down the hall. He saw nothing.

A flash of irritation flashed over Hasel's face which quickly cleared. He indicated the room again. "I have told you we will not harm you. It is truth." Pause. "We will be here for a time until others arrive and go to safer places. No one is hurting you, and all will be clear." He cocked his head. "I have told more than I should. Now...please?" He held his hand out.

Salim's dad sighed and entered the room. Salim followed. The door closed with a hefty bump and the metallic click of the lock.

Bare walls. A wooden plank floor, scuffed and worn down, though it seemed clean, if a little dusty from lack of use. The walls had been painted with little care: defects and worn spots could be seen in the plaster behind. A bare bulb, unlit, was fixed in a cheap socket in the middle of the ceiling. A conduit ran down to a switch box beside the door, and from there to the floor. Two other conduits ran along one of the four walls to an electric socket. A small window was set in the wall opposite the door, up high, within a few inches of the ceiling. A large bucket sat in one corner.

Salim's dad flipped the switch up, down, then up again, with no effect. He checked the window, but could barely reach it. There was no latch to open it. The glass was thick, and even if not, it appeared too narrow for escape, even for Salim.

Opposite the bucket in the corner were two plain wooden chairs, with slotted backs, between which sat a small plain side table with spindly legs. A few books lay on the table, covered in a layer of dust. Salim leaned down to read the title of the top volume: *Le Compte de Monte Cristo*—it was an old printing based on the cover styling. He picked it up and noted the precise line of dust left on the book below, an old illustrated version of *Pinnochio*. Salim picked it up in his other hand. The third book was quite thick, with a long title in Italian. It looked like one of the academic book which lined the shelves of Herr Doctor Weissweich's office in his home back in Heidelberg.

"All the comforts of home." Salim turned and looked at his dad, standing in a corner, who was staring down at a stack of blankets on the floor. They appeared to be clean and new.

Salim went over. *What is going on? I am scared. What are they going to do with us?*

His dad looked down at him, and his expression softened. His dad nodded and put his hand on Salim's shoulder and led him to the chairs. They sat.

"I am a little scared, too, Salim, though not for our safety. I believe these men are from a group called the Sword of God. If true, I am pretty sure they will not hurt us. But they won't let us go home." He leaned forward, cocking his head to the side. Another familiar gesture, this one meant that what his dad was about to say held great conviction for him. "They will not hurt *you*. I know that."

Salim searched his eyes and believed him. *But*, he signed, *why is this happening? Did you do something wrong?*

His dad's gaze lingered on him for a moment, longer than was comfortable, then looked away. Salim sensed an internal debate. Not with anger, but a fair struggle. *Had* his dad done something wrong? He waited with an ache in the pit of his stomach.

His dad finally sighed. "No, Salim, I haven't done anything wrong. Not at all. But other people have. A lot of other people. And we're caught up in it."

Salim waited for more, but his father did not continue.

What does it have to do with us? Why are they doing this to me and you and mom?

He glanced back at Salim, then up and to the right. He sighed and scratched his cheek. "I don't know."

π

The door opened again about an hour later, as near as Salim could figure. They leapt up from the chairs where they had been dozing. Gerhardt entered, carrying a large brown cloth bag.

"I have brought a dinner." He set the bag on the floor. Before they could say a word, he was gone and the door was closed and locked.

They opened the bag and took out sandwiches, bottled water, a plastic container filled with cut carrots, cucumbers, and broccoli heads. A wax-paper-wrapped item turned out to be two chocolate-filled pastries. Salim would have been thrilled with such a bounty were it not for the circumstances.

They sat at the small table and ate in silence. About halfway through, Salim's dad spoke.

"Salim."

His dad's face was worn and tired. Like it did when Salim's grandmother died.

"Salim, I need to tell you something. This is very important. If the chance presents itself, you need to escape. Even if it means leaving without me."

Salim started to shake his head and protest.

His dad held up his hand. "Now listen. Neither of us are in physical danger. They will not hurt me. They will not hurt you, even if you try to escape and they stop you. You must believe me."

But they already did hurt you and mom!

"Those were not the same people."

Salim digested that for a moment. *You mean more than one group is after us?*

"Yes. I am afraid so."

Why?

His dad looked uncomfortable, then looked away. "I don't—I—" he looked back at Salim. "It's too complicated to explain right now."

Salim had learned that adults said this—about things being too complicated—when they did not want to tell what they knew.

"If you can, get away. But don't go back home. Go to Vienna, to the university there. Ask for the departmental head of the bio-research department. I know that seems strange, but trust me."

Vienna? Why?

"Do as I say, please. Please, Salim?"

The kidnapper told him not to go home. The woman on the train told him to go to Colmar. His father tells him to go to Vienna. And none of them would tell him why. His brain so was muddled with confusion, he did not even know what to say to his father.

He nodded in agreement.

"I hope it won't come to that, Salim. Perhaps the police will find us. Or..." He hesitated and sighed. "Perhaps the police will find us."

8 June 2032

They were startled awake by the sounds of voices outside. Loud, angry, and growing louder. Salim and his father looked at each other, and both stood. Yells, a scream, and scuffling, which faded away with distance. Silence.

What was that?

His dad shook his head. "I don't know. Police?"

Footsteps sounded, and a key turned in the lock. The door swung open and slammed against the wall with a bang. Salim and his dad were standing beside their blankets

A man strode in. Salim noted the fine thread count and silken sheen of his tailored suit, visible even in the low light. As he came into view, Salim gasped.

He stopped before them with his hands on his hips. Two other men came in behind him, dressed in casual, dark clothes. Both were large.

"Yes." He smiled and looked at Salim. "You thought your little trick on the train would allay us, boy?" He turned to the men behind. "Why did those idiots bring them both?" He turned back and took a step towards Salim's dad. "You are supposed to be dead."

The man held his father's gaze for a moment, then turned to the men. "Take him to München. Leave him at the Englischer Garten. Incapacitated."

One man looked shocked. "Won't the police find him?"

"Yes, exactly."

The man opened his mouth as if to say something, then closed it. "Very well, sir." He stood, looking at the floor.

"Tie his hands so he doesn't overpower you during the journey through your incompetence. Iudicio redimetur."

"Sir," Salim's father said, "please don't take me from him...I can provide—"

"Shut up. He'll be safe with us." He leaned towards Salim's dad. "As you well know, *father*."

Salim's father blanched. "Who are you?"

The man laughed.

"You are not the Sword of God?"

The man raised back up and paused for a moment. "Yes, indeed we are."

'Where are Hasel and Gerhardt?"

"Other business. I'm in charge of this phase of the operation."

"Let me stay, please...for his sake. He's afraid."

He motioned to the two men. "Take him."

The men stepped forward and took the arms of Salim's father. When he didn't move, they pulled him with ease towards the door. Salim's father struggled as they dragged him. "Please, have some compassion..."

Beaknose laughed. "Compassion?! *You* say that? *Tu quoque!*"

Salim's dad looked back over his shoulder. "Remember what I said."

Salim heard them struggling down the hall until a door slammed and there was silence. He tried to still his heart. He was sweating and afraid to move or speak.

The man walked to the door and turned around. His beaked nose gleamed white in the dim light.

"You will be taken care of. You are quite precious, you know." He smiled. The smile found on a smarmy car salesman who just made a huge commission. An attorney who had just received a significant windfall from a successful case. There was no pity or compassion in his eyes. "You won't be leaving us—there are no traitors to help you this time. Cat's out of the bag, boy."

What did that mean?

Another man entered. "Perimeter guard in place. No sign of pursuit. Nothing on the wires. Extraction team on the way."

"Good. Make sure we are ready for their arrival. I expect tracking within the day. Probably the Americans or British, but who knows. We're ready for them all this time. Get the doctor in here."

"Yes, sir." The man left.

Salim stood. Tears came to his eyes. He pointed out the doorway and then mimed a badge on his shoulder.

Beaknose smiled. "The police? Your father will tell the police? I count on it. And they'll waste their time chasing the Sword of God." His smile grew more broad as he turned towards the door. Before he pulled it shut, he looked back at Salim.

"By the way, the man who just left here is not your father. And your mother died right after you were born. So quit your sniveling."

π

Salim wept in the dark. What kind of evil man said such terrible lies? He'd thought his mom was dead, but his dad and the police both said she was alive. And why did he say dad wasn't his dad? Because they looked different? Salim had heard those comments—and some taunts—all his life. But for an adult to say it...

He was young when he realized that his bone structure and skin color were different from that of his father or mother, and his eyes were a deep brown instead of blue-green like both of them. People guessed that he was a mixture of European with Asian or Semitic. It made him wonder if he was adopted, and he got up the courage to ask his parents. It was an awkward conversation. They told him that they both had ancestors from those places, and sometimes genetic lines reinforced each other to make a child look different from a parent. Unusual, but it happened.

He was satisfied for years until he began to read about genetics. Their explanation seemed unlikely, but when he asked outright if they had adopted him, they answered with a definitive "no."

He woke several times during the night. Each time, the feel of the hard floor beneath the blanket and the musty smell caused a flood of memories from the last few days like water from a broken dam. *I'm in Florence. I'm a prisoner. My father is gone. My mom is hurt or dying.*

The feelings of loneliness and fear were almost overwhelming. He sobbed every time he woke from his fitful sleep.

It was still light when he got up. He went over to the table and looked through the books again. He could not read the Italian one. It looked dry and dull anyway—a long, detailed table of contents, dense text throughout, and very long sentences. Lots of footnotes. He amused himself for a while with the *Pinnochio* book. Apparently, there was some connection between the story of *Pinnochio* and Florence. It also was in Italian, but he could look at the pictures and guess at some of the captions. Florence was mentioned, as well as the Duomo and the Ponte Vecchio. He tried to read some of *Le Compte de Monte Cristo*, which was in French. He had studied French and had visited Paris twice a year with his parents. Still, literary French was more than he could handle. He tried to distract himself by working through a sentence here and there.

One man brought him lunch and a little portable toilet to replace the bucket. It appeared to be a medical device—for the elderly, maybe. A button on the side rendered the waste into an odor-free liquid, encased in a block for easy disposal.

Salim explored the room again. The window was too narrow for him to get out, even if he could break it. He tried anyway, using the voluminous Italian tome, thinking he could yell for help, but the glass was too thick. The door was sealed well, and the lock was a deadbolt. There was no interior knob, screws, or hinges that could be removed, even if he had any tools.

He thought again about Beaknose's words about his mom. It was mean-spirited, but why would he say she'd been dead a long time?

He replayed the attack on his mom, trying to notice details that might be relevant. With the pain of memory, he heard the crack of the bat, saw the blood under her head. It could have been fatal. Meant to be, perhaps. It sucked the breath out of him to think about it. He tried to recall if he had seen her breathing as she lay there; If there had been a fluttering of the eyelids, a moan, or any little movement. He saw none. He hoped his excellent memory was failing him in the moment's trauma.

Still, his dad had said she was okay. He had never known him to lie to him, though he had kept things from him a few times, purportedly for his own good. His dad obviously knew a lot more than he was telling him about this sitaution.

Salim stood and clapped his hands together. This internal debate was useless. It did not further his knowledge or add up to a plan. He did not have enough information to come to any conclusions. He could think and recall and rationalize and replay conversations and still could be no more sure of the truth.

What he could do was focus on the present and work on an escape. As his father had asked him to do. He had to remain calm and observant and wait for an opportunity.

He picked up *Le Compte de Monte Cristo* again and began puzzling out chapter 20.

RECOVERY

8 June 2032 07:33

He was startled awake when the door was opened. Beaknose entered, followed by a man in a white coat and a woman in a white uniform dress. Each carried a medical bag.

"Salim," Beaknose announced, "this is Doctor Dundheim. He's here to make sure you are healthy."

The doctor was older than his dad, maybe about the age of their neighbor, Herr Doktor Weissweich. He was portly, with thin black hair flecked with gray. He smiled at Salim awkwardly. The woman, who had come in behind the doctor, was also looking at Salim and seemed surprised. She was younger than the doctor, and thinner. Her blonde hair was cut in a conservative manner.

The doctor, seeing Salim's gaze, spoke up. "This is my assistant, Frau Hohen. I understand you are mute?"

Salim nodded.

"Frau Hohen speaks sign language and if—"

"This is just to make sure you are in good health...as I told you," Beaknose interrupted. "We wish to take good care of you." He turned to the doctor. "Isn't that correct, Doctor? We want to take the best care of him."

Salim heard a parent saying things in front of a child to make him believe their words. "Isn't that right, dear?"

"Nothing to fear, my boy," the doctor said. "Just a simple examination."

Salim looked at Beaknose. *I don't need a doctor. I am in perfect health. Thank you anyway.*

The nurse translated, and Beaknose said, "Please reassure him, Doctor."

"Young man," the doctor said, "I won't do anything that I don't explain first, and not anything you do not feel comfortable with. I am only going to take vital signs and draw some blood."

"For tests," Beaknose added, "to run some blood tests on your health."

Why is he so nervous? thought Salim. It seemed out of character. He looked at the nurse.

She smiled. "It's fine. All standard stuff. I'm sure you've had it done before."

The doctor moved closer and set his bag down on the ground. The nurse stepped back and did the same.

"First, my boy—Salim, is it?" Salim nodded. "First, I shall listen to your heart with this stethoscope. Is that okay?"

Salim looked up at Frau Hohen. She nodded.

He took a tablet out of the bag and then removed several sensors, which he placed on various parts of Salim's stomach, chest, and upper back. The tablet beeped with each one. "Now, take a deep breath...good."

He sent the tablet aside and took out another instrument. "Now, to check your blood pressure. I am sure you are fine." Salim nodded. As the doctor wrapped the cloth around his arm and watched the display on the tablet. As it hummed and vibrated slightly, Salim looked at Frau Hohen again. She was looking around the room as if she were cataloging it—just like Salim had done. He was getting a strange feeling about her, though it did not feel dangerous.

Beaknose stood in front of her, intent on the doctor's every move.

The doctor looked up from the tablet. "Yes, quite good for a young man such as yourself." The woman looked back at Salim. Intent.

Something was going on.

"Now hold still a moment." He began to loosen the cloth band, and as he did so, the tablet tilted to where Salim could see the screen.

It was dark. Blank.

This was a sham. Why?

The doctor grunted and took the band off and put it away. "Now, the last item." He began to remove items from the bag: two vials, a tube, a needle package, and a needle gun. What if they were going to give him drugs? What if they were going to kill him? Salim gasped.

The doctor looked sharply at him. "Just drawing some blood. It is nothing to worry about. You have had blood drawn before?"

Salim looked at the woman. While the doctor was attaching the tubes and vials, she stepped back slightly and signed to him—down low, just at her waist.

Do not respond. Are you okay?

He shook his head slightly.

"I will put this small electronic band around your arm, it will inflate automatically. I will place the needle gun against your inside elbow. The computer will release the band and engage the needle. You will hardly feel it. Just a little stick, then no pain. You have given blood before, yes?"

Salim nodded. He began, and Salim glanced at the nurse again.

Stay calm and alert, she signed.

Was she another spy? Mole, as Beaknose had called the man in the van? Beaknose's organization was like a sieve. Salim wanted to laugh, in spite of the situation.

"Okay," the doctor said. "Ready?"

Salim nodded. He watched the instrument for a bit, then back at the woman. She looked at Beaknose, who was still watching the doctor. He seemed almost...excited. She turned back to Salim.

They aren't going to hurt you. But you must escape.

The same thing his father said.

Salim saw his blood flowing down the tube, filling the vial. Needles did not bother him, but he decided to look nervous and panicky. Seemed like a proper act, and he'd have a reason to watch her. "It's okay," she said aloud, "this is the easy part now. Relax."

When the vial was full, the doctor fitted another and filled it, then tapped the gun. The needle withdrew and excreted a small bandage over the spot and beeped. The doctor put the instruments away. He handed the expelled needle and paper wrappings.

Beaknose turned to the nurse. "I'll take those."

"They need to be disposed of properly and safely," the nurse said.

"I will take those." He extended his hand, and the nurse shrugged and handed him the materials. He turned to the doctor.

"The vials."

The nurse signed watch me and stepped forward. "They need to be sealed and labelled properly first. Otherwise, they could be contaminated and become useless. It's also required under the law."

Beaknose paused. "Very well. Quickly."

She stepped close to the doctor and took the vials. Right before she did so, she signed at Salim so quickly, he would have missed it if she hadn't told him to watch her.

Make distraction

She took vials from the doctor and went back to kneel down beside her own bag.

Salim stood and swayed, then stumbled into the doctor with enough force to push him back into Beaknose. The doctor fell to the ground, and Beaknose stumbled back. Salim regained his balance and walked to stand right in front of Beaknose*I want to make a phone call. You can't just keep me. It's illegal.*

"Ah, ah, careful boy!" Beaknose tried to take a step back and push Salim away. As the doctor climbed to his feet, Salim pushed Beaknose away with enough force to make him crumble back again.

"Eh, you idiot child." Salim scrambled back and tried to go around Beaknose, opposite the side where the nurse was working, as if trying to get to the door. Beaknose grabbed him by the shoulders. The doctor was at his side, his hand on Salim's shoulder. "I—I don't know what happened. It was not enough blood to make him dizzy. Unless lack of sleep or food—"

"It wasn't the blood, doctor," Beaknose grinned. " I know what he's up to." He leaned down into Salim's face. "Really, boy? There are guards all along the corridor and every entrance. You are supposed to be smart." He laughed and pushed him away.

Behind Beaknose and the doctor, the nurse stood. Salim backed up more, hands up, signing, sorry. Beaknose shook his head and turned to the nurse. She handed him the vials. He left the room.

As the doctor straightened his coat and finished packing up, the nurse took a few steps to the table. She picked up one of the books with both hands, then placed it, back down.

"*Pinnochio* is a fine classic. The Dumas novel is wonderful, too, and it is the complete edition."

She approached the doctor and picked up her own bag.

Beaknose returned, without the vials, accompanied by another man.

"Thank you, doctor. Nurse. My man here will escort you out." After the door had slammed shut, and the footsteps had retreated, Salim stood, reviewing everything that had just happened. Who was Frau Hohen? Why did she need a distraction?

After a time, he went to the table and straightened the book that the woman had picked up.

A scalpel lay on the table behind the stack of books.

8 June 2032 08:01

The door opened, and an arm appeared, dropping a bag of food and a bottle of water. Salim waited ten minutes, then got to work. The books went on the floor. The table he slid under the window; chair on top of the table. Standing on the chair, he was chest-high to the window.

Salim inspected the wooden frame. As he suspected, it was caked with paint and putty and multiple repairs, like in so many of the old houses of Europe. He found a small spot at the bottom right corner where a lot of putty had fallen away. He picked at it with his fingernail, and more fell to the floor.

The wall around the window frame was plaster. The window was small, just an open rectangle left in the middle of the bricks and stone. It probably had hinges attached to the inside with wood shutter doors when the building was constructed. In modern times, someone had pulled it out and set a frame inside the opening with a glass window. The window was too small for him to get through (even if he could open it), but if he could remove the entire frame, he should be able to squeeze out.

He retrieved the scalpel and began chipping away. It was tedious work, but in about fifteen or twenty minutes he had one side of the frame exposed to the stone. He worked along the bottom, then the opposite side. Bent over, prying and digging, was hard work, and he sweated with the effort. His arm began to tire.

He glanced back at the door. If patterns held, they would not open that door for another four or five hours. But they had said they wanted him out of here, so there was a possibility that they could come back at any time.

He renewed his efforts. Once he had worked his way across the bottom and opposite side digging and scraping, he could feel the whole structure moving each time he pried into the plaster.

He set down the scalpel on the chair at his feet, grabbed the bottom of the frame, and pulled. The top held, but a crack appeared all along it. He yanked, and it loosened more, raining paint chips and plaster shards down over him. He worked the frame back and forth, then pulled again. It still held at the top.

Frustrated, he renewed his grip and gave a mighty yank. The whole window and its frame came loose. He dropped it and grabbed for the opening to balance himself but too late. The window frame, glass, chair, table, and Salim came crashing down in a heap.

His wind knocked out of him, he struggled to scramble to his feet. The fall was loud—at least inside the room. If anyone were outside the door, they'd hear. He set the table upright, retrieved the chair and place it on top, climbed up (wincing at a pain in his side and arm), and stuck his upper half through the opening.

He was looking up out of a small, square hole in the ground, reinforced on all sides by a concrete window well. Using his elbows for leverage, he wriggled the rest of his body out into the small space. He stood and looked around. He was in a narrow alley with no one in sight.

As he scrambled up out of the window well, he thought he heard a noise behind. He ran, now noticing a sharp pain in his left side and burning in his left knee and elbow. Taking deep breaths, he sped up.

He turned a corner, and a shout caused him to glanced back. Two figures, at the other end of the block, running in his direction.

He sped up and turned down another alley. Old cities like this were laid out in a grid: he saw it in his mind, with the locations of the two men and himself superimposed upon it. What pattern of turns would confuse them the most? He played the scenarios in his head. It was like an old game he used to play on his first tablet.

It was likely that they would assume he had turned down the next alley, either left or right, with a chance they'd split up, with going the wrong way. They'd expect him to run away from the place of his imprisonment, not parallel or towards it.

At the next street, he turned left, back towards the original road, then right again before he reached it. Surely everyone in the building would go out in search of him. They'd know how to canvass an area. If they were thinking right, they'd send people out to cordon off the area to hem him in—if they had enough men. This was a variable he did not know. He went through every face he had seen, every voice he had heard since he'd been there. Eight maximum. But he couldn't be sure there weren't more—a lot more, even. He had to outrun any cordon before it was set.

He turned right, now parallel to the street he had escaped onto, but in the opposite direction he had first run. That should help—they would not expect a kid to run *back* in the direction he escaped. Now he needed to find a place to hide that was unexpected and still had a lot of exits.

Two blocks past his place of imprisonment, he turned onto a wider street. A few people were walking here and there, but not as many as he wished. Being close to dusk, most people were either at dinner or preparing it. He considered entering a shop and asking to be hidden, but a young boy running away from adults would garner suspicion and waste time if it didn't work.

He entered a square and slowed down to avoid attention. More people milling. There was a small chapel to the right. The door was open, and a sign out front read:

Allessandro Francesco funeral
8:00 pm
8 June
Burial at Saint Stefano Chapel Cemetery
Noon, 9 June

He continued up the steps and approached the large doors. As he entered, a man was walking up the aisle.

"Oh, hello, young man. You startled me." He was an elderly man, dressed in a suit. "Are you here for the funeral? It does not begin for another thirty minutes. Everyone is in the meeting hall next door." He waved to the right. "I was just going out for a bit of air while I wait."

Salim nodded his thanks and turned, walking out and to the right, moving behind a large pillar, thankful that most people usually offered more information than was necessary.

He watched as the man walked out into the square and down a street, then scooted around the pillar and back inside. He walked down the dimly lit aisle and glanced back into the square.

Three men stood at the center. Crouching behind a pew, he examined them with care. As one talked to the other two, he pointed in three directions and then at the chapel.

It surprised Salim that they were already here. They must have a lot more people than he assumed.

He ran along the aisle and down the side of the church. A door to the left of the altar was locked. Another door was on the opposite side, but he was running out of time, if that pointing meant "you go search the chapel."

He ran across the transept, behind the coffin and row of flowers, risking it. No one at the chapel door yet.

The door was locked. He was trapped.

He crouched and ran back to the center of the transept again, scanning the entire room and above. There was a balcony, but he saw no entrance from here. Back up front, perhaps? Behind the locked doors, more likely.

His heart pounded. They were going to catch him.

He looked down at the coffin. Three little lock switches on this side, each for one section of the tripartite lid. He turned foremost and lifted the lid.

He had seen dead bodies twice before: at a neighbor's funeral and then at the funeral of his mom's co-worker. In a coffin like this. He had peered in at both events, curious. They had looked more like wax mannikins than people. Once, when Salim was in the city with his dad, they came across a car accident. An elderly man had been struck and killed. He was lying in the street with medical and police personnel all around. He *looked* like a dead person. The body was so still—too still. It *felt* dead. Before his dad hustled him away, he noticed the gray pallor, the eyes open and unseeing, the jaw slack.

This was not gruesome. The man was small and thin. Salim was even smaller and thinner. He climbed in, trying not to think too much, slid his legs and torso down beside the body, and allowed the lid to shut over him. The smell of embalming fluids and whatever else the preparers used was strong. He breathed through his mouth to avoid vomiting.

He turned to his side, facing away from the body, and pushed his mouth and nose into the soft padding, using it as a mask to breath through. Better. His back was against the corprse, and by pushing with his back, he could move it a little to the far side. There was no warmth—he tried to pretend it was not a dead body.

He held still and listened, but heard nothing inside the padded box. How long should he stay? When would it be safe?

Since the interior doors were locked, it would not take long for the man to search the sanctuary. Maybe ten minutes to run the room and look under the pews? At most?

He lost track of time, straining to listen.

After a time, he heard voices. Low. Murmuring. Footsteps clumped on the steps and transept floor, causing the coffin to shake slightly. The humming of voices grew louder.

The funeral attendees were arriving.

8 June 2032 09:48

Salim had no sense of how long the event lasted. Talking, singing, periods of silence. He may have drifted off into a shallow sleep a few times. Once, he felt an urge to cough, but stifled it.

The sound of shuffling of feet and vibrations brought him to alert. The coffin was jostled. *Oh, no!* A public viewing!

It wasn't. The coffin was lifted and carried. It tilted, evened out, and began a slow, rhythmic jerking. They were taking it out of the chapel. Unlike many churches, this one, in the middle of the city, did not have a graveyard. So where were they going?

Soon, with a jolt, the motion of his morbid capsule ceased with a clunk. A car door slammed. Then three others. He held his breath in the silence. The coffin began to vibrate. An engine.

He was in a hearse.

After five minutes, he sensed motion as the vehicle drove. Whether it was panic or lack of oxygen, his breathing became labored. Claustrophobia set in. He had to get out of here. Turning onto his back, he pushed up on the lid.

Air. Fresh, cool air.

He waited. No sounds or voices, only the hum of a motor and wheels on pavement. He pushed the lid higher and pulled himself to a sitting position, head out.

He was facing the back of the hearse. Through the window, the city streets and buildings moved by on either side. He leaned out and craned his neck to looked forward. Like a limousine, there was a partition between the drivers and the back of the car. The window partition was blacked out.

The lid would not go all the way up because of the roof of the car, so he had to crawl out head first, like a snake slithering out of a box. Once out, he crouched beside the coffin, taking stock. Besides the large back door, there was a side door, where the back passenger door would be on a long limousine.

He waited. After a time, the hearse slowed and stopped. He grabbed the handle of the door and yanked, worried that might only open from the outside. But it swung wide with more force than he intended.

No time to worry about it. He slipped out and slammed the door behind as he ran to the rear of the vehicle. Glancing back, he briefly spotted the driver in the side mirror, staring with wide eyes.

8 June 2032 12:45

Oblivious to everything around, he stared at the note.

The woman on the train had saved him from the kidnappers. She had done as she said she would, and her plan helped him escape. She told him to go to Colmar.

Of course, she also didn't tell him *where* to go in Colmar. Now, here was a note with an address.

The man in the van helped him escape. The woman on the train helped him escape. The nurse helped him escape. And now a foreign college student, dropping a note.

They had to be a connection. And he was sure it was not the Sword of God or the Beaknose crew.

What to do? *What to do?!*

The board showed three trains leaving for Colmar within the next two hours.

He moved through the crowd to platform 6 and took a seat inside one of the sheltered benches, pulling a newspaper out of the bin next to it and pretended to read. He watched as people came to stand nearby, waiting for the train. Searching their faces for furtive looks, questing eyes, hunched shoulders.

The train pulled in and the passengers disembarked. Salim waited, watching the platform clock and the new passengers boarding. As the clock ticked to one minute before departure, he stood and strode across the platform, boarding the train just before the alarm sounded and the doors closed.

He went to the first train just behind the food car. If there was trouble, he could get the attention of the staff. He took a seat by the door and slid over by the window.

The rear door swooshed open, and a woman came and sat beside him without even glancing at him. He started to get up and she put her hand out.

"Not yet."

Oh no. Not again. He turned and watched out the window.

The train pulled out, and the woman took out a tablet and began scrolling, tapping, and reading. He watched her, trying to assess the danger. Light, angular features. She appeared to be in her late 40s. Dark hair in a no-nonsense bob.

She dropped the device to her lap and turned to him.

"You are a difficult person to keep track of."

He stared.

"Which is good. You've done quite well."

What is going on? Where is my father? Is my mother okay? he signed.

"We're safe for now, Salim. I'm taking you to a secure location. But there is a lot for you to learn, and it will not be easy to hear."

Who are you?

"Someone trying to make up for her sins." She glanced around the train car, tapped her device for a bit, then, seeming satisfied, said, "Follow me."

She led him through three train cars and into a compartment in the sleeping car. As they entered, he thought he saw her nod at someone down the passageway, but when he looked, the person was gone.

It was a small compartment, with two bunks on one side and a bench seat on the other. She indicated that he should sit.

"This is going to be difficult and it will take some time to process. I wish you could hear it in better circumstances."

His mind told him he should be suspicious, but his heart said she was genuine. He nodded.

She took a deep breath. "I have rehearsed this speech many times, but now that the time is here, I find I do not know how to begin." She pursed her lips. "Okay. The simple version."

She took his hands in hers. "A long time ago, a brilliant scientist had some theories about how to engineer traits in humans: physical, mental, emotional, social, and more. He worked for many years and was finally ready to test it. He needed human subjects, an expensive lab, and a lot of scientists with different areas of expertise. This would cost a lot of money, and while his University was willing, they needed more than their entire endowment. They put him in touch with a woman who was experienced with organizing large biological research projects. Some said she was the best in the world. She saw that this project—if successful—would produce a windfall, and therefore attract a lot of private companies, governments, and other organizations. Does this make sense so far?"

Salim nodded. A fear began to grow in his belly.

"The woman was wildly successful. Companies that tripped over themselves to fund the staff, equipment, drugs, bio-printers, subject researchers, investigators—you name it, they wanted in. The goal was to eradicate disease, strengthen health and mental abilities, and so on. You can imagine how much money could be made by those who could offer such benefits. Everyone would want the procedure: not only private people, but employers, military, research facilities—everyone would benefit. It would be like the discovery of the polio vaccine, the 2026 cure for cancer, or stopping a pandemic—except instead of stopping something bad, it would be a positive benefit."

Some of his earlier memories. Things his parents said. Things that—

"But the woman was not entirely honest about the project to all the funders. It was not so much a procedure that anyone could undergo, it was a complicated set of procedures that required the selection of two people—a man and a woman—of certain genetic characteristics. They would undergo a series of genetic processes, the scientists would artificially inseminate the woman. Do you understand this?"

Salim didn't move. He knew.

"The fetus would also undergo several procedures: DNA modifications, genetic synthesis using—well, I need not go into that. Anyway, after many unsuccessful tests—over about ten years—a successful fetus was produced and the baby was born."

She sighed and looked off in the distance, as if she was no longer speaking to him, but to someone else. "The entities funding the project—over a billion dollars every year—came in, took over the project, and kicked out most of the original scientists and staff, bringing in people of their own choosing. Some fought the changes, both the university-appointed administrators and the people most involved in the project. They disappeared."

Salim sat up. *What do you mean?*

She shook her head. "Oh, I don't think they killed them. I think they sent them away and gave them a lot of money and threatened to ruin them if they didn't stay quiet. But other groups wanted this information, too. Black marketers, rogue companies with less than stellar ethics. They wanted their hands on this project—this child—too. Once the University people were squeezed out, the project became something quite different. And some of those who wanted it just *might* kill for it. The potential value was stupendous."

He felt a clammy sweat on his skin. *Why?*

She shrugged. "You're smart, you can guess. Military purposes, super-soldiers. A monopoly on the most-wanted medical procedures in history. Lawyers for these companies had IP and copyright figures dancing in their heads. Even religious groups popped up, wanting to destroy the project because it was a terrible sin to play god." She waved her hands. "I am getting too much into the weeds. Here is what matters. After they kicked the primary staff out of the program, various groups vied for control and power. In the midst of the power struggle, the project staff took the baby away. Few people know what happened after that, but the baby disappeared and has not been found. Until recently."

She turned to him and took his hands in hers. "Salim..."

He pulled away. *I'm that baby.*

A sad smile played across her lips. "When did you know?"

He shook his head. *I didn't until just now. But I knew something wasn't right—*

He stopped. It was too much. His brain began playing back words, events, faces, conflicts, changes—all of them clicking into a place into a nice neat diagram that lead, quite simply, to one thing. It even made sense of his father's actions, of—

His mind reeled, and the train car flickered as if he was in a dream. He was stunned, but the diagram floating before him from his mind was beautiful, symmetrical, and the answer to everything.

Almost everything.

She took his hand. "I'm sorry, Salim. There were people who argued, at the beginning, that the whole approach was unethical because the child—you—would be part of an experiment with no say, which, they said, violated medical and scientific ethics. But money and power often override ethics with rationalizations that convince even the well-meaning that they are working for the greater good."

Stop. If I am a genetically modified human, why this flaw? He felt like his muteness was irrelevant in light of the other information, yet for some reason, he wanted to know.

She nodded. "No one was sure, because it was not apparent until after you were born. Then everything went to hell and you disappeared. However—this a bit of good news—there are people who continued the research as best they could, hidden away, unknown. They think they found the reason, and a remedy. It involves a bit of genetic modification and some bio-nano-surgery. And speech therapy, of course."

He looked away, thinking. Then back at her. *You are the woman who did the funding.*

"Yes."

And part of the group who continued the research, and you are located in Colmar.

She sat back nodding. "I sure hope our enemies cannot make conclusions like that with as little data as you do."

It's not data. It's my life.

She nodded. "Good point. Sorry. Salim, Colmar is where my lab is located. It is a safe place, and a stepping stone to finding a way for you to be safe forever. If you agree. And, we can easily perform the procedure to give you a voice."

Will my parents be there?

She turned back to look at him and he thought he spotted pain in her eyes. "I think so."

8 June 2032 09:30

I sat on a bench at the Gare du Nord, waiting for my train and pretending to read a newspaper. I was watching the crowds, especially the people who looked to be trying to blend in. It was exhausting to be always on alert. But it was part of my training, and practice was essential.

The train pulled in and the passengers disembarked. I waited, watching the platform clock and the new passengers, making my way aboard just before the doors closed. I settled into a private car in First Class. I had bought all four seats, as usual. I settled back to read a report from Tasta's intelligence team, and barely noticed when the train pulled out of the station and made its way through the outskirts of Paris, picking up speed as it reached the countryside.

A tapping on the door startled me into high alert. The door slid open, and a woman stepped in, nodded, shut the door, and sat down opposite me.

My hand strayed near the small taser inside my jacket. She wore a white button-up shirt, a skirt, and carried a small purse. No place to conceal any kind of significant weapon. She set the purse at her feet, leaned back, and placed her hands on the seat on either side of her. If she was some sort of operative, she was signaling that she meant me no harm.

"Excuse-moi, Madame. C'est mon compartment. Mais…" Was my bodyguard sleeping in the next compartment?! I pay a lot of money to be shadowed when in public.

Delicate features. Middle-age. In good shape. Blondish brown hair.

"English, Pate. I have a message."

I frowned. Someone was tracking me well enough to find me on a train, though the fact it was a public place and not at one of my locations was a good sign. But I never used my real name for booking, renting, buying, or anything.

"Do I know you?"

"No. The boy is okay, but kidnapped and being held in Firenze. He will escape. You need to be ready."

I feigned ignorance. "The boy?"

She smiled. "If you don't find him soon enough, he will probably try to get to Colmar."

"I don't know what you are talking about."

How could this woman—or who she worked for—out-intelligence my people?

"I know of no boy. I don't know who 'she' is. You must have me confused with someone else."

She smiled again. It was not a condescending smile or a patronizing smile. It was like they were sharing a secret.

She nodded. "Yes, yes. Perhaps so. I guess the Sword of God and the Blackguard Co-op mean nothing to you as well." She stood. "Sorry for the mistake." She smiled once again. "One other bit of information." She lost her smile and leaned in towards me. "You need to prepare for more enemies than you think."

I was up and grabbed her arm with far more force than I intended. The room spun. "Who the *hell*—"

She yanked away in one smooth motion, slid open the door and stepped out. As she shut it, she said, loud enough for anyone nearby to hear, "My apologies, sir! It is the wrong car!

I stared at her through the compartment door window. She nodded firmly, then turned and left.

I stood motionless for some time. Someone was one step ahead of me *again.*

My phone beeped. I pulled it out of my pocket and sat down. Tasta appeared in the air above the device.

"Good news, boss. We've located him. I have our assets on the way."

"He's in Firenze?"

He balked. "I—How did you know?"

"And the Sword of God had him, but now the Blackguard Coop?"

He frowned. "Who do you have on your team who's better than me? I'm insulted." He laughed. "We *just* got—"

"I think I just met our mystery party. The boy is going to escape, and we need a *lot* more people. And Tasta?"

"Yes?"

"Your bodyguards are terrible."

8 June 2032 09:33

The smell was becoming overwhelming, and he was feeling light-headed. Were coffins air-tight? Would he run out of oxygen?

He had a vision of the funeral service coming to a close and the lid opening to allow friends and family to pay final respects, only to find two bodies inside. It was both disturbing and funny.

If he began to suffocate, he'd have to push the door open. Which was also disturbing and funny.

What if the men were in the crowd, waiting until it was over, so they could search the entire chapel, breaking down doors if need be?

He did some relaxation exercises and felt his heart slow down. He relaxed. It was warm and comfortable. Everything was fine. He could wait.

As long as there wasn't a viewing.

8 June 2032 10:01

"Our team is just about to arrive in Florence! And you want me to reroute them to Colmar because some stranger on a train told you to?" Tasta was shaking his head.

"Yes, I do," I said.

"Pate, we are as close to the target as we've been in thirteen years. We have exceptional intelligence."

I grimaced. "You do, my friend. But I think her team—whoever they are—has even better intelligence."

Tasta fell back in his chair. "Look. I am familiar with every major ops organization in the field—legit and not. I don't know who these people are. It could be a trap."

"True. It could. But I don't think so."

"Why?"

I shrugged. "Call it a hunch."

Tasta shook his head. "This is no time for hunches. Facts, Pate, facts. You know that."

"The hunch *is* based on facts collected over two decades of experience. Call it a reasoned decision based on disparate facts if it makes you feel better."

Tasta raised his eyebrows. "Hope it's a good hunch."

"Me, too."

8 June 2032 11:43

Ten minutes after escaping the hearse, the morbidness of what he had just done hit him. It felt like bugs were crawling all over him.

He found a city map and located the train station. If he could get on a train with no one spotting him, they would not know where he'd gone.

But where should he go? He'd been told not to go home. Go to Vienna. Go to Colmar.

He didn't know who to trust.

A a pang of regret touched his heart. He should be worrying about what happened to his father, but for some reason, he was sure he was fine. His mother—that was another story. If he could get to her, then she'd tell him the truth. He could trust her. But he was certain they were watching his home. Whoever "they" were. To go back would put his mom in danger. Again.

It hit him that he was at the center of all this insanity. Not something his dad had done. Not his mom. They were in jeopardy because of him.

And he did not understand why.

When he arrived at the train station, he was pleased to see it was busy, which would make it easy to get lost in the crowd. Yet it also made it harder to watch everyone. The important factor was not to *look* nervous. Blend in. He was just a normal kid, who did this sort of thing all the time.

He stood off to the side, near a pillar, examining the train schedule board. Where to? The woman on the train told him to go to Colmar. Why? He knew no one there, he'd never been there. It made no sense.

Yet she had had helped him escape, and she and the nurse were the only people he'd met during this Kafkaesque adventure who seemed concerned for *him*. He wondered if they were working together. He'd have to explore that later.

Still, he could trust no one. No matter who it was, whatever anyone told him, he had to do something else. Something unexpected.

Again, where to? He wracked his brain for someone—anyone—he might know outside Heidelberg. There was a friend of his who's family had moved to Hamburg a few months ago. Maybe he could find them. His fourth grade teacher, who had been fond of Salim, had gotten married last year and they lived in Füssen.

What would happen if he just showed up at the door of either? With a crazy story of near-fatal attack, kidnapping, escape, his father's strange behavior, and imprisonment in Italy—they'd call the authorities. And after München, he didn't trust the police.

He put his back against the pillar and slid to the floor. It was as if some evil god had decided to throw dice for the events of his life. Nothing made sense, he couldn't count on anyone, and he had—

"Excuse me, are you lost?"

He looked up. A young man, dressed in jeans and a t-shirt, with a backpack and earpieces. One of thousands of college students traveling across Europe, with unshowered bodies, hostel food, and stars in their eyes.

Salim felt stupid. The first rule was not to draw attention to himself. Here he was, in tears at the foot of a pillar in plain site. "No, I'm fine. Just waiting for a train."

"Ok, bud. Have a good day." As the student turned, a paper fluttered to the floor beside Salim. He picked it up and stood, scanning the crowd for the man. But he was nowhere in sight.

He looked down. It was a mere scrap, torn out of a notebook. Written in a sloppy hand were the words:

Colmar. 3495 Rue de Tiefenbach. Destroy this.

8 June 2032 13:30

"Excuse me?"

"Yes?" She frowned.

"I have a message for you."

"Have I met you?" She knew she hadn't as she examined the woman. Elderly. Simple clothes, rather plain.

"No. You need to go to Colmar. As soon as possible."

"I'm sorry, but you have the wrong person. I've never been to Colmar, and I don't know anyone there."

"Yes, you do. You just don't realize it yet."

She grabbed the woman's arm. It has taken a lot of work to be invisible. "Who the hell are you?"

"Please. I am just delivering a message." She took the woman's hand and removed it from her arm.

"Leave me alone, or I will call a manager."

The woman took a phone out of her purse, tapped a few times, and held it up before her face.

Her mouth dropped open.

9 June 2032 10:05

Sergei Prokov pulled his wool cloak around him as he stepped from the limousine into the chill air of St. Petersburg. He hurried across the sidewalk into the glass and steel skyscraper of Medezin Research, Inc. He nodded to the guard sitting at a bank of television monitors, strolled to the elevator, waved his hand over the security lock, and tapped the button for the top floor. The hum and silence comforted him as car rose smoothly skyward. He took a few deep breaths. This was his calm space, his moment of the day to relax and gather himself. It only lasted a few minutes, but that was all he needed.

Because when the door opened, secretaries and underlings would accost him like ducklings around their mother. Each believed that their issue was not only the most important, but by bringing it to his attention, they would gain gravitas in his eyes. He would ignore them, all part of this daily play, and head straight to his office—his elegant, plush office of wood and steel and fine cloth, in the corner of the building, with beautiful views of the Neva River, the Spit of Vasilievsky Island, and the Peter and Paul Fortress. His secretary would bring him an espresso laced with a splash of vodka.

He'd check his messages, schedule, and personal notebook, then call his secretary into his presence to brief him on the essential matters of the day. A summary results of the latest genetic and bio-tech research, sales figures on current products, projection for new products, information on the negotiations with various governmental agencies, current status of lawsuits, and so on.

He loved it.

The elevator came to a gentle stop and the door snicked open.

The lobby was empty and quiet.

Confused and concerned, he stepped onto the plush landing and hurried through the foyer and into the offices. Everyone was in their place, working, and each one looked up at him and back down at their work. He could feel the tension. Something was wrong.

Of course, he would not show any concern, panic, or worry. He strolled down the aisle towards his office, looking neither right nor left, ensuring his face betrayed no emotion. Just a normal day. The issue, whatever it was, did not faze Mr. Prokov, CEO and Chief Research Officer.

He entered the anteroom to his office suites.

"Good morning, sir." His executive assistant was as imperturbable as he was: no emotion, nothing revealing that anything was out of order. "I will have your espresso for you in a moment. Mr. Skolinkovich is waiting for you. Shall I bring him one as well, sir?"

That was it. Skolinkovich had *never* been to the offices or labs. Not once in fifteen years.

"Yes, thank you."

He opened the ornate door, entered, and closed it behind him. Mr. Skolinkovich was standing with his back to the door, looking out the huge plate glass window. His ever-present personal assistant was absent. People said he was never without him—some claimed he even slept on a cot just outside Skolinkovich's bedroom.

"Welcome, sir. It is an honor to have you visit," Prokov said.

Skolinkovich turned, and Prokov was shocked to see that his eyes were crinkled with joy. Or amusement.

"My friend! What a wondrous view you have here!"

"Yes...yes, it is, sir. Our facilities—"

"Pacem has been found."

Prokov stared. His mind was spinning. Hundreds of events, people, possibilities, questions. Over ten years...

His mouth opened, but no words came out.

Skolinkovich chuckled. "Yes, my reaction as well." He moved around the desk and clapped him on the shoulder. "Sit."

Prokov found his way to a chair in front of his desk. Skolinkovich sat in a chair next to it.

He recovered his voice. "Do we have him?"

"Oh, no. Not yet. But we will. He popped up on our systems three days ago from a report we saw by the police in München. He had been kidnapped by the Sword of God and lost when some other faction got involved. Perhaps the British or the Americans. All the old players came to life and began a massive search, each of us watching the others, trying to get the jump. What did the old British detective say? 'The game was afoot!' But we located him just hours ago on a train, and I have people ready to move once we know his disembarkation point."

"Who knows of this reappearance?"

"In addition to those I mentioned, the Austrians, German intelligence, maybe the French. Several other research labs, too, we can assume. And Vienna, for certain."

"British Genetics?"

"Probably."

"What about the KGB?"

"Of course."

Prokov always suspected that much of the work undertaken by Medezin Research was supported and encouraged by the KGB. A good thing, since their intelligence and strike teams were among the best.

If Medezin could catch him, and Prokov could get his team up to speed...well, it could give their research a monstrous leap ahead of everyone else. He'd call Dr. Abramov and his team back from Namibia, and then retool the Alpha Lab with the new—

He looked up at Skolinkovich, who was watching him, still smiling.

"What now, sir?"

"You tell me."

Prokov took a deep breath and told him everything he'd been thinking. "...and we should pull the bio team from the SyncroBrain project to help. We'll also need to lock down the lab tighter than the Kremlin—"

"Yes, that part is already in place, ready to implement. You tell me when. We're not going to lose this time. We dumped a lot of money into this project for a return that was far below what they promised. With the subject in our hands, there will be no *accidental* deaths or loss of data and samples."

Prokov cringed, and memories of a decade ago flooded his mind. Chief researcher dead. Three Russian secret service agents, dead. An innocent little girl and boy, dead. And the explosion and the fire—the official report was a boiler explosion, but well-sourced rumors said it was no accident. This was supposed to be science, technology, medical research, and—most importantly— economic windfall. Not spy stuff and murder.

All the same, Androvich had been killed, the lab destroyed, and every bit of data gone. The child dead—though no one ever believed that. For over a decade, Skolinkovich—and all the other investor-competitors—had been searching.

But now Prokov's years of promising results was about to come to fruition.

8 June 2032 21:02

As the train approached Colmar, the woman pulled clothes out of her bag.

"Put these on." It was a hoodie, a hat, and glasses.

I don't wear glasses.

"I know, They are not prescription. Just to make it more difficult for anyone watching CCTV feeds. The clothing has been embedded with nanofiber to alter what appears on video."

She asked him to turn around. When he turned back she had on a different skirt, with a new jacket and a winter beanie. Her hair was dark. She appeared younger and heavier.

The announcement for Colmar came over the speakers.

"Ready?"

He nodded.

"We'll go back down to the next car and exit there. Inside the station, we will meet a man and a young girl who is a few years older than you. Take off the hoodie and the cap when I tell you. There will be a taxi waiting."

All this subterfuge was dizzying.

The events went as she had described. The man appeared to be about the same age as the woman. They approached each other and hugged, kissed, and locked arms as if they were husband and wife. The man shook Salim's hand and made a joke about his hoodie, as if they were family. The girl playfully punched him in the arm and laughed, then flounced along beside him.

Once the four to them were inside the taxi, the woman appeared to relax. "Good work, everyone. Pierre, any news on the other targets?"

The driver spoke. "Cami sent a message right before I picked you up. On their way."

"What about the outsiders?"

"No sign yet. Most of their assets are still following up in the four other cities. Massandro is antsy, though. He has a hunch that one of them has info that he was on that train. No confirmation, though. He thinks they've upped their game and are running silent."

"Governments?"

"American and British on their way. They are more concerned about the black market people than the legit."

She nodded. Salim was baffled. All of this over his genetic background.

His parents would be there, though! At least some normalcy would return. He didn't care about the strange behavior of has father, he just wanted to be together again. The woman implied that they would have to move somewhere and maybe even undergo identity changes. That was okay with him.

They pulled into an alley, around a block, and then down into an underground parking structure. They took an elevator *down*, which surprised Salim. The man, the girl, and driver got out at one floor, but the woman indicated that they he was to stay with her. Salim watched the floor indicators tick down to B8.

The doors opened to reveal a white lobby, with corridors stretching back on two sides. Glass doors lined each side, with trays and medical instruments lining the rooms. The desk in front looked like a nurses's station.

The woman stopped him with an arm. "Now, Salim, I know this is confusing and perhaps alarming. It will all unfold, some of which will be even more difficult to hear than what you already know. For now, I ask you to be patient."

Where are my parents?

Another woman approached from down the corridor, and the woman turned to her. "Dr. Schneider, this is Salim."

"Hello, Salim. It is nice to meet you."

He nodded. *Nice to meet you.*

"Dr. Schneider is going to take you and give you a medical exam. I know you have some injuries. She'll tend to you and then we'll have a late dinner together and talk. Is that okay?"

He nodded again, wondering what she would do if he refused.

8 June 2032 21:47

"You have some bruised ribs and some contusions, but nothing broken. I can fix you up quickly. The bruises will take a while to heal, of course. She ran an instrument over the scrapes and his skin tingled. He jerked a little.

She smiled. "Biological nanobots. Nanobiots, we call them. Helping your body repair. Rather new technology we are quite proud of. They work from inside, then become waste through your bloodstream and digestive tract. You'll never even know." She gave him a brief injection near the bruised ribs, placed a self-sealing bandage over the scrapes.

She checked his vitals, and then led him to a small cafeteria where the woman sat waiting. A bowl of soup and some bread had been placed opposite her.

He sat and began to eat. He had not realized how hungry he was. She said nothing until he was mopping up the last of the soup with a morsel of bread.

"Better?"

He nodded between bites.

"Good. Have you thought about the treatment?

He sat back and wiped his mouth with a napkin. *Already? Why the hurry?*

"I just thought you might want it. We have some time. Not long."

Are there any side effects or dangers?

"No. Other than it might not work. But I am pretty sure it will."

Then I want to do it. Wouldn't you?

"Without a doubt. Okay, we can begin this afternoon. As I said, you'll need therapy and it will take a while for a full recovery. Do you have any other questions?"

No. When will my mother and father be here? Can we go back to Heidelberg?

She sat back, and her mouth opened, then closed. She closed her eyes and her face took on a pained look. "Salim, I think you misunderstood, and that is my fault."

He felt his body heat up in panic. *Are they dead? Did you lie to me?*

"No, no. They are both alive, though your mom is in critical condition and it will be months before she can leave the hospital. But she is getting the most advanced care in existence. I made sure of it."

You made sure of it? Who are you exactly? How do you know my parents?

"Allow me to tell you this most difficult part first. They are not coming. Their role is finished."

You did lie to me.

"Not...exactly..."

A flash of memories shot through his mind. A myriad of events, words, and faces, from the years of his life, coalesced into a pattern. The lack of relatives. The way they took holidays. How he felt around other kids. What the kidnappers said on the train. What the men in the car, and the man in Firenze, had told him. His mind saw it all, structured now into a three-dimensional pattern of connections, probabilities, and one, almost surely correct, conclusion.

He looked up at her with tears in his eyes. *They are not my real parents.*

Her shoulders dropped. "No, Salim, they are not. Not your biological parents. But they did raise you and take good care of you." She sat back with wide eyes. "Hm. You really *can* extrapolate quickly." She shook her head and blushed. "I'm sorry. That's irrelevant at the moment and rude of me. If by 'real' you mean 'biological,' then yes, you are correct. They are not your parents in that sense.

I don't care They are the only parents I ever known.

"True...and normal circumstances that would make no difference, because...because they were chosen by me to hide you. To protect you. It was never a long-term solution. And now they cannot protect you any longer. Their job is done. She shook her head. "I know how heartless that sounds. It is a terrible thing to do to a someone. But I had no choice."

He didn't know what to say. She reached out and took his hand, but he pulled it away. *What do I need to be protected from?*

"It's a long story."

I want to hear it. All. Now.

She held his eyes for a moment. "Okay. You deserve that at least." She took a deep breath.

9 June 2032 06:17

"This will take about an hour, Salim. Follow me."

His mind was still reeling from the conversation with the woman earlier. Salim had long known that he was not normal. Things were not quite right in his world. At first, he chalked it up to being young—everyone feels that way to some extent.

What he had learned made sense of it all—but it was a confirmation that reconstructed his world into something foreign. He was still Salim, but the universe he inhabited had taken a dramatic shift.

He didn't feel much of anything. Shock, he imagined.

"Here we are." The doctor showed him into a lab room where an assistant was waiting, a young man with dark skin and hair, like Salim.

"Please lay on this bed, Salim. It was like a dentist chair, with armrests. He crawled up and laid his head back against the rest.

"I'll expedite the procedure. We'll give you a sedative. The procedure is not complicated or lengthy, but it does involved some rather long instruments and several injections. We'll follow up later in the day with some monitoring tests and some oral nanobiots. Okay? May we begin?"

He nodded, feeling some trepidation.

The assistant put a mask over his face and tapped some places on the holo floating above the bed.

π

He woke up in the same chair with no memory after putting on the mask. The doctor was bending over him.

"How do you feel?"

He tried to speak, or at least what he thought speaking would be like. Nothing happened. *I can't talk.*

She smiled. "No, not yet. It will take some time. The nanobiots are rebuilding your vocal cords, though they'll finish soon. Others have already made the proper connections in your brain, diverting or repairing some key synaptic pathways. Right now, though, most of the nanos are the healers, strengthening and supplying what your body needs to speed healing. But you'll need therapy to learn to talk."

Do you know if it will work yet?

She smiled. "Unless something goes wrong, there is a 95% certainty.

Salim felt a moment of excitement, but it waned quickly. It did not feel like a time to celebrate. And he had no one to celebrate with.

No one.

9 June 2032 10:15

Tasta stood up with me as the train pulled into the station. I put my arm in front of him.

"Get out the next car back. You and the bodyguard follow. I need to look like I'm alone. I'll signal if I need help."

"And if they shoot you dead? Will that be my signal?"

"If they shoot me dead, none of this matters and you can go enjoy all the money I have given you. But they won't."

"Wish I was as sure as you."

"Team in place?"

"All signaled green at their locations. Wish I knew what to tell them to look for."

"Don't know yet." I tapped my earpiece. "I'll tell you anything I learn, but I think we'll all recognize what to do when it's time. Quite soon."

"Not the way I like to operate, Pate."

"I appreciate that. None of this is normal."

He moved off down the aisle and I stepped out of the train car, taking in the motion of the crowds in the broad view and the individuals in a micro view. I saw nothing unusual, nor anyone moving toward me or tracking me.

I went down the platform, and as I turned I took a quick glance to to see if Tasta was near. No sign of him. *Good*, I thought. *If I could see him with a g lance, he wouldn't be doing his job.*

I needed to appear as if I was going somewhere, but I didn't know where. But if my hunch was right—

woman brushed by me, carrying a large bag. She looked back, "Pardon," she said, and kept moving. I watched her until she disappeared into the crowd ahead. No, just an innocent interaction.

I moved through the turnstiles and passed by the ticket counters. It was not too crowded, but there were enough people to mask my movements and keep me alert.

"Excuse me, young man?"

An elderly man, stooped over a cane, held out a paper. Trembling a bit, he appeared embarrassed. "Could you help me read this? I can't find the platform number."

"Sure." I looked at the ticket. "Platform eight to Nancy. Go down this way." I pointed.

"Thank you." He bowed, and as he drew close, he said, "Taxi. Black and white. Human driver." He took the ticket and headed towards his platform.

I stared after him. *Really? An elderly man?* I tapped my earpiece. "Get that, Tasta?"

"Affirmative."

I moved outside and soon spotted the black and white taxi. It was the only one with a human driver. I hurried over.

Before I got in, I tapped my earpiece. "On me?"

"—team two black and white taxi with a human driver—" crackled back. I took that as a yes.

The driver turned back to glance at me. He was also wearing an earpiece. "Where too, sir?"

"You tell me."

"Leave it to me."

"—have eyes on Pate. We're good on tail—"

The driver pulled out and drove downtown first, but then turned twice and headed back in nearly the same direction, but farther out. We entered an older section of the city. Soon, he turned into a narrow alley and said something that I did not catch.

"—problem, Pate...police traffic stop...may be intentional...trap..."

We turned into a smaller driveway and a door rolled up and admitted the car into a dark tunnel, illuminated only by the vehicle's lights.

"—losing signal...give us a ping, Pate...power...can't—"

I took out my device out and tapped.

No signal.

We descended at least four or five levels. Dangerous, but Tastas' men should be able to find my last location. Shouldn't take long to get in or get a signal through.

The ramp opened into a surprisingly large underground garage. The driver parked on the far side and shut off the engine. I jumped out as three people approached from a doorway nearby.

The two in front were paramilitary, wearing kevlar and holstered guns. They approach without a word and searched me, finding the thin knife and the personal EMP. I allowed it.

The third figure stepped forward. A youngish woman, dressed in a business suit. "Hello, Pate."

"Nice welcome."

She shrugged. "Necessary. As you know. Follow me."

"Can I ask who you are?" I said as we walked.

"Sure." She kept walking in front , the two goons behind.

Ah. A smart aleck. "Who are you?"

"Cami." The ringlets of her long dark hair bounced as she walked.

"Was hoping for a little more."

She glanced back. "Second-in-command."

"Second in command of what?" This dramatic stuff was irritating.

She looked back and smiled. "You'll see. I know a lot about you, though we never met. You're about to be surprised."

"Why don't you stop being so obtuse and just tell me who you are and what is going on?"

"Not my place. But I am taking you to someone who will."

All right. Let it play out. Tasta can't be too far out. I check my device. Still no signal. One goon cleared his throat and Cami glanced back.

"No need, Pate. We've got people contacting Tasta as we speak. We'll bring them in. We're going to need them."

I was surprised, though I refused to show it. How could they be so knowledgeable about my operation? I hope it just meant they were far better at this that my other pursuers.

In any case, I was finished talking to this woman. She was relishing her role, and if this is what I think it is, it's fine.

The three led me down a hallway, made a few turns, and then descended a set of stairs to another hallway. She stopped at a door.

"Wait in here, please. The boss will be with you shortly."

The two men entered with him and indicated for me to sit on the couch.

It was a conference or waiting room. A round table, a little kitchen and bar, a couple of couches and cushioned chairs. No windows, but a few generic pictures on the walls. European city-scapes.

One man went to a small refrigerator and retrieved bottles of water. He offered one to his buddy, and then to me. I shook my head. Not until this played out.

My device still showed no connection. No cell, no satellite, not even internal wireless. Maybe this was a mistake, and I had just walked into an enemy lair.

A loud boom startled me out of my thoughts, and I rolled to the floor as the two goons unholstered their guns out and ran to the door.

The building shook with another boom. Closer. Both men were on their comms.

I jumped up. "What have we got?"

One man shushed me with a hand and spoke to the other. "You stay. I'll get her. Boss is on the way with escort."

"Affirmative."

The first stepped out the door, scanned both ways with gun out, then shut the door behind him.

"What is it?" I asked again.

The man shook his head. "Not sure. Could have been an accident—this place is old. Could be an incursion. We'll know—" he stopped and put his hand to his ear.

I considered my options. I did not know the layout or size of the building. I could find my way back to the garage, but without knowing more, it was probably best to trust these people until I had reason not to.

The door flew open and the second goon returned. He shoved her in and she stumbled to her knees.

"Sit rep?" The first goon said.

"Incursion. Standing by for instructions."

The woman straightened up and looked at me.

My heart stopped. "Eris?!"

9 June 2032 10:45

Salim sat in the cafeteria, waiting. When she came in, she sat, and, without looking at him, tapped and read her tablet. Finally, she smiled and looked up. "Excellent. Not long now. Are you okay?"

What do you think? He was surprised at his boldness, but he was beginning not to care. Others had devised and controlled his entire life. That would now change.

But it hurt. A lot.

She paled. "I meant about the procedure." She sighed. "I'm sorry. I'm trying to make it right and hope you see that someday. I really do have your best interest in mind."

By hiding me from my bio parents, taking me away from my real parents, and turning my life upside down?

She looked hurt. "Yes, I deserve that."

He shook his head. *Well. You didn't kidnap me, you helped me escape. You didn't turn my life upside, a bunch of scientists and money-hungry people did.*

"The first is true." She hesitated. "The latter is...not. I played a big role in the Project. As you know. And I was all in...until I wasn't. I am to blame. And I am trying to do right. A lot of damage is done that cannot be undone."

So how are you going to right it?

"Salim, I think what we did came from good intentions, but we rationalized a lot. We hired some people that did not have good intentions. And it went to hell, and I got fired."

So it's their fault?

"And mine. They fired me, but I received a significant payoff with a serious non-disclosure agreement. So I took the money and set up my own research lab with my own people. No outside influences. No deep-pocket investors. No drug companies or governments. It's a secret—or they'd be coming after me. I wanted to continue the research, because I think it is important, but I am doing it like Androvich intended. I wasn't a scientist. But I knew how to get the best out of scientists."

Okay...what does that have to do with me?

"Look, the original intention of the Project was good and worthwhile. I can't undo what happened to those who volunteered as subjects. Some of them are dead. And I can't undo what was done to you. We created a human for an experiment, who became a pawn, and had to be hidden to keep him safe."

You did that? You hid me away?

"Myself and others. If you think it was a terrible thing to do, I'm sorry, but if you had fallen into the hands of others, it would have been worse. We didn't know how else to do it except rely on the best re-identity people in the business." She leaned forward. "Salim, one of the largest black market drug organizations came within seconds of getting you. You'd have been a guinea pig in a lab for the last twelve years—if you survived. We feared someone would find you eventually, and we were monitoring you."

Did my parents know all of this?

She pursed her lips. "Yes."

They were in on it?

"Yes."

Salim set his jaw. All his life…a lie. And his parents were in on it.

"When you turned 18, we were going to reveal everything to you and give you a choice. The first choice you ever really had. But the others found you and forced our hand."

What is that choice?

"There are three. First, you stay here, with us, at the lab. Join the project—as a volunteer, not as a subject. Offer as much or as little as you want of yourself. You'd be safe. And we'd give you a salary."

And give you a big boost on your research and light years ahead of everyone. Which could mean a lot of money.

"Yes. True. There is some self-interest. Though I do want to keep you safe."

The other options?

"You can just leave. Do what you want. Go wherever you want. Back to your hometown and your parents. I know they would take you in, even though they are also aware people will come for you, and this time they might not survive. We'd go back to protecting you again. But we can't prepare and defend against every contingency."

That choice sounds like it comes with a guilt trip.

"I'm just telling you the truth. The last option is to go away into hiding somewhere else."

I'm thirteen years old. I don't have any idea where to go.

"Well, this is not something you have to decide right now. Stay here for a while, let us do some tests and other research on you. We'll pay you enough so you can go wherever you choose and do what you want. When you are ready."

And the third?

"Similar. After you disappeared, before I had the idea to start my own research lab, I was planning a way to spirit you away. Go somewhere with people who care about you that would be difficult to find. We could do some editing to make you all look different."

And who are these people who care about me?

"Well, I was about—"

A boom shook the room. Salim ducked and saw panic in her face. "Oh, no no no not yet—" She grabbed at her device. An alarm sounded, the lights dimmed, and a red light began flashing. Another boom sounded and plaster fell from the ceiling.

"Come on!" She jumped up and grabbed his arm, pulling him after her into the hallway and down the corridor. Two men rounded a corner fast, dressed in what looked like military gear.

"What's the situation, Massandro?!" the woman said.

"Breach. Not sure who yet." Both stopped in front of them. The man speaking put a hand to one ear, listening, then dropped it. "Blew the elevator doors to ingress. Team is on its way."

"Where are our visitors?"

"Being escorted to quarters the last I heard."

"Code Alba. Take Salim to the emergency point. Get the Alba packets!"

"Yes, boss." He stepped away and touched his ear, talking.

"Salim, go with these men. They will protect you and get you out of here. I'll meet up with you later."

Salim protested, but she was already running down the corridor.

"Come with me, Salim," the second man spoke. "Rodgers, get the packet and meet us at the garage."

"Affirmative."

The man hustled Salim through a door. The halls were dim and the flashing red lights were disorienting, like an amusement park ride.

Salim had never liked amusement park rides.

More booms and people yelling far away, echoing through the air ducts. They took several turns, went through more doors, and up one flight of stairs. They burst out into the underground garage, where a few vehicles were lined up along the nearest side. A taxi sat in the middle of the space, engine running.

As the man pulled Salim towards the taxi, a woman came out of a far door towards them, carrying a bundle. She met them as the soldier opened the back door.

"Get in." He turned to the woman. "Alles klar?"

She nodded and slid in. He scooted over to give her room as the guard shut the door.

A driver sat in front. "Ready?"

"A moment," the woman said. She turned to Salim and pulled something from the bundle she was carrying and raised it to his head. He flinched.

"I need to put this on you." He allowed her to do so. It was a short-haired, blonde-brown wig. She tucked his own, longish hair into it.

"Damn!" She said. "You still have scrubs on. Here..." she fumbled once more in the bag and pulled out a leather jacket. "This may be big, but it must do." She turned back to the driver. "Get us out of here now. I'll call and see if someone can meet us with more clothes."

"Yes, boss," the driver said. "Hang on."

The car sped up as the man drove the car out of the garage, up a curving, indoor ramp, and then down a long tunnel. As they approached the end, a door rolled up. An armed man beside the door waved them through.

"I'm your Aunt Emma, by the way."

Salim stopped putting on the jacket and stared.

"Oh...I'm not really your aunt. Sorry! I'm Cari." She touched his shoulder. "But Aunt Emma for now."

Where are we going?

"It's important that you do not sign for the rest of this trip. You are not Salim. You are Pablo, a boy traveling with his aunt. Lean in and pretend to talk to me every so often. Stay close to me. Act like I am a family member. Hold my hand through the airport."

Airport?

"Yes. We're getting you out to a safe place."

You guys tried that before and it didn't work

She hesitated. "True. This time is different." She gazed out the window. "Quite, quite different."

9 June 2032 14:48

Salim disembarked from the tiny plane. The flight across the Celtic Sea from Dublin was not pleasant. The craft only held thirty people, and it was about half full.

He walked across the tarmac into the little terminal and located the lockers. In Dublin, they had changed clothes again, and his "aunt" had sent him off on the tiny plane, telling him, at the last moment, to find locker 34 inside the station at his destination. It would be biocoded to his fingerprint, she said.

Locker 34 opened to his thumb. He pulled out a small metallic packet with a thumbprint plate. It held a printed note and an envelope.

> *Cab to docks.*
> *Ferry to Garbh Eilean*
> *Small boat named the Lynnberg. Find Captain J.B. Holland and tell him you need passage to*
> *"Pacem."*

The envelope was a stack of Euros.

Salim sighed. He did not know who he was, where he belonged, or why he was here. Nothing about his life was as he thought it was.

Despite what the woman said, he was not free. Just in a different kind of imprisonment.

He shrugged. All one can do is the next thing.

9 June 2032 11:14

"Pate?!"

"Eris?!"

"But you're dead," we both said at the same time.

"I…I saw you., she stammered. "In the lab. Dying. I saw your *grave*."

The surrounding room began to shrink. "I saw *you*…dying after giving birth. I found *your* grave in England."

"I haven't been back—" She stopped, both of our minds spinning, trying to make sense of it all. The truth dawned on us. "Bastards," she said.

"I'm gonna—"

Another boom shook the room. She stepped forward and I took her in my arms. It felt like a dream.

"Is it really you?" she said, anguish in her voice.

"Yes."

She pulled away and looked into my eyes. "I can't believe it. What the hell are they doing to us?"

I felt anger rising. "I'm not sure. What happened to you?"

"After you died…after I thought you died, they paid me a lot of money and set me up in St. Petersburg. Made me sign a rather hardcore NDA, but I didn't—"

"They gave the money to you? Then where did—"

"—and with you and the baby dead, I—"

"Eris."

"What?" She narrowed her eyes.

"The baby's not dead."

She stepped back. "*What?!*"

"They lied about that, too."

"Where? Do you—"

Another boom made us jump, this time accompanied by gunfire.

The goon with us, who had been talking on his headset, grabbed us both by the upper arms. "We have to move."

He ushered us into the hallway. Yells, footsteps, and bangs echoed near and far. We reached a dead end, the goon tapped on a plate on the wall, and a recessed door opened inward. He shooed us in and ran back the way we came as the door closed behind us.

Our eyes adjusted in the dim small room in time to see two figures approaching from a dark opening on the other side. Their features resolved into another guard and a woman.

"Director!" Eris shouted.

"Hello, Eris." She turned to me. "Are you surprised to see me, too, Pate?"

"No."

She laughed. "Well, that is disappointing. You haven't known the whole time, I hope."

"No. A few days. How do you know so much about my operation?"

"Good God, Pate, are you that stupid?"

I stared at her as a grin grew on her face.

What an idiot I'd been. "You put a tracker in me."

"A bio-bot monitoring device, manufactured from your own DNA. Almost undetectable. Still, I was always afraid you'd discover it and have it removed."

Eris spoke. "You made me think Pate was dead. *And* the baby! How dare you! *Why?!*" She clenched her fists at her side.

"Wasn't me, Eris. I fought it, was fired for it, relocated, and forced to sign a ridiculously stringent NDA. And more."

Gunfire again, this time much closer.

"We have to get you out of here."

"Where's my *baby*, Director?!"

"Safe. Come on!"

We left the room and hurried down another dark hallway, lit only by dim emergency beacons. Soon there were no more lights, and we navigated by flashlights in the Director's hand and mounted on the gun of the goon.

We reached a door, and the Director placed her thumb on the pad and it opened into the parking garage, empty except for two barrels and a crate.

"Bastards, they aren't here yet."

"Do you know who these attackers are?" I asked.

"No. Maybe through my tracking of you, or your son. Or perhaps time just caught up with me."

"This is your lab?" I said.

"Yeah. They gave me a lot of money to shut up and go away. After a while, I hired some people to help me find out what happened. If you recall, I successfully argued for them to let you come see Eris—who *I* thought was dying, too. While there were complications to the birth, they also gave her combo of drugs and circulatory biots, plus some good old-fashioned fake medical displays, to make it appear she was dying. Then they took you—"

"And they took me for some fake tests and did the same so that Eris would think *I* died."

"Yes. I discovered you were still there the next day, even though they were keeping it from me. I recognized something was up, but I didn't know what. So I had Dr. Patterson implant the biomonitor."

Eris spoke, calmer now. "They did all this subterfuge so we'd go away and leave them alone, thinking the project was all over?"

"I'd ask why all the deception, but I guess I know," I said.

"The root of all evil: money and power. It drives people to do terrible things and rationalize it. And even the best of us get caught up in it. When I found out that the baby was alive, I assembled a team and went after him. I wanted to take him from the bastards." She turned to me. "And so did you."

"That was you? In Istanbul?"

"Yes. I couldn't contact you or tell you, because it would risk my plan for Salim."

"Salim?" Eris said.

"That's the baby's name. Who is not a baby, but a teenager who is quite an amazing young man."

I looked at Eris, who had tears in her eyes. "Oh my God, oh my God..."

I hugged her to me. "I suspect we're not standing here waiting for the world to fall upon us, Director. You have a plan. Unfortunately for you, I have my own plan. Or, rather, three plans to choose from. I had hoped that you and Eris and Salim would stay at the lab with me and—"

"He's *here?!*" Eris said.

"Not any more. You'll meet up later."

"Why this lab?" I said.

"I set it up to continuing the project with more accountability, scientist-driven, and no money-hungry bastards controlling it. To finish the work as Androvich envisioned it."

"But *why?*" Eris said. "It's a horrible—"

"No. The concept behind it is sound, Eris. It would be a great benefit to mankind. Great benefits can be misused—space flight, atomic energy—"

"No way, Director." I fixed her with a firm stare.

"Pate, listen. I planned for this. I have a duplicate lab in —"

"No. The project ends today. And you know it has to."

She scanned my face. "But the *loss*—"

"Is that loss worth the life of a boy? The lives of me and Eris? The rest that you all lied about to us?"

"That's a philosophical discussion that is—"

"Look, Director. We're not talking Hobson's choice here. It's not a choice between a few people dying to benefit others, or sacrificing one life for another. This is asking someone to sacrifice their life for a potential upgrade to humans—which will come someday, regardless. There's no reason to sacrifice lives just to be the first."

She held my eyes for a long time. "Maybe."

"Whether you agree or not," Eris said, "Pate is right. It ends now."

The Director nodded. "Okay. I guess I'm still trying to hang on—"

Engine sounds came from the tunnel and a car appeared with a diplomatic license plate.

"All right, then," the Director said. "Plan C."

"What's plan C?"

"Same as your plan. Mostly."

"You know about that? I went to great lengths to make that deal and make sure it stayed secret!"

She smiled. "You thought Powers was working for you?"

"My real estate guy?"

"The same. I didn't interfere with your clandestine purchases, I just enhanced them. It's ready to go, Pate. Secured, untraceable. Off the grid, but loaded with secure technology. We've been working on it for months. If you had decided to help me continue the project, we'd have used it as a remote safe house."

He shook his head. "How were you so many steps ahead of me all the time?"

"I told you. I'm the Director of you. Get in."

I slid into the back seat beside Eris and grabbed her hand. She squeezed mine back. "This is so surreal."

She smiled. "But so much more—"

A barrage of gunfire spittled the car. The Director fell forward against the door she had just opened and slid to the ground.

Eris screamed. The driver floored the accelerator, causing the blood-covered door to slam shut.

9 June 2032 12:09

Salim and his "aunt" moved through the airport with the rest of crowds. Being just after noon in a summer month, it was busy. He wore the wig, a jacket that was a bit too big, and pants retrieved from a locker. These people worked fast.

He felt silly, but he played the part, walking close to the woman and occasionally, when the crowds got thick, reaching up to take her hand.

At the security checkpoint, a clammy sweat break out on his palms. This experience—the revelations about his life—it made him paranoid and unsure who to trust.

"Hang on for a moment." She pulled a packet of papers from her purse and rifled through them, glancing up at the departures board every once in a while.

"Ah. Here we go. Perfect." A single sheet came out and she and stuffed the others back into her purse.

"It should be a nice trip to Dublin."

Ireland? Why Ireland?

"Flight leaves shortly. Let's get to the gate."

She grabbed his hand and hurried him along, arriving ten minutes before boarding. Some passengers were already lined up . Salim and his "aunt" took seats near the back of the waiting area.

He looked at her and pantomimed writing.

A tablet was produced out of her bag and passed it to him. He tapped a notepad open and wrote:

Why Dublin?

"Not the final destination."

Where?

"Don't need to know yet. But a long-planned location, carefully vetted. You will be safe. And with people who care about you and have your best interest in mind."

He turned off the tablet and handed it back.

"And you will be happy there, Salim."

He doubted it.

9 June 2032 11:45

The driver spun the wheel, causing the car to fishtail, wheels squealing. Aimed back at the garage entrance, the four gunmen raised their guns. As the car accelerated, I shoved Eris down and covered her with my body. Bullets ricocheted off the car. Two bumps, a shudder, a jolt, and the gunfire stopped. I looked up as we shot out into a vacant lot, bouncing over debris. We pulled onto a street, drove a short way, joining a line of cars on the primary road.

"Where are we going?" I asked.

The driver picked up two packets sitting in the seat and handed them back to us. "Dropping you both at separate locations. One at the airport and one at the train station after a car change. Inside are instructions and tickets for each. Different—" the men grunted as if in pain as he made a turn.

"What?" Eris said.

"Took a bullet. Not serious. Follow the directions exactly. *Do not deviate.*"

Eris leaned over to me. "He's not okay."

"No."

"Do you know what's going on?"

"Only that a lot of people have been looking for our child for a long time, but the Director had hidden him. A black market pharmaceutical organization found him—perhaps my fault. And they will do anything to get him."

"To reverse-engineer?"

"That would be my guess. As for where we are traveling...well, if the Director was telling the truth, everything will be okay. If we make it."

"You aren't going to tell me?" She gazed into my eyes, mouth tight.

I took a breath and started to speak, but she put a finger on my lips. "I get it. If I'm caught, you don't want to compromise the location."

The packet was a metallic-mesh security pouch with a biometric sensor. I placed my thumb on it. Nothing. I handed it to Eris and picked up the other one, which popped open at my touch. Inside was a train ticket to Bern, a plane ticket to Gatwick, with a connecting flight to Glasgow. The instructions included the number of a locker at Glasgow—also secured with my biometrics.

Eris was looking through her papers. I glanced over and saw she was flying into Charles de Gaulle. I looked away. If I didn't make it—

She was crying. "I...I am so...I don't know...I thought..."

I kissed her cheek. "I have an advantage because I've been working on this. Or something like it—" I stopped, surprised that I was choked up. "She's dead. But all these years, she was— His voice caught.

"Saving us."

"I was going to say 'directing us,' but yes. Saving us."

"I can't believe—"

The car swerved as the driver slumped over the wheel.

9 June 2032 12:15

The driver jerked back up and grabbed the wheel, breathing heavily.

"Pull over!" I shouted.

"Got to get you to locations first...ah!"

"We won't get there if you kill us. *Pull over!*"

The man navigated to the curb, stopped the car, and leaned back into his seat with a moan.

I jumped out with Eris behind me.

"Pate, put him on the sidewalk and call emergency—112 —on his phone. I'll drive!"

"Got it."

I dragged the driver out the passenger side by the shoulders. He yelped in pain and passed out. The right side of his shirt was soaked in blood.

I laid him carefully on the pavement, glancing up and down the street. There were few people, but a middle-aged man standing in a shop nearby stepped out and headed towards us.

"Help!" I said. "He's injured! Please call 112."

He nodded and ran back inside the store. I jumped in the car. "Go."

Eris drove, not too fast, but quick enough. "Where to?"

"Let's see." I leaned in to study the navigation display. "Looks like the airport is *here* and we are here."

"Don't set directions!"

"I'm not an idiot. Keep straight on D201 to D83. It'll be on our left in a few miles."

"Are we going together?"

"No, we should to follow the plan. Her plan. Pull over—" I looked at the screen again "—after the roundabout on Avenue de la Foire aux Vins and you go into the airport and adhere to your instructions. I'll drive the car to the train station."

It took about ten minutes. She turned to me.

"See you...wherever."

"Be careful."

"You, too, Pate."

"I love you, Eris."

"I don't want to leave. I lost you once."

"Not long this time. Go."

She got out and I forced myself not to watch her walk away.

9 June 2032 15:44

She disembarked and went to the lockers outside the train station. The flight over was fine but crowded. It made her nervous, though she tried not to let it show. The entire way, she tapped on the pouch she carried.

Would she really see her child again?

Did she want to?

At the airport, she opened the biometric package and frowned as she read the directions. A train and a hired boat? Interesting. Had Pate set this up? Or the Director?

A sigh escaped her mouth. She had become so used to merely going through the motions of life. Working at the library, believing that Pate and her child were dead. Accepting that happiness would always elude her. She read, ate, slept, and worked.

She was not so naïve to think that a decent life wasn't possible for her. Maybe she'd meet someone someday. A life that could satisfy her. Perhaps even have children. It was a serviceable life. A life without drama.

Now, her life was upended once more. It might work out; it might not. Maybe Pate wouldn't make it. Maybe the boy —Salim—wouldn't make it. Maybe she wouldn't make it.

With a start, she sat up straight. Maybe she *shouldn't* make it.

The thought hurt her heart, and she slumped back into the seat with a sigh.

Right now, all she could do was the next thing.

3 October 2038 15:01

He stood at the top of the green cliff a half a mile from the farmhouse, gazing out over the ocean. The sun was not down yet, but the shadows were long . The soft lap lap lap of the waves was mesmerizing. A gannet cried out high overhead.

Across the deep rich blue he could see the mainland. It wasn't really the mainland, just a few of the myriad of islands making up the Outer Hebrides. Beyond those isles lay the verdant hills of Scotland.

The air was crisp but not bitter. He breathed it in.

A shout made him turn to see a figure jogging up the hill, weaving in and out between the scattered boulders and tuffs of heather. The genetic modifications had done their work, and he looked older, with light skin and reddish-brown hair. His long hair bobbed back and forth as he ran.

He arrived at the cliff top, hardly out of breath.They were both in excellent shape. Running the farm on this sparsely inhabited island was good for the health, even for those who were genetically superior.

"Beautiful, isn't it?"

"Yes, I never get tired of it."

"One of the few things in life that stays the same. And yet it, too, is constantly shifting. Subtly and slowly, but changing."

They stood in silence, side-by-side, watching. A few fishing boats were just making their way back to the port in the waning day. Most were small, wooden crafts. A few were larger, but nothing like the commercial ships found on the greater islands or the mainland. The wind was starting to whip up.

"Do you ever wish to go away, son? To travel? Would you want to live in a city with lots of people your age?"

"You ask me that all the time, Dad. I'll let you know if my answer changes. I love it here. I love the work. We have enough contact with the other farms and the people on Mull and Skye."

His father nodded. "I appreciate that. Still. It isn't really fair."

"As you often tell me, life's not fair. And I prefer living out the truth in seclusion to living a lie in a city."

His dad turned and examined his face. "Do you?"

"Don't you?"

He turned to look back out at sea. "Yes. Yes, I do."

They pulled their cloaks tighter as the wind increased.

"Dad? Do you think they'll find us? Come for us?"

He sighed. "I'm sure they're trying."

"What will we do if they show up?"

His dad smiled. "They'll find out what happens to people who try to control others."

"The Director controlled us."

"She said so. But she was directing, guiding, and protecting. Not controlling. Besides, humans control so little in life. We tell ourselves we do. But we don't."

"Is that a statement about the futility of planning?"

"No. We still need to plan. But most of the time, all we can do is the next thing. And enjoy what we have."

There was silence again as the sun settled into the sea at the horizon.

"Dad? Do you think she's alive? That they have her somewhere?"

He took a deep breath. "I don't know. They couldn't have known where she was going that quickly."

He nodded. "I miss her."

He sighed. "So do I, Salim."

About the Author

Markus McDowell is an author, editor, and researcher. He has been writing fiction since he was eight years old. He has a Ph.D. from Fuller Theological Seminary and a law degree from the University of London, and is the author of *To and Fro Upon the Earth: A Novel*, *Onesimus: A Novel of Christianity in the Roman Empire*, and *The Sky Over Chaos: Short Stories by Markus McDowell.*

Get a free collection of short stories by joining the newsletter at https://markusmcdowell.com/newsletter-2/

Visit the author's website at https://markusmcdowell.com

About the Publisher

Sulis International Press publishes select fiction and nonfiction in a variety of genres under four imprints: Riversong Books, Sulis Academic Press, Sulis Press, and Keledei Publications.

For more, visit the website at
https://sulisinternational.com

Subscribe to the newsletter at
https://sulisinternational.com/subscribe/

Follow on social media
https://www.facebook.com/SulisInternational
https://twitter.com/Sulis_Intl
https://www.pinterest.com/Sulis_Intl/
https://www.instagram.com/sulis_international/

More from Markus McDowell

So Deep in Shadow
Mortals As They Walk
The Sky Over Chaos: Short Stories
To and Fro Upon the Earth
Onesimus: A Novel of Christianity in the Roman Empire

Markus also writes book reviews, restaurant reviews, and articles on writing and life. You can read these on his website at www.markusmcdowell.com.

9 781946 849687